you
look
nice
today

you
look
nice
today

a novel

stanley bing

BLOOMSBURY

Published by Bloomsbury, New York and London
Distributed to the trade by Holtzbrinck Publishers

Library of Congress Cataloging-in-Publication Data
has been applied for.

ISBN 1-58234-280-6

First U.S. Edition 2003

10 9 8 7 6 5 4 3 2 1

Typeset by Palimpsest Book Production Ltd,
Polmont, Stirlingshire, Scotland
Printed in the United States of America
by R.R. Donnelley & Sons, Crawfordsville, Indiana

to the excellent corporation,
where this kind of nonsense never happens,
or is settled out of court

contents

The company will not tolerate any form of harassment on account of race, color, national origin, religion, sex, age, sexual orientation, disability, veteran's status, marital status, or height or weight. Insofar as sexual harassment is concerned, the company's guidelines list three criteria for determining whether such acts are unwelcome sexual advances, requests for sexual favors and other verbal or physical conduct of a sexual nature constitute unlawful sexual harassment. They are: (1) submission to the conduct is made either an explicit or implicit condition of employment; (2) submission to or rejection of the conduct is the basis for either continued employment or for decisions affecting pay, benefits, or advancement opportunities; (3) the conduct has the purpose or effect of substantially interfering with an individual's work performance or creating an intimidating, hostile, or offensive work environment. The company will investigate any issue as it arises and will take appropriate action. Any employee who engages in such harassment by any means, including in person and/or through the use of E-mail, voice mail, telephone, audio or video devices, and/or computer or hard-copy documents, will be subject to discipline, up to and including termination.

—Corporate EEO Policy

No good deed goes unpunished.

—Anonymous

book
one

Carole Anne

1

My name is Tell. The events I want to pass along to you took place at the end of the century just past, as the world was somewhat nervously preparing for a future millennium that was as yet unknown. The prospect of change does strange things to all people, but it affects each of us differently. Myself, I don't like change. Now that we are here in that very same future, however, I find that there was no point in being either nervous or excited about the big transition after all. Much has changed and much has not, and what has changed is mostly that which we have not foreseen. And except for the occasional digital television set you see now and then, and the sense of perilous insecurity that now underlies all daily existence, the occasional waiting line to which we now are subject in airport, train terminal, or museum, the conviction, underneath it all, that we could be erased by the contents of one small suitcase, nothing of substance has been altered at all in our daily lives. We rise, go to work, return at the end of the day tired and as happy as our innate spirits will allow. Everyday life proceeds in this century as it did in the last. And that has made a significant difference, at least to those of us who worship stability.

But I get ahead of things. I should probably at this time more properly introduce myself in true corporate fashion—by function as well as by name. I am the executive vice president of what used to be called Personnel, now referred to more cryptically and certainly less informatively as Human Resources, at a multinational conglomerate that employs slightly more than two hundred thousand people, mostly in Chicago, but also in New York City, San Diego, and Pittsburgh, Pennsylvania. We have satellite offices around the globe, in places as marginal as Benin, Belize, Luxembourg, and Omaha, Nebraska, the latter in a honeycomb of cubicles beneath a million-acre field.

At some point in the middle of 1997, a woman I will from this time forth call CaroleAnne Winter joined our corporation in the financial services group in Chicago, first as a temporary secretary, then, shortly thereafter, as an ultra-high-level administrative assistant. The circumstances of her abrupt and surprising promotion are quite interesting but must wait for a few moments while we take care of some final backgrounding.

The function of the business operation that concerns us was to find enterprises in which we as a corporation might place our capital to good effect. Let me put that another way: Its purpose was to lend money. Money costs money. Whatever the money costs at any given point in time is our gain. It's a large segment of our operation, and quite profitable, but it depends for its success on the sobriety, judgment, and maturity of the individuals who staff and manage it. The importance and irony of that statement will become clear to you as we move forward.

CaroleAnne was at that time a rather young thirty-six years of age, and I believe it would be remiss of me, if not almost criminally disingenuous, either to skip or somehow disguise the striking quality of her physical beauty. Perhaps she was of that group of Americanized Hawaiians who have moved to the mainland and lost their ethnicity, or a child of a marine who did his duty in the South Sea Islands in more ways than one, I don't know. The effect was exotic but not outlandishly foreign. Her skin was a very light shade of copper, with slightly red highlights at the apex of her cheekbones, which were pronounced. Her eyes were large and brown but cantilevered slightly upward at their edges, which lent her a Brahmin look. Her hair, which she wore in no particular style, or rather, to be more accurate, in every imaginable one, was the deepest of black, lustrous and plentiful. Her nose was small and tipped ever so slightly upward, and covered with an attractive spray of virtually imperceptible freckles. Her lips were full but not overly ample, and extremely expressive, particularly when she smiled, which was quite often. One would have to say, on balance, that the face as it came together was rather odd, except that, in its mélange of types and qualities, it achieved not only balance but also loveliness.

Her voice added to this overall impression, being generally well modulated, somewhat deep in register, and—how shall I put this?— almost artfully cultivated. It was as if at some point in her life, CaroleAnne had taken control of this aspect of her personality and eradicated all traces of her original form of expression, replacing it with something far more perfect, aesthetically pleasing, and managed. This fine musical instrument was the tool she used to convey what were invariably subtle, intelligent, and thoughtful comments that showed a keen mind exquisitely aware of the world around it and a sensibility capable of evaluating, judging, and testing reality against some internal standard. Here, then, was above all a rational person in full command of herself. Such an individual is always a pleasure to have around, particularly in an environment where such qualities are not always evident in those with whom we are compelled to work.

About the rest of her physical makeup I will do my best to be descriptive without being prurient, believing, however, that this subject is not peripheral to the story but rather an integral part of the events as they played themselves out. CaroleAnne was small . . . not short but quite slight of build, lithe and willowy, and she gave off a strong aura of fragility. There was about her carriage a curious sense of reticence and delicacy, a quality that made women want to take her under their wings and mother her, and men to shelter and care for her in a somewhat less familial way. She was, as I have said, slender, but she was also quite ample for a woman of her size in both her chest and her hips, and when she was not careful to dress with discretion, as sometimes was the case in those early years, she could quite literally stop corporate traffic. Add to that her disconcerting tendency occasionally to be somewhat too liberal with a chosen scent, and her flamboyance was enormous within the gray confines of an organization where a patterned shirt could elicit widespread comment.

I feel it is not inappropriate to mention our subsequent discovery that CaroleAnne hailed from a small hamlet outside of New Orleans, one to which plumbing and electricity only recently were provided. Her people, it turned out, were quite impoverished and subsisted, I believe, via some combination of farming and, when it could be found in the somnolent, minuscule central city of their parish, light office and domestic work. I note this fact not only informationally but also to indicate to what lengths she must have gone, at some point in her early life, to wipe out all relics of her provincial upbringing. If one had heard she was a native of London, New Delhi, or Cancún, it would have come as no surprise. She had made of herself a citizen of the world, appropriate and necessary to the home office of any global enterprise.

It was on a Wednesday she first made our acquaintance—Wednesday the 7th of May, 1997. I made a note in my datebook, as I sometimes like to do when something extraordinary is presented to me. I don't have the memory I used to, so these devices help me a great deal as I work to make sure that my entire life does not, as it were, slip away in a cloud of forgetfulness and preoccupation. At any rate, that is why, throughout this telling, I might seem to have some omniscient power of recall. Nothing could be farther from the truth. I just make notes, that's all.

"CaroleAnne Winter," I wrote at the time. "Very quiet and attractive young woman with superb support skills. Interesting job history."

It is curious to me, looking back now, that I did not go farther into this particular aspect of CaroleAnne's background, since if I had it might have provided me with some insight into her remarkable character as it later revealed itself. But then again, she seemed so . . . well, so *wonderful*, like a vision sent down to us from the corporate deities, in fact, that none of us, least of all I, who am often accused of tying everything up in useless red tape, wanted to poop on this parade.

It was clear from her rather gnomic and cursory résumé that she had held no fewer than five jobs in three years and lived in as many cities, having set down temporary roots in Cleveland, Detroit, Los Angeles, and Garden City, Long Island, before finally planting what seemed to be a more final flag in what we denizens of this region refer to as Chicagoland. That was her final destination as far as I know. Unless something has substantially changed without my knowledge, she lives here still.

At each prior work location, she had held a substantial position in which she was placed by an exclusive agency, and from each place she had fled. There was some upset in her past that one could see not only in her peripatetic curriculum vitae but also, more importantly, in her eyes, along with a sense that behind that well-masked turmoil lay a quiet and admirable determination to forbid the past to rise up and wreck a future that was moving decisively to meet her.

On Wednesday the 7th of May, 1997, we in the financial services group were in the middle of what might variously be called a feeding frenzy, or possibly a Chinese fire drill. It's hard sometimes to tell the difference, but there is one. In a feeding frenzy, the group of predators roils about, falling on its prey, snapping at each other in a paroxysm of greed that transcends rational or physical need for sustenance. So . . . it was sort of like that. In a Chinese fire drill, on the other hand, passengers in a closed vehicle, who find themselves stopped at a traffic light, exit the enclosure and run about the conveyance in a mad dash, with the objective of returning to one's seating position before the light turns green and it is time for the car to start moving again. The feeding frenzy is vicious and serious. The Chinese fire drill celebrates the fundamentally frivolous nature of all human activity. Each is pleasurable and terrifying in a very different way. We were then alternating between both, and when we weren't alternating we were doing them concurrently.

In short, our business on that day visited upon the members of the group a barely controlled hysteria that smote us from seven-seventeen A.M., when the first phone rang, to nine twenty-seven P.M., when the last of us straggled out of the electronic doors and passed our key cards through the elevator call pad for the last time.

Our group, as it was constituted then, consisted of one department head, a fellow by the name of Richard Podesky, with a title of executive vice president, two senior officers, three middle managers, a couple of submanager-level professionals, and two implacable administrative assistants who in their own way ran the operation.

In the corner office, as I said, was Executive Vice President Richard Podesky, whom everybody called Dick. He was a man then entering the later years of his seventh decade, which made him about sixty-eight years of age, for those who have trouble counting decades. Dick was the bedrock upon which the department had been founded, but he was ailing. You couldn't tell it by looking at him, though. He appeared each morning, except those in which his difficulties kept him in bed, in an absolutely invariable gray suit, stiffly starched white shirt, and club tie held close with a gold bar, his thin gray hair oiled and brushed neatly back to accentuate what was left of his widow's peak. Much of his time he spent in his office, bent over papers. When he wished complete privacy, he closed his door, but never for more than twenty minutes or so. Privacy was an issue in our offices anyhow. Either by design or simple insensitivity, the architect had supplied each door with a glass panel that enabled anyone to peer into an executive's inner sanctum and see what he was up to. This made napping, among other personal pastimes one might want to pursue, impossible. This is not an idle consideration, as you shall see.

What ailed Dick was an ulcer. He was dying of it. Still is, as far as I know. He retired last year, after a series of parties that very nearly killed men and women half his age. He soldiered through them all, then was hospitalized for several weeks at a quiet, luxurious mausoleum upstate. Up until the moment he departed, he was in titular control of the department, however, and nobody questioned his overall authority, even if he wasn't always the first person we came to for day-to-day advice. That role was ably filled by a fellow I will call Robert Harbert, for that was very nearly his name. Harb, as he was affectionately called by everyone from the custodian to the chairman of the board on the sixty-fifth floor, was the director of the department and later its vice president. At the time in which our narrative begins, Harb was in his forty-fourth year.

I would like to state that Harb was a prepossessing person, with a straight back, a clear, judicious eye, and a nerve as rock-steady as his washboard stomach. Alas, none of these statements would be true, except perhaps for the quality of his eye. He did possess the gift of all great senior managers—the ability to judge the strengths, weaknesses, and potential energy of other people and, more often than not, the capacity to make others do what he wished them to do while at the same time allowing them to think they acted on their own initiative.

As a physical specimen, however, Harb was issued something short of a full load. Not that he was ugly or misshapen in any way. There was no feature in his face or body that declared itself too strenuously. And that was it. Harb was bland, bland to a level so profound it was almost a personal statement. He was essentially thin, with narrow shoulders that arced backward slightly, like the wings of a bird, and not a noble bird, either, but one more closely related to the most ubiquitous fowl of all, the chicken. His chest was not broad or deep, but rather slender and a trifle, well, sunken, as if he had been ill as a child and never quite recovered. He had, since we are in the pursuit of truth, a bit of a stomach growing as he entered the full blush of high middle age. Mercifully, he had kept the greater part of his hair, although when one wandered behind him at a business meeting and looked down at him as he doodled on a yellow pad, one might catch a glimpse of scalp beneath his whorl. In the front, thankfully, the effect was more ample, a shock of sandy brown shot with occasional white falling boyishly over his high, domed forehead, wandering constantly into his eyes as he tried to work, which for him, I believe, was all about seeing. Lips small, in the middle of his face, quite thin. Good straight teeth. Unfortunate chin, though. Just a little too small for the evocation of true, manly virtue. Now that I come to think about it, there was something perhaps overly sensitive about that face. Perhaps it was in his eyes, which were, as I have said, his best feature, very large and brown, spaced rather widely apart, with big lashes and brows that one could read, if one chose, as a meteorologist might read a barometer. I have his corporate head shot before me as I write this now. Harb is looking at me, straight on, a small, professional smile on his lips, his bulb of a nose a little red, even in black and white, his gaze boring directly into the camera in spite of the organizational front the man is attempting to put on. Dog's eyes, that's what they were. A dog can't keep what he's feeling a secret. Neither could Harb.

Now, I will do my best as we move along to stick to the facts as much as I can, because there are certainly enough of them. There are, in fact, almost too many facts. I wonder if it is possible that the more facts one has at one's disposal, the farther one is from arriving at the truth.

2

That morning in 1997, the final stages of activity had arrived vis-à-vis the Fett/Wiedenbaum situation, a complicated deal involving the mutual assured destruction of two once-proud, independent corporations that could no longer compete with each other and had therefore decided to merge. The only individuals who were likely to benefit from this transaction were the senior management of both entities, several very large shareholders (who had some idea of the "strategic plans" of the firms and therefore had worked out the best possible "investment" strategy that would guarantee their immediate profit when they flipped the stock in a timely fashion), and we who were providing the capital.

The losers, as always, would be the employees of each existing corporation, tens of thousands of which would forfeit their jobs, and, eventually, the smaller and certainly less well-informed shareholders of the new entity, who would suffer when the eventual value of the new, bloated, unfocused company was inevitably perceived aright.

It's odd. No matter how hard you work on a deal, how organized you are—planning each step in meticulous detail, doing flowcharts and work schedules with military precision—the final days and hours leading up to the passing of final paper are always a nightmare. You see the mettle of individuals in such circumstances. Some people achieve a marvelous, cool-blooded calm, serenity imparted by the size of the stakes at hand and the knowledge that each job can be accomplished only one task at a time. Others turn beet red, lose control of their hair and eyeballs, and begin barking orders and imprecations like children about to be deprived of their nightly bottle. Dick Podesky, our executive vice president, always the most equable and civilized of men in the best of times, particularly after lunch, invariably turned into a monstrosity when we were required to fire with live ammunition, fussing and simpering in his kennel like a spoiled shih tzu about the most minor of momentary hitches, emerging at frequent intervals only to gaze around himself like Richard III in search of his horse, muttering such dark forebodings at his senior managers as, "We're gonna have to change the way we do things around here" and "I wanna see you when this is all over."

We ignored him at such times, partially because we were required to do so in order to get the job done, and also because we liked Dick and didn't want to force him to display himself at his worst by placing him in a situation that was not to his advantage.

Harb, on the other hand, appeared as if this was a day much as any other. No glitch in the proceedings surprised him. No problem was worth spilling coffee over. The worse things got, the quieter grew Harb, until, as the height of the crisis swirled about our ears, he achieved a level of placidity normally associated with ancient Japanese relics of the Buddha, sitting stolidly behind his desk in perfect tranquillity, a tiny smile playing around the corners of his mouth, his door wide open to welcome any passing concern from large and subordinate player alike—this as opposed to the entry to Dick's lair, which often slammed shut when things grew as hairy as they were that morning.

This was it: Someone had lost the diskette holding the chairman's final revisions of the executive summary that covered the consummating contractual document that would seal the Fett/Wiedenbaum agreement. This package—the executive summary and the massive contract it covered—was even then supposed to be flying its way crosstown to the offices of Shea & Bumpus, the firm representing one of the parties in this matter. I forget whether it was a party of the first or second part; it's not important.

A hard copy existed of this executive summary, which was designed to make reading the companion material unnecessary. At approximately three thousand words in length, the summary traced the history of the association between the two companies whose merger we were financing, outlined the structure of the pending deal, offered conservative (and almost wholly fictional) projections as to the monetary consequences of the enterprise, and closed with our chairman's heartfelt emotions attending the happy outcome of this matter. At its current length, and covered with the chairman's characteristic chicken scrawl, it was only about 300 per cent too long but could not now be changed without further discussion with the big dog himself, who was known to be satisfied with the document—as amended by him, of course.

And now the diskette holding all those changes was lost. Naturally, the old man had an electronic copy in his computer, or more accurately, in the computer of Betty, his assistant. But anyone wishing to procure that copy would have to call and ask for it, and then the old man would find out, and depending on his mood . . . well, it was thought that reentering the hard copy into our department computer might be a better option.

This presented certain difficulties. First, we had less than thirty minutes to get that portion of the job done—the packet was supposed to be delivered in about that time frame, but there was of course fifteen minutes leeway to allow for traffic, confused or psychotic car services, or the possibility that the messenger decided, as was often the case, to stop for a joint in the park. So speed was of the essence. While this should not have been a problem, alas, it was. Dick Podesky's administrative assistant, Shelly, was several years his senior and had arthritis. She was scheduled to retire when he did, and not a moment sooner, and that was unquestionably the way it should have been. Nobody wanted to force Shelly out after all her years of service simply because she couldn't walk, file, or utilize a computer.

The other department secretary, Louise, was very young, very pretty, and very nice.

After the latest round of cutbacks, it was deemed that two support people in our department were sufficient, and I was hard-pressed to argue, being the author of and designated apologist for much of that painful process of productivity management. Louise, then, was responsible for virtually all serious activity that took place among our leadership cadre, and most of the time that worked out all right. We all had our own computers and were fairly proficient at everyday keyboarding and E-mailing. We all had cellular phones and faxes at every location at which we might conceivably be found, and sometimes places we didn't want to be found. Truthfully, the role of secretary had devolved in our group into that of low-level personal servant and receptionist, and Louise liked that fine. And we liked her a very great deal indeed.

This did mean, however, that several senior officers, including Harb and myself, were forced essentially to operate without serious secretarial support. If we had a big job, we brought in a temp.

Knowing it was going to be a large and indigestible hair ball of a morning, I had the presence of mind the night before to request just such assistance, which had to be booked through Shelly, Dick Podesky's assistant. The exchange was typical.

"Shelly," I said at approximately four-thirty on the afternoon before the following day, "I think we should book a temp for tomorrow morning."

"Now?" said Shelly. She was then engaged in filling out Dick Podesky's expense report by hand, in pencil, a portion of her job that occupied fully 90 percent of her time in any given week. As always, she was neat to perfection and smelled of baby soap. Her gunmetal hair was up in a tight bun that could have been baked freshly just five or ten minutes ago, even though I knew it was done more than ten hours prior, when Shelly rose for the day, in a condo community just outside of Glencoe, Illinois, at the first minting of the newborn sun.

"Yes, Shelly, it would have to be now since we're going to need this person tomorrow."

"Dick would have to authorize that," she said, not contentiously. This was the rule of all rules in Shelly's world, particularly when it came to the expenditure of money. Strictly speaking, however, it was not the case. Both Harb and myself had signatory authority, me up to $150,000, Harb's virtually unlimited.

"Shelly," I said. What was the point of getting annoyed? It would not move things along any faster. "Dick is gone for the day. We cannot get his approval. And we can't wait for tomorrow, since by then we're going to need to have this person in place."

"I see," said Shelly and looked at me.

"I will take personal responsibility for this expenditure," I said after a time.

"Okay," said Shelly with a little grin. "What was it you wanted again?" She was kidding. Nothing got by Shelly. She saw everything and, more important, had an opinion on everything, an opinion born of staunch moral principles and an obsolete hierarchy of virtues and scruples. I mention this because it will be important later on.

It was at the height of our consternation about the missing diskette that our temp appeared. It was CaroleAnne. She was late.

I will never forget the impact that CaroleAnne made in that first instant in which she entered our department. Keep in mind, please, that large emotions and reactions are alien to a true corporate work-place environment. We seek sameness. A great business milieu is like crème brûlée, with the tasty custard down below and a fine glazed topping up above, sweet and hard, that obscures what is beneath. CaroleAnne violated that crust immediately. She was all custard.

She was dressed in a flowered . . . garment that wrapped around her upper torso and was tied at the waist by a belt. The two . . . flaps, I guess you would call them, met at a point well north of her navel, but not quite north enough. There was some breast exposure is what I'm trying to say as delicately as possible. I wouldn't even mention it if I didn't think it was a subsequent factor in some way. The skirt of this piece of apparel was also alarmingly short, revealing a pair of dramatically long, muscular legs sheathed in dancer's tights. On her feet were a pair of shocking red sandal things that tied at the ankle.

"Hello?" said CaroleAnne, gazing coolly at the collection of stressed-out individuals who stood, somewhat agape, before her, each at that point trying mightily to work out a strategy by which his or her career could be salvaged without, each hoped, injury to anyone, but not necessarily.

"And you are . . . ?" It was Harb, who had exited his office just a bit and was standing in the doorway. A smile of pleasurable surprise played across his mouth and a glimmer of amusement lit his eye. Whatever reaction he was having, it was immediate and positive, in some prejudgmental sense.

"CaroleAnne Winter," said CaroleAnne. "I'm the temp. Fortunately for you, I'm the best temp you'll ever have."

"Oh, good," said Harb, evenly assessing this show of quiet bravado. I could tell he appreciated it, saw it as an attempt to put us at our ease when we clearly needed such an effort in our behalf. He further emerged from his office, rolling down his sleeves and buttoning them as he went. To most, this action would mean little. But I knew Harb, and I knew what it signified. It meant that Harb would have liked very much, at that moment, to look his best.

"Good," he said. "Could you come over here for a minute?" He casually sat on the edge of Louise's desk. Louise looked up at him with some interest. "Louise?" said Harb. "Could you see if Dick and Shelly have everything under control at this point in time?"

"Sure, Harb," said Louise. She got up without any sense of urgency and, with a polite smile at CaroleAnne, who was then standing in very close proximity to her, moved across the office to Shelly's desk. "She's not here," she said upon arrival.

"She's not?" said Harb, who had watched this rather bovine emigration with admirable sangfroid, given the perilous nature of the situation at hand. "Well, then, have a seat and man the fort, Louise. Man the fort."

"Aye, aye captain," said Louise, selecting the wrong branch of the military for her witticism. I wondered, and not for the first time, whether she knew how funny she was. I suspected she did. This made me somewhat nervous. You like to know the bottom line of the people you work with.

Louise sat. Harb turned politely to the new temp. You would never have known from his demeanor how much was riding on the outcome of the next twenty minutes. I'm sure the rest of us, however, looked somewhat the worse for wear.

"Now . . . CaroleAnne is it?"

"Yes, sir," said CaroleAnne, looking at the floor. "That's one word. With a capital *A* in the middle." From the tipping of her ears and the slightly tilted aspect of her head, I could tell she was listening intently, and this impressed me and, even at this early date, inspired something close to affection. Here was a woman who in spite of her rather outlandish getup held herself quite modestly, going so far as to avert her gaze becomingly when a superior officer aimed an order in her direction. There were many in more traditional outfits who popped gum and fielded snazzy glances when tapped for duty. Not this one. She exuded a certain willingness . . . no, a barely suppressed eagerness . . . to get down to the challenge at hand and master it. A certain electricity hit the entire group of us at that moment. I noticed that Blatt, our junior executrix, who generally made herself scarce at the slightest indication of danger (or any physical labor that involved more than moving her chin up and down, for that matter), had popped out of her cubicle and was settling in to watch what would perhaps be the most important show of her young career.

"CaroleAnne, then," said Harb, motioning the young woman to sit at Louise's workstation. "We have something of a situation here." He was holding the hard copy of the chairman's executive summary in one hand. He held it forth to CaroleAnne, who took it while continuing to gaze at him with almost preternatural concentration. "We seem to have lost the diskette that held the marked revisions you see on that document. It is of some three thousand words in length. The entire thing will have to be inputted as quickly as possible, with the marked revisions intact, and no errors. You will note that on page four there is an embedded bar chart, which I believe was accomplished in Excel and then imported into the master document, which I assume was produced in Microsoft Word and then brought into Quark Express. What would you say the possibility would be that this job could be accomplished in, say, thirty minutes?"

"Huh," said CaroleAnne. A small line of concentration appeared between her eyebrows, which were arched high and exquisitely tweezed. She paged thoughtfully through the paper, then propped it up on the little metal stand provided for that purpose and began to type. Each member of the permanent office staff turned to one of his counterparts, shrugged a shoulder, found something to do. For his part, Harb simply stood off to one side and watched CaroleAnne as she went about her business.

I have heard typing in my time, but nothing like this before, although I heard it many times since, and always from the same source. It is a beautiful sound, the noise that perfect, mechanical, technical typing creates. I judge that the clickity-click of Carole-Anne's work production was generated at a rate of some 150 words per minute. I have seen Wayne Gretzky in his prime score a hat trick. One time I was fortunate enough to be present when Fleetwood Mac played an entire set during a rehearsal for an upcoming concert, because we were arranging financing for the hall in which they were playing that night. The feeling of awe that true mastery of a given craft produces is like none other. That is what I personally felt when I heard and saw CaroleAnne spew forth that executive summary on a computer that, until that moment, had been used for the most part to play solitaire.

"This is a mother," said CaroleAnne, almost to herself. After that, she did not speak for some time.

At one point while this demonstration was progressing without incident, I strolled around behind CaroleAnne's chair as she sat there with perfect posture, her head inclined to read the master document, her bottom perched at the very edge of the desk chair, her back perfectly symmetrical, her torso bent forward into the task. The words appeared as if by magic on the luminescent screen, flowing onto the CRT like water into a virtual mountain pool. Harb was still standing several yards behind her, watching with a gaze I

18

couldn't quite read. Then he looked up at me, and I got him all right.

Any man who has been with his fraternity brother at two in the morning at a cocktail party or random social gathering stuffed with neat, pristine girls from out of town knows the expression that I beheld that morning on Harb's crooked face. It was the kind of admiration that can easily be misperceived, or at least misunderstood. "This girl is the one," is what that expression says, and there is nothing sad or smarmy about it. It is the face of hope. Put simply, Harb was in love, and that is all, in love with the idealized object of his most profound desire at that moment, with the perfection of this masterful woman who was right then saving our lives for the grand sum of $11.55 per hour, with no benefits, promises, or strings attached. Some may not call it love, but they would be wrong. Mix equal parts of admiration, respect, gratitude, fear of abandonment, and physical excitation, and . . . well, if you can think of another word for it, good for you. I cannot. It may not be the kind of love that lasts forever . . . but then what kind of love does?

"I'm going to need coordinates for this bar chart," said CaroleAnne in a voice so calm it filled me with a tiny electric thrill.

"I don't believe we have any," said Harb. "Do we have any coordinates around here, Mr. Tell?"

"No," I said with some sadness. "We don't do coordinates on this floor."

"Do you think you can estimate the actual numbers to create the same general parameters on the graphic itself?" Harb asked. He might have been asking her whether she preferred a Beaujolais nouveau to a classic Chianti as an accompaniment to a hearty stew.

"Hmm," said CaroleAnne. "I guess so. Rather funky as a general practice, however, don't you think?"

And sure enough, that's what she did. She had to mess around with it for a while, of course. But when she was done, it was an almost perfect replica of the original, without the financial underpinning that would have provided it with honest economic credibility. The resulting chart was simply an empty illustration, whipped up to provide the illusion of intellectual depth and rigor, which is generally all that is required in what we do—the illusion, that is. As CaroleAnne noted, as a way of presenting things it was rather funky. It was also exactly what the doctor ordered.

The finished product (at right) was not much to look at, I grant you. But it had the benefit of appearing completely legitimate and was considerably more than any secretary south of the fifty-eighth floor could do on a moment's notice, I can tell you that.

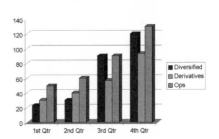

The document was completed on the screen with some three minutes to spare. I use that precise measurement because the messenger was scheduled to arrive at that exact time, and we assumed that he would do so, simply because we had threatened the top officer in Corporate Services with immediate termination should his winged Nike fail to perform as required. Senior management having been brought to the field, the lower tier quite naturally was the epitome of compliance. In short, the guy was there when he was supposed to be and the document was whisked on its merry way without further incident.

Afterward, the office seemed oddly quiet. Julianne Blatt, sniggering slightly for some reason, retreated to her spare, cluttered little office to do whatever it is she was supposed to do at that moment based on a direct order issued by someone of whom she was afraid not more than two hours prior. An analyst and professional middle manager, she was never required for active duty in real-time situations, which I presume she felt gave her the right to look down her nose from her ivory tower at anyone who actually had a function in a firestorm. Dick Podesky, for the first time that morning, emerged from his cubby, his eyes slightly squinting with the brightness of the common-area fluorescents like Punxsutawney Phil on the verge of a great climatic discovery. "What are you doing here?" he said to Louise, who was still seated at Shelly's desk. Without comment, Louise pointed without any visual inflection whatsoever to the new denizen of her ergonomic chair.

"Hi," said CaroleAnne. She was carefully adjusting her makeup in an old-fashioned compact that held a mirror and some rather weathered pancake base. "That was hairy," she observed to nobody in particular. Harb laughed, a short, sharp bark that was gone almost before it escaped him.

"Hello," said Dick Podesky. Then he stood there for a while, looking at CaroleAnne. Several times, he appeared on the verge of clearing his throat and issuing an executive utterance, but then thought better of it. After a time, he said in his best basso profundo, "Mr. Harbert, could you see me for a minute?" Then, without ascertaining whether Harb was either in the room or had heard his request, he turned and went back into his office, stopping for a moment to check a piece of paper that was hanging around on an adjacent desk before disappearing into his well-appointed den. "Hmm," he said, picking it up and taking it with him as he went. Even at the distance at which I was standing, I could tell what the document was: the cafeteria lunch menu for the rest of the month. It was interesting . . . but not that interesting.

Harb made his way over to CaroleAnne and put his hand lightly on her shoulder. "Stick around a bit, wouldja?" he said.

"Sure!" said CaroleAnne. She did not look surprised. A tiny smile of . . . what was it? . . . triumph? pleasure? postshow excitation? . . . vibrated around the corners of her mouth.

Without any sign of hurry, Harb dislodged himself from the space he was then inhabiting and crossed the distance to Dick Podesky's office. "Who is that woman?" was the only thing I managed to hear before Harb swung the door shut.

CaroleAnne joined our department as a full-time administrative assistant two days after, at a salary of $53,500, reporting to Harb and myself, but in truth, from that time forth, she worked only for Harb. Louise went to work for Julianne Blatt, where she afterward was able to observe events without the interruption of distractions

21

like typing, filing, and taking dictation, due to the indeterminate nature of Blatt's job, for which she was well prepared at Wharton. I, too, was able to watch. But then, that's what I do. You'll excuse me then, if, as we move forward in this thing, I dispense with every justification for my seeming omniscient status. Suffice it to say that I was there. I saw. And what I tell is true.

3

Every story has many beginnings, but very few have just one. It's necessary, to maintain both the appearance of cohesion and the fiction that life has describable shape and form, to start at a place and, presumably, to end somewhere as well. I'm going to try to do both, although you will forgive me if I point out that life does extend infinitely in either direction, back into the past and forward into the future—until it does not, of course.

For purposes of this chronicle, we will place ourselves not within the confines of our office, where much of the subsequent events took place, but in a small garden apartment in a suburb of Chicago located in quite a marginal section of housing not far from the town of Deerfield, Illinois. We are in an apartment complex populated primarily by working people of modest but respectable means. For it is here where CaroleAnne Winter lived at the time we first met her, and here where the person we thought we knew awoke each morning, at least for the first year or so in which our story takes place, before Harb and his good intentions got to her and changed her life for the better, or so I'm sure he thought.

The building in which CaroleAnne's apartment could be found was in one of those low brick enclaves that cluster in no particular pattern around a central green. This plaza, as it were, was cut with asphalt paths leading to the front door of each building in the compound. Dotting the grassy common were benches for sitting, and simple wrought-iron lampposts were strategically placed up and down these walks to provide light for those returning from work after dark, or those hustling back to their apartments after dinner at a nearby beanery. A majority of these lamps were broken, the globes shattered by rocks, jagged shards of glass poking up in perpetuity, presumably, since the devices had obviously been attacked and rendered inoperative long, long ago. Rust climbed up each pole, eating through the heavy black weatherproof enamel that had been laid on when most of the inhabitants of the village were building the great dream after the Second World War, or teething.

Likewise, the paths that scored the parched, weedy front yard of the living quarters were still functional, but a variety of spiky, hardy plant life had burst through the cracks, pulverizing whole sections of asphalt, which was bordered in crabgrass and dirt.

The squat buildings were two stories in height, with white trim and dark green shutters. The brick appeared to be in good shape although badly in need of pointing here and there. The paint had long ago become a shadow of itself. Air conditioners stuck out of many front windows like teeth uncorrected by orthodontics.

This is not to say that the entire effect was one of squalor. It was not. It was, rather, an atmosphere of dejected low-bourgeois faux affluence, a testament to the noble striving of every human being to live in pleasant, dignified circumstances. Small window boxes filled with geraniums were only one of the signs that spoke of this continuing effort.

How many people can live in four rooms? Well, there was CaroleAnne, and a friend of hers whose name I do not recall since it is of no importance except to say that it was this friend who had offered her accommodations when she moved into town, and there was CaroleAnne's husband, Edgar. Edgar was not a very nice person. He'd been disappointed with life and had to smoke a lot of pot to forget about that. Also in the apartment were a couple of Edgar's cousins and their retinue. The total number of inhabitants of this living space, then, numbered at any time between eight and fifteen, depending on who was visiting or who had gotten lucky the previous evening.

And the day arrived when CaroleAnne came into the office dressed in what was obviously somebody else's clothing. Several articles did not match, and the blouse was excessively revealing, in that it was not buttoned at the neck, nor even at the thorax. As always, she was late. She seated herself at her desk, tears flowing behind enormous sunglasses.

None of us could touch her, let alone speak with her. She was strung tighter than catgut on a brand-new tennis racquet. It felt like if you got too close, she would pop from her moorings and start whipping around the room. We all felt bad for her, but Harb? Harb was stricken. I could see it in his big doggy eyes.

God, did he want to help her!

He made his way to the desk where CaroleAnne sat in inviolable misery and simply stood there for a time, looking exquisitely uncomfortable.

"Can I get you something?" he said eventually.

"No, thank you," said CaroleAnne. She was sitting stiffly at her desk, staring down at her hands with great concentration. She did not look up.

"Is this something you would care to talk about?" said Harb. He waited.

"No, Harb," said CaroleAnne very quietly. Then she turned her head up to face him and looked through her gigantic sunglasses into his eyes.

"What would I see if I took off those glasses, Cee?" he said.

"Please don't," she said quite firmly and went back to regarding her knuckles with great intensity.

"All right," said Harb. He went to the door of his office. "You up to making some coffee?"

"Yeah, sure," said CaroleAnne with, I thought, a certain amount of appreciation. "Coffee sounds good."

She kept her sunglasses on for the rest of the day. The next day, she wore a smaller pair. Harb began to refer to her publicly as Madonna, which I suppose was his rather quaint idea of a person who walked around in sunglasses all the time. By the end of the week the glasses were gone, replaced by perhaps too much makeup around the upper portion of her face.

People studiously avoided referring, even among themselves, to the possible implications of this incident. But a certain amount of empathy went out to CaroleAnne which had heretofore perhaps been lacking, as are all relations in a formal environment such as ours.

It may have also helped that any job she was given to do was done superbly. In that regard, she was the soul of consistency itself.

This efficacy was more important than ever, for during the fall days that first year, before the cold set in for good, November 10 to be precise, Harb was given a large promotion, one that generated a host of new job duties while, ironically, dramatically cutting his number of direct reports, narrowing his everyday world to a mere handful of devoted lieutenants and teammates, myself included.

Harb was named executive vice president of corporate process and procedure, which was a fancy way of saying he was now in charge of the establishment and maintenance of Quality nationwide. Quality with a capital Q is now sort of a laughable concept, but back then it was a huge, huge deal.

The program in our establishment was called 2P/3G, which was pronounced all in a mouthful just that way: "Two Pee three Gee." It was never said with anything approaching a smile. Two Pee three Gee was dead serious. The clever designation, invented by the Old Man, our chairman, stood for "Profit and Performance—Going, Going, Gone!" It didn't matter what stupid thing you called it. It was our holy grail, and we were expected to bow down before it.

There was some business reason behind the Quality exercise in its most simple and least baroque form. The corporation was growing beyond its means to manage its service to customers, so Harb was in charge of nothing less than the future well-being of the entire company. It was all about delivering to our customers on the promises we had made to earn their trust. Is there anything more important? Obviously not.

Harb had the ear of senior management. He was hot.

It was the late 1990s, in the days before the most recent serious market adjustment, if you remember. The bulls were running free in the streets, goring the insufficiently gung-ho and those who weren't prepared to run fast enough. There seemed no end to the possibilities of capitalism driven by the hedonistic, crazed, idiotic stock market. All things seem not only conceivable but also imminent. IPO's! Internet companies trading at an infinite multiple of their nonexistent cash flow! Stock options issued in 1995 were now worth roughly ten times their value. Ones from before that were coming together in no great number to form summer houses and BMWs and even an occasional trip to Stanford or Brown. Nobody exercised these options, though. Were you kidding? There was no place to go but up, right?

Harb, among others, did consider exercising a few of his stock options, to help pay for the new house he'd just purchased in order to live in manorial splendor with his admirable wife, Jean, and his kids, one boy, one girl, I believe. No, no. I'm quite sure of it. Charles, whom they called Chas, was the elder child, and . . . what was it? . . . oh, that's right. Katherine. He called her Kiki. She would often call during the workday, and Harb would sometimes interrupt his meetings to discuss things with her. The boy called less often and was, I think, more serious. Jean called almost not at all, but he at times called her. She was younger than he, and more attractive, and rarely attended corporate events and social gatherings, possibly because she had to care for the children, as he said, or possibly for other reasons. I've never enjoyed those events much myself, and I work here. I don't blame her for staying away is my point.

Where was I? Oh, yes. Options. This was quite interesting and spoke of Harb's new status. He announced his intention, via the corporate hot line dedicated to this purpose, to exercise some of his more valuable options—issued when the stock was at sixteen dollars—when the price of our shares hit thirty-five dollars, as it was expected to do in the next several days, given market conditions and the creeks refusing to rise. He declared to me, with a greedy glint in his eye that I recognized as not dissimilar to my own each morning as I opened the stock page, that he not only intended to help pay for his new patio, he also wanted to buy both Chas and Kiki new computers, "real screamers," as he put it, and buy Jean a new Leica camera, which she had been drooling over for several years but could not afford to purchase while they were still trying to build a college fund and Harb was not yet earning fuck-you money.

That morning, Harb called to exercise ten thousand or so of these valuable options. It was approximately eleven A.M., and the stock had hit thirty-four, and he decided not to wait any longer. Several minutes after he hung up from the ostensibly confidential call, there was a knock at Harb's door. It was this fellow from Finance, Mooney. He was one of those nice guys, the ones with the rosy, chubby cheeks who would love to play golf with you the morning before they surprise you after lunch by eliminating your secretary. The details of this conversation are unimportant, but the gist was simple: As the corporate official in charge of helping senior officers manage their money, Mooney had an opinion about the wisdom of Harb's impending stock divestiture, i.e., that it would be an ill-considered move, that the stock was headed for fifty dollars!—and also bad for morale if it became known that he had exercised a bunch of options right in the middle of the booming market, which was certain to keep on booming as long as influential senior people did not unload their shares in a show of low confidence in both the company and the overall economy.

Harb certainly did not want to betray any nonexecutive levels of confidence. So he did not exercise his options at that time.

Of course it is understood that Harb didn't bother CaroleAnne with his financial dilemmas and CaroleAnne did not burden Harb with her personal problems, but when he probed, she let him know what was going on with her. She wasn't a shy person, and when scratched, she gave. One might say that, once primed and flowing, she was even quite demanding of emotional investment in her own way, without the truculence that colors so many assertive contemporary personalities. Sometimes, it was true, she upped the ante by weeping. Harb took to having a large box of extrasoft tissues on his desk for such eventualities, and CaroleAnne depleted it with some regularity.

I walked by Harb's office door one summer afternoon and heard the following bit of conversation, which I will divulge even though I am aware it is not my particular right to do so.

HARB: Come on now, Carrie.

CAROLEANNE: Never mind. *(Sobs)* There's nothing that can be done about it. You love someone and you think you know him, and then it turns out you don't. And he proves that again and again . . . and yet, you have hope. The hope is what makes the whole thing so . . . pathetic. *(Sobs)*

HARB: Come on, Cees. Life is too short. *(Puts his hand on her shoulder. She weeps more. Harb hands her a tissue as she sobs into her open hands, a look of extreme hatred calcifying his features, which he takes no pains to hide.)* We'll take care of this thing, don't you worry. Don't you worry now. Don't you worry.

CAROLEANNE: Oh, Harb. I try and try. But I just don't . . . see . . . see a solution to any of it. You just can't stop loving someone simply because he's not worthy of your love.

HARB: Come on, Cees. The guy is a loser.

CAROLEANNE: Yeah. Well. And I'm still there.

Harb then made a noise that was hard to interpret, a mixture of pity and disgust at the entire situation, I think. CaroleAnne had stopped crying. She sat staring vacantly out the window while Harb went back to his desk and pretended to sign documents.

After a couple of minutes, she seemed to be breathing somewhat easier. Harb continued to sign things, I have no idea what, since we don't really need to sit and sign things for hours. It sure made things quiet and peaceful. He appeared pretty careful not to be looking at her while he was about his official duties. Eventually I had to admit I had no reason to be loitering around in those environs. I made a noisy display of finishing my soda and getting back to my office.

Aside from these occasional summer storms of emotion, what separated CaroleAnne even then from the general tenor of our little group was how strikingly individual and revealing were her overall aspect and behavior. Many people cloak their true selves, if such a thing can be said to exist, reserving their genuine personalities for other locations. CaroleAnne appeared to be always 100 percent whatever person she appeared to be. When she was merry, she was wreathed in smiles. When troubled, dark storm clouds hung around her brow like thunderheads over Parnassus. When a thought crossed her mind, she expressed it. If she had nothing to say, she was comfortable existing in silence. She had a way of making one feel quite comfortable, because it seemed she was completely comfortable with some inner self over which she had command. What you saw with CaroleAnne was evidently what you got. Not one member of our group believed otherwise.

Especially Harb, who was suddenly a different level of big shot. I remember the party we had in his honor when his new office was established at the end of 1997. Total Quality had just been given the dry, slightly medicinal kiss of the Old Man himself, and boy, did we get loaded! Scotch! Beer! Wine! Sangria!

Not CaroleAnne, though, for CaroleAnne, incredibly, was not drinking. I wondered at the time, munching on the last olive in my third martini, if that lonely purity altered her perception of us. What was it like being the only sober person at a party jammed with drunken imbeciles caterwauling and lurching around the dark and smelly watering hole around the corner from the office?

What do you think?

4

The trappings are better for guys in charge of achieving productivity. Harb's new phalanx of officers was completely expanded and renovated as befit the importance of the process of which Harb was duke. What was created almost overnight with Sheetrock and prefab soundproofed dividers was a huge battle headquarters virtually devoid of human life, stretching the best part of an enormous floor at the dead center of our enterprise. We all had more room than we knew what to do with. Televisions and Bloomberg machines in every office. Drab postmodern art that you couldn't object to because it was so nondescript. The works.

Harb had migrated to a major corner, with a terrific view of the lake. As his right hand and sword, CaroleAnne now merited a gigundo space, one pretentious and awesome in its implications. There were staff vice presidents who had inferior territory to hers, and certainly the junior members of the department like Blatt could have fit their offices into her area three or four times over, and don't believe they didn't notice it.

The Quality hounds didn't spend a lot of desk time, though. The meeting schedule was intense. The travel was intense. A lot of the time, I had to get out on the road too, and I won't lie to you and tell you I didn't enjoy it. The road is fun, especially for a party animal. I'm not saying I conform to that description, but I assure you I can handle a cocktail or two when called upon to do so.

It's impossible for me accurately to enumerate exactly how many times I traveled with Harb. Here, however, is an estimate:

Business Destinations

Joint Travel: Robert Harbert and Fred Tell

City	# of Times Visited
Houston	12
New Orleans	9
Los Angeles	23
New York	35
Bonn, Germany	7
Paris, France	6
Rio de Janeiro, Brazil	5
Skokie, Illinois	4
Sun City, South Africa	3
Riyadh, Saudi Arabia	2
Other cities (i.e., Bridgeport)	1,134

Most of the time, it was amazing how little content there was to our journeys. Classically, we would fly in, either just the two of us or with a somewhat larger group, and check into the finest hotel in town. This was often not the Elysium it seems. Hotels can put you in spaces called deluxe that are actually converted broom closets, especially in pretentious, recently renovated places in major cities. No-smoking floors can smell like the inside of a camel's mouth. Wake-up calls do not come. Public conveyances can be dangerous and inconsistent.

But whatever its hazards and annoyances, the traveling life was the one most of us now called our own and we kind of dug it. You get into the swing of it after a while and lose your desk self, which is not always unpleasurable. You feel somewhat footloose. It's not a bad thing, if taken in doses. If you're not sufficiently centered, however, the road can present certain dangers. You have to know yourself and keep certain things in mind pertaining to the inevitability of return, or you can get yourself into some trouble.

The churn of executive movement could produce an assortment of weird personnel issues back at the home office, as one cluster or another sallied forth and another contingent stayed at home, creating temporary realignment of power vectors throughout the workplace. This was most true when Harb traveled without the assistance of CaroleAnne, leaving her at home to fend for herself in an office that was mostly, but not entirely, congenial.

For there was one corporate soldier who remained for the most part off the road. Dick Podesky stood fast, ever on the job, with no function to speak of but with an executive title equal to Harb's. The only reason this became somewhat important was that Dick did not like CaroleAnne, not one bit. No, Dick did not buy CaroleAnne's act at all, unfortunately. This led to the first unhappy conflict, which seemed so silly at the time but upset CaroleAnne much more than any of us could possibly suspect.

Harb had been away for an incredible ten days, leading a Quality symposium in a succession of one-restaurant burgs, but I was in, having just returned from something I forgot the moment it was over. That's true of so much as you move forward through life, don't you think? I view it as a blessing.

During the time Harb was away, I could see Dick growing more and more impatient with CaroleAnne—her style, the sound of her voice, her relentless cheerfulness, her chattering on the phone during downtime, even her occasional tendency to give herself a shot of Binaca after a smoke downstairs. She just seemed to grate on his delicate nerves, first thing in the morning, when he was stone cold sober, and after lunch as well, when he was not. He held his tongue. He arched an eyebrow. And he waited, one slightly yellow, rheumy, glistening eye trained on her for something that he could use against her when the time came. Executives are rarely happy unless they are either reacting to or creating some crisis or other. Many require anger in order to function. I could see Dick whetting his blade for a little action, but there was really nothing I could do, short of being obviously friendly to CaroleAnne, thereby indicating on which side of the issue I was likely to fall.

I knew Dick would wait for Harb's return, since corporate etiquette stipulates that one executive of the same rank may not assault another's subordinate but must raise the issue with that executive during the normal course of business.

Harb returned, exhausted and vague, as one can be after more than a week presenting the corporate face. Dick greeted him warmly, as did we all. A day or two went by. Then Dick found his opportunity and made the most of it.

What happened was this: CaroleAnne was on the way one morning to get everyone some coffee. This was not part of her job description, but she was accustomed to doing it anyhow, without complaint. Often I would see her, singing a quiet song to herself in her fetching little contralto, brewing a potful of java at the Mr. Coffee. That morning, just at the moment she was passing by the office of Dick Podesky, the door to that room opened, and Dick himself emerged, shined and buffed for the new day as usual, with a pair of Japanese businessmen in tow.

"Good morning, Dick!" CaroleAnne sang out.

I knew it was trouble right off. Not that people didn't call Dick Dick. They did. Certainly nobody called him Richard. But when visitors were in the office, it was sort of assumed that, when he was in the mood for formality, support staff would refer to him by name either not at all or as Mr. Podesky. Louise, as confused as she was by many aspects of corporate life and work, at least had known this much. Shelly, certainly, had this portion of her duties down cold. CaroleAnne, on the other hand, seemed to have the unfortunate belief that everyone within hailing distance was if not her friend, then at least a working peer. It's a nice illusion. I was sorry she was about to lose it.

Unaware of the storm that was about to strike her tiny dinghy, CaroleAnne breezed insouciantly by, and I took a quick peek at Dick to see if my initial reaction was justified. It was. The Japanese dignitaries having departed with the traditional orgy of bowing, Podesky had walked very slowly and thoughtfully to the center of our main work area with an expression of implacable calm and just stood there for a long while. This was a bad sign. It meant that Dick was trying to think seriously about something, and that exercise always made him trend toward a certain meanness of spirit.

After a few moments, back came CaroleAnne again with the empty coffee cups in her hands. This was her routine. She would go to the vestibule where the department coffeemaker was ensconced, set up the brew, retrieve each person's mug and bring it to his or her desk, including her own and Shelly's. Several minutes later, when the coffee was done, she would retrieve the pot and go from desk to desk, dispensing. As each cup was filled, she would invariably say, "God bless," in an unpretentious but somewhat overly serious way, and depart. I believe she invented this system in the very first days of her employment, after trying out the method of bringing out individual cups one by one (too time-consuming and servile, I would guess) and transporting a number of portions out together on one tray (chance of a major accident that could possibly ruin one of the few officeworthy outfits in her possession).

I don't know about anyone else, but I appreciated the fact that CaroleAnne was willing to do this. It did not demean her in my sight. She was hired to be a support person. Coffee is an enormous support, is it not? The knowledge that there was someone so unassuming about herself that she was willing to act out this part was also a blessing in a world full of unhelpful self-aggrandizers. It made me think more of her, actually, not less.

At any rate, CaroleAnne was breezing back with the empty coffee cups. She detoured around the inert form of Podesky, who was standing there, doing his version of fuming ostentatiously.

"Excuse me, Dick," said CaroleAnne with exquisite deference and bad timing.

That seemed to do it for Dick. He snapped to attention, looked around him as a man who had just awakened from a lengthy trance, went into Harb's office and closed the door. I heard voices, then louder voices, then some shouting. The shouting was all in Dick's voice and I knew that he was treating Harb to one of his deplorable yelling episodes. Awful things they were, really. A grown man, blown up like a distended puffer fish, expelling air at high volume simply because no one would challenge his right to do so. I've always found such yelling in the office to be distasteful. Not everyone does it, but those who do cannot, I fear, be dissuaded. I believe they think it speaks of power. It does not. It testifies to nothing but petulance and weakness. Of course, that's just my opinion.

I went to the closed door of Harb's office and leaned against the outer credenza, pretending to read a memo. The conversation from that vantage point was quite audible. Across the room, CaroleAnne was cringing with the coffeepot, her eyes as big as Frisbees.

Dick had stoked himself up quite a goodly snit by that point. "Damn it, Harb! I won't have it!" he choked out through the closed door.

"Quiet, Dick. Please," purred Harb. "There's no reason the office needs to hear you."

"I don't want her calling me that." So that was it. The Dick thing.

"Dick," said Harb.

"It's disrespectful!"

"Dick." Harb was impossibly temperate. "I don't know how to convey this message to you. Everybody calls you Dick. Nobody calls you Mr. Podesky. How should I tell her that all of a sudden she's the only one in the whole building who's got to call you Mr. Podesky? It's going to confuse her, hurt her feelings. There's no reason for it."

"If you don't tell her, I will," Dick thundered. "She's your reportee and I don't want to interject myself, but I will if I have to. In private, perhaps we can make exceptions here and there. In public, I don't want her calling me Dick!"

"Okay, Dick," said Harb.

Dick strode to the door of Harb's office and swung it open with such ferocity that I barely had time to get out of the way in a nonchalant fashion. He went into his office and slammed the door with some flair. Harb sat there for a while, his office door ajar.

"CaroleAnne," he said, very low.

"Coming, Harb," said CaroleAnne in a barely audible murmur.

She went in and they closed the door. They were in there for a long time. After a while, CaroleAnne emerged. She went immediately to her desk and sat down, trembling. I thought I might try to make things better.

"Don't worry about it, Cee," I said to her, placing an avuncular hand on her shoulder. It felt as if I had touched a bunny fried on an electrical fence, and I removed my hand immediately.

"Oh, I'm not," she said, in a queer, constricted voice. "This is not the kind of thing a person should have to worry about."

"Well," I said. "I agree." I was glad to see she was handling things so well. Except for the big, salty tears that were coursing silently down her cheeks, one would have thought she had taken the entire incident in stride.

"The Lord will take care of his own," she said. Then she buried herself in some clerical chore or other, and that was all she would say to anyone, including Harb, for the rest of the day. The next morning she called in sick.

She never made coffee again.

5

We were now in the pleasant time between Halloween and Thanksgiving of that year. The frost was on the pumpkin. The ice crept over the corners of the pond outside my house. It was my very favorite time, a time of impending good fellowship, of incipient peace on earth and all that.

My dogs like to walk in the leafy forest on the weekends, and I've been known to accompany them, wandering far from home with a cigar in my mouth for several hours. There are days when I truly regret having to go to the air-controlled office on Monday mornings.

For a period of several days immediately prior to the four-day Thanksgiving weekend that really signals the beginning of the season of joy and redemption that invariably transforms our city into a triumph of holiday marketing, Harb came to a decision. CaroleAnne had been arriving at work later and later, and in increasingly disheveled condition. She never complained, nor did she make specific the situation that produced these injuries. But we all could guess. It didn't take a lot of imagination. Edgar was a brute and he was expressing the overall outlines of his character on her physical person. It was deplorable.

One morning she came in with a lump the size of a golf ball disfiguring her jawline. She sat stiffly at her desk, shuffling papers as if nothing were wrong. A mucilaginous silence descended on the office, with people tiptoeing around the whole area as if a shameful secret was being shared. After a while, Harb breezed in with his usual White Rabbit gee-I'm-so-very-late act and blew by into his office. A few minutes later, he emerged, sans coat and jacket, rolling up his sleeves and otherwise signaling that the time had come for some form of work or other. He strolled out and stopped to say good morning to CaroleAnne, who did not look up. She was trembling at a very high frequency, and a hectic glow suffused her cheeks.

"What's that, Ceece?" said Harb quietly, after looking at her for perhaps three seconds.

"It's not something I can really talk about, you know," said CaroleAnne, staring before her calmly.

"Did . . ." said Harb. He started over. "I mean . . . what," he said. Then he stopped and just sort of gazed at her, at a loss.

"There's nothing to talk about," said CaroleAnne, and turned the full force of her most mesmeric gaze upon him. Her eyes were enormous pools of despair.

"Yes," said Harb, his own eyes suddenly brimming. "I see that." He went back into his office and closed the door. After a couple of minutes, CaroleAnne went to the coffee area, where I believe Louise had brewed a horrible pot, got a cup of high-test, added Harb's specific requirements vis-à-vis nondairy creamer and Sweet'n Low, took it to his closed door and, throwing it open without ceremony, entered the office of the executive vice president.

"Come on, Harb," I heard her say. "We're up to our ass in alligators and you can't be moping around in here."

Further evidence of the desperation of CaroleAnne's position was forthcoming. Telephone calls from a threatening outside entity came with increasing regularity. I answered several myself. The voice, quite gruff, would ask to speak to CaroleAnne and would brook no opposition. If CaroleAnne was not at hand, the voice, dripping with hostility and suspicion, would demand to know where she was. On those occasions when she was available and would get on the phone, the conversation was all one-way. She would say, "Yes," and sometimes "Yes, baby," these responses becoming ever more infrequent, until all that could be heard in the quiet office was the sound of a person at a very great distance, barking like a dog into a telephone line. After these calls, CaroleAnne was no particular good to anyone for perhaps an hour. After that, she was completely herself and quite agreeable, I think, for one in her predicament.

The only difference in her comportment, perhaps, was a tendency to sit and stare into the middle distance without expression when she believed no one was looking at her. I was, however, and the general effect this expression produced was truly pathetic, even in an individual as hardened to employee suffering as am I.

I should note that her performance continued to be simply fantastic. She had now graduated to the de facto role of office manager, although she did not enjoy either the title or the money that came along with true recognition of that responsibility. She attended a considerable number of Harb's meetings with him, to take notes and capture actions that would perhaps need to be taken as a result of the discourse. Her output was impeccable. She still looked rather bizarre at times for a corporate setting. But beyond a little ribbing now and then about her tendency toward unpunctuality and her somewhat flamboyant attire, she was quite appreciated by everyone except, perhaps, for Dick Podesky, but he had less and less to do with the mainstream life of the operation, so this was not intolerable. Everyone has enemies. The ability to sustain your existence in an environment in which you are hated by one or more persons, some more powerful than you, is what marks the survivor from his less fortunate counterparts.

Harb now avoided the aforementioned Podesky altogether and, in essence, no longer reported to anyone. Now and then he received a call from the executive floor and went up to have discussions and receive instructions. CaroleAnne never went to those meetings, of course. None of us did. Naturally, I had my own opportunities on the big floor as well with my ultrasenior officers, so I was not ignorant of the general sweep of things.

We were doing okay, in other words, or perhaps in exactly those words. We were doing okay. In a context such as ours, doing okay was a huge thing. There was no middle ground, and the only alternative to doing okay was clear: not doing okay, the consequences of which were immediate and dramatic.

CaroleAnne was a big part of us doing okay. And she was a lot better than okay herself. She made coming into work more entertaining and eliminated a huge layer of uncertainty that had previously made every day an unwelcome adventure. I was proud to have her in my department. And Harb . . . Harb was so gaga about the woman I was fearful for his safety. When she entered a room, he went all gooey inside. She made his heart race. Of course he never showed anything, not in the way you are perhaps thinking about at this moment. He would sooner have cut out his own tongue. His feelings about CaroleAnne were deeply embarrassing to him, because they gave him the kind of pleasure that does not belong in any workplace. She made him happy.

At any rate. There came an evening when CaroleAnne loitered at her desk long after the time at which she was accustomed to depart. She seemed unwilling to go. Harb and I were used to staying rather late and having the office pretty much to ourselves. But there was CaroleAnne. "Give me a minute," said Harb to me. I could tell that a determination to engage on some human level was rising within him and could not be checked. He had the look of chivalry on his face. I didn't like it.

"Harb, man," I said. "You can't solve everybody's problems."

"Not everybody's," he said, and I saw he was committed. As I have said, he didn't have a strong face, but when his mind was made up about something it acquired a mild, pugnacious look that was not unpleasant. It was the demeanor of a small but feisty child who intended to do something much larger than his size would warrant. "Come in, Annie," he said to CaroleAnne. It was a name he used for her when he was at his most tender. None of us followed suit, but I assure you at the time it didn't seem inappropriate. Are loyalty and affection ever out of place? I think at this point we could all say with some definition that the answer to that semi-rhetorical question is yes, of course they are. Back then I thought differently.

They left the door open, as they almost always did. I moseyed by only once, to get a stapler I didn't need. CaroleAnne was bent over in her chair, her head in her hands, sobbing quietly, her entire frame shaking. Harb was standing well away from her, across the expanse of his desk, simply staring at her grimly.

"You have to do something," I heard him say. "I can't solve this thing for you. I can help. But it's gonna have to be you."

"It's easy to say," CaroleAnne said, speaking down into her hands, which were now folded in her lap. "I don't know why I can't pull the trigger. I know I have to. But . . . every day goes by and nothing changes. Maybe nothing ever changes. Did that ever occur to you? That it's all a big illusion? That there's no change . . . there's just . . . fate?"

"Gee," said Harb, "I hope not." Then there was a truly massive pause that made me increasingly nervous as it maintained itself. What was going on in that silence? "It's not always easy to get out of somewhere you don't want to be," said Harb at last.

Then there was a great deal more silence. If I didn't know any better, I would say that inside that silence was the sound of a man snuffling into a handkerchief, but at the time I found that too incredible to believe. I didn't dare look into that office, for I knew that what was going on in there was totally out of proportion to anything I had ever encountered in a business setting. It left me quite unsettled and badly in need of a drink, which I secured at the earliest possible moment.

About a week later, CaroleAnne moved to one of the company-owned apartments in town. This was no big deal for an employee, by the way. We own quite a few housing complexes in the Chicagoland area and, indeed, around the world. But there is a waiting list for quality domiciles in the city. This one was in a reconditioned area that was quite sought after. I figured the normal waiting time for such a space would be, say, five to ten years. She moved in just before Christmas.

I saw the place, at a little housewarming gathering CaroleAnne threw for herself. I have to say it was done up beautifully. Harb seemed proud of it as well. I got the feeling that he chose much of the furniture himself, but it's possible they had a decorator and worked with him.

6

It was Christmas at last. The office was full of wassail, even rather early in the day, and I'm generally a big wassail supporter. That year was no exception, perhaps because I felt certain storm clouds gathering. The daily doses of booze and too much lunch take care of those kinds of thoughts, making it easier, nay, possible, I guess, to sustain the mandatory jocularity and forced religiosity of the season, which ends in perhaps the most depressing of all enforced holidays: New Year. Ah, New Year! A time of reflection and self-investigation, of celebration and comradeship—or not.

I did not mean to imply that the obligatory lack of temperance is not effective as a tonic for the demands of those weeks. It is, at least for me, and makes what we now in our deracinated day refer to as "the Holidays" perhaps the nicest time of year for those who do not happen to be laid off, even better than the summer, when people generally expect you to work a little bit.

The discrepancy between what is and what should be, however, is always most garish at that time of year. So naturally Harb began to have some trouble at home. He didn't talk about it much, but I could tell. He often arrived a little earlier than usual and in what was for him a rather foul mood. One time I asked him about it.

"Hey, man," I said to him one morning as he sat staring disconsolately into his coffee cup. "What happened to the can-do corporate Quality warrior whom I always found to be such a pain in the ass?"

"What's your deal?" he replied, staring at me with stony lack of amusement. I could see he was in no temper for badinage, so I got out of there. I'm too old to deal with stuff that's obviously going to be an immediate bummer right from the get go.

It could be the work, I thought, as I fortified myself with a little breakfast eggnog. The tasks at hand were massive and disorganized, due to the peculiar form of idiocy inherent in their makeup at the end of the year. But I knew it wasn't the work. It was something closer to where the real man lived.

Observing my testy friend from a distance those days, I saw him eating quite a bit of aspirin and drinking perhaps too much coffee. We spoke somewhat less than usual, and to tell you the truth, I began to feel a little neglected. He was, after all, my pal. The fact that he didn't feel comfortable discussing his problems with me caused me pain. I tried again in the elevator one Friday afternoon.

"Big weekend?" I inquired affably.

"Nah," he said. He stood there, briefcase in hand, staring at the doors of the elevator with unseeing eyes. After a moment, he turned that canine gaze on me, and I got a little chill. "We got nothin' goin' on," he said, and turned once again to the stainless steel a foot from his expressionless face. "Perhaps we'll go shopping for a garbage can at The Container Store," he added with a truly odd flatness I couldn't quite read. Then the doors opened and he got out and split for the revolving doors in the lobby with a perfunctory wave over his shoulder. I don't think he meant anything by it. He just didn't want to give me any more of himself right then. I tried not to be hurt, but it did sting a little.

I did, however, figure that whatever was going on at home, I would find it out eventually. Whatever it is, I always do.

As often happens, discord and misery on the personal front go hand in hand with professional achievement. Harb was spending a lot more time on the executive floor now. It was clear something either very good or quite the opposite was in the works for him, for us. I was guessing it was good, because of the level of stress it seemed to be imposing on him. Remember, when things were bad,

Harb looked good. Now, honestly, he looked quite terrible. So things must have been getting kind of great.

I should probably note for the record that at the time I processed Harb's W2 for the year, his total income fell just short of seven figures. Perhaps a half dozen executives in our multibillion-dollar corporation earned more than Harb. His options, too, were significant and would be certain to produce real long-term wealth if he was not for some reason forced to leave the bosom of the enterprise, which was very capacious, warm, and perky as bosoms go.

As was normal in times that presaged a certain kind of very visible success, Harb chose this moment to lose control of his back. Once it started acting up, Harb's back, it just didn't quit. When I first met him, he was one of those guys whose backs would go out every now and then, leaving them a huffing, whining invertebrate trembling in discomfort on the floor. He would be doing something completely innocuous—reaching for the phone, turning to pick up a calendar—and suddenly his whole frame would be wracked with pain and he would collapse in a heap, moaning. We got used to this after a while. Several of us would gently help Harb to his feet, walk him gingerly to his office couch, lie him quite flat, with no pillow beneath his head, and leave him lying, frozen, waiting for the horrible spasm to subside. After several years of this, Harb had gone away for a while, but not a very long while, and reemerged, completely healed, after arthroscopic surgery of some sort. There ensued several years of moderate comfort for him, or at least I believe it to have been so, because he never thereafter complained. Until that winter. Then, on one December morning not too far from the deadest week of the year, when all major duties had been accomplished and there was little left to do but relax and think about the days ahead, Harb came to work one morning almost completely bent over into a human question mark.

"Oh, no," I said to him. Harb's skin was pure white, with a slightly greenish undertint. His hands shook. He walked with exquisite

46

tenderness and placed himself in his chair. I sat with him for a short time, and then I had to leave. I can't stand watching somebody in pain, and that's the truth. It's a weakness in my character; I freely admit it.

That afternoon, I happened to walk past Harb's door looking for either a pencil or some decent conversation, whichever came first and, truthfully, to see whether Harb was fit for human consumption. CaroleAnne was in Harb's office with him.

He was on his stomach, facedown on the floor, fully dressed. CaroleAnne was walking on his back, strolling slowly and carefully up his poor, damaged spine. When she came to the base of his neck, she turned around carefully with a graceful half spin and headed back in the other direction. She had removed her high heels, obviously, and through the darkened tip of her panty hose I could see each of her individual toes digging into a different vertebra. I know this will sound somewhat incredible, but there seemed nothing wrong in this scenario to me. We had all tried to help Harb in one way or another. Perhaps, I thought, this exotic method of CaroleAnne's would prove more effective than the cup full of scotch I had offered him one September afternoon several years ago, which almost got him fired when he was called into an upstairs meeting shortly after its consumption.

The door was open and there was nothing clandestine about this episode, by the way. As I said, Harb had his shirt and tie still on, of course, but his jacket was off. More businesslike yet, in CaroleAnne's hands were a pad and pencil, which she was using to good effect as she walked across her human terrain with perfect balance, writing. As I got a little closer I could hear Harb speaking as he lay facedown on the carpet. He was dictating.

"Hi, Fred," CaroleAnne said as I entered. "I didn't get that last little bit about the purchasing pipeline vis-à-vis the controlling function," she said as she carefully inserted her heel between two of his vertebrae.

I must have looked a little shocked.

"Don't worry, Mr. T.," said Harb. That was his name for me

when he was in a very good mood. His voice was muffled because his face was in the carpet. "You can have one when I'm done."

"Hey," said CaroleAnne, "I'll be the judge of that."

Even if she offered, of course I wouldn't have taken one. I have worked in this place for a long time and not once, beyond a perfunctory nudge in the elbow or insincere shoulder squeeze, has anyone touched me, and I guess we're going to keep it that way.

Right before the first of the new year, Harb gave the entire department its performance reviews. I went over them all with him. That's the way we do things. We have standards, practices. These aren't just whims we act upon, you know. I had to agree with him that there was in fact no performer on the entire floor superior to CaroleAnne. She was absolutely indispensable to our operation. She was worth ten of anyone else. We looked at what she was making, as compared, say, to a worthless MBA like Blatt, and together we authorized a 25 percent raise for her.

This still brought her to less than seventy grand, however—sixty-seven K, to be exact. On top of that, she was not yet eligible for the bonus pool. So, unbeknownst to me, Harb wrote CaroleAnne a personal check for three thousand dollars to help make up that deficit to the big, round number. This is quite uncommon, and if I had known about my friend's generous impulse, I would have advised against it. That is perhaps why he didn't ask me. There is nothing wrong with it in actuality. But it carries the appearance of impropriety to those who see bad motivation at the root of all human behavior—which these days includes just about everybody, don't you think?

With this money, it turned out, the grateful CaroleAnne was able to plan a visit to her ailing mother who now resided in Baltimore. Unfortunately, it turned out that the cost of the plane ticket would significantly eat into this unexpected windfall from Harb, which would sort of defeat the purpose of this, her only cash award of the bonus season. To solve this problem, and to assure that CaroleAnne's relatives in Baltimore received the gifts she, as a dutiful and beloved family member, had selected for each of them, Harb gave CaroleAnne something truly remarkable. True, it was something he no longer had any need for, an object that was all but worthless to him at the moment it was given, but as a demonstration of friendship and true affection I have yet to see it equaled.

"Here," he said on that frigid, gunmetal gray winter afternoon, giving her a bundle of keys and standing proudly away from his plate glass windows, pointing down to the street below. "It's over there. See?"

CaroleAnne pretended not to understand, but I'm pretty sure she got it on the very first try. "What?" she said.

"See?" said Harb again. He pointed to an elderly Nissan automobile, one that I happened to know Harb had been using to get to the train on time for the past ten years or so. It had been washed for the occasion and driven in for this little ceremony. "Behind the graffiti-covered panel truck. It's a piece of junk. I'm taking a deduction on it. Just don't sue me when the wheels fall off."

"Harb," she said. "Thanks." She looked out the window. Then she said, "Thanks, Harb," again. Then she turned to him and put her hand on his cheek. It was at the end of the day and I saw he needed a bit of a shave, not a huge one but certainly a touch-up. "You're a sweet, sweet man," she said and planted for just one second, and certainly no more than five, a soft little kiss on the side of Harb's face. Harb blushed.

I can tell you now, as I have already told others time and time again, that there was absolutely nothing sexual in that kiss. Nothing at all. But I won't lie and tell you that there was no love in it. Love is what that season is all about, for goodness sake.

For those who see nothing but either purely charitable or thoroughly dastardly intentions in Harb's act, I must point out that for himself he bought as a replacement a new BMW Z3 roadster, in red, which he also loved very, very much. And so we were all very happy indeed that holiday time. Oh tidings of comfort and joy!

The next day CaroleAnne went to Baltimore for a two-week vacation. While she was gone, the entire office function fell apart. She returned on January 18, glowing with relaxation and happiness. Christ, it was good to have her back!

7

New Year's came and went, and with it the level of energy and resolve that always attends beginnings. The Quality Process was in full cry. Meetings took place across the nation. Meetings and meetings and meetings, and still more meetings, then meals that were nothing more than disguised meetings, then more meetings to plan subsequent meetings. Anyone who endured this at its height lost forever his taste for meetings.

One afternoon, after a truly grueling and stupid day where we quite literally saw each other over and over again for a sequence of gatherings whose discrete purposes were increasingly unclear, Blatt posted a humorous sign she had retrieved from a business magazine.

"Are you lonely? Hold a meeting," said the sign. Under the headline there was a graphic of people sitting around a conference table drinking coffee and yakking. The text then went on: "You can see people draw organizational charts, feel important and impress your colleagues, eat bagels, all on company time. Meetings, the practical alternative to work." And that was it. I thought it was pretty clever, actually.

"What's this?" CaroleAnne said to me somewhat later. She was looking at the sign and scowling.

"It's a joke," I said to her.

"I don't think it's very funny," she replied with surprising asperity. "I wonder at the things people do around here sometimes."

I disregarded this tiny outburst. We all get on each other's nerves on occasion. You can't pay attention to everything. The sign, it turned out, stayed up for many years, with certain consequences that will later become apparent.

51

The work went on, and with it the travel. Month after grueling month, back and forth and back and forth again, weaving through the great, chaotic tapestry of America, Harb traveled. Sometimes I came along for the ride, in conditions both good and less so. I feel about travel the way I feel about Sambuca. At first, it's sweet. After a while, it becomes sticky and disgusting, even when it has a coffee bean in it.

Most of the time, Harb was crushingly, amazingly alone. Perhaps that is why he began to take CaroleAnne with him with some regularity. On his own or with her help, he led hundreds upon hundreds of Quality conclaves, exhorting wary employees, fearful of noncompliance, to achieve the appearance of ever-greater levels of Quality, Customer Satisfaction, and Productivity.

At night in the fine hotels, whisper quiet and bathed in luxury, Harb lay awake, the flickering of the pay-per-view movie playing out across the room on a television too small for the space it was intended to fill. CaroleAnne was not next door. No, she was on another, lower floor, as befit her standing. But he could feel her in the hotel . . . almost smell her in his room. Why shouldn't he be able to smell her? He had been with her without interruption for more than eleven hours, from the first morning meeting to the end-of-day wrap-ups over dinner to drinks and salty trail mix at eleven P.M.

And what about those drinks? For Harb, it was martinis, mostly, although sometimes, to minimize the effect of the constant, daily onslaught of road life upon his liver, he switched over to beer over ice.

It was hard to escape the end of the day without these semi-informal nightcaps. Often they were conducted with a group of chattering, garrulous wahoos, with Harb at its dead center, the guru, the magnet, the best friend of everybody. But a fair amount of the time, particularly on the last day of a three-day Quality bender, it would be getaway night, and Harb would find himself unwinding with just a few trusted subordinates, and more often than not, only one, and that one would be the kind of person with whom you could truly drop all pretense and, for a few moments, be your real self, and generally, if that one person was there, in that city, at that time, that person would be CaroleAnne.

It is difficult to measure the significance and importance of this rite to those who don't have to work in costume for a living. The day is done. The tie is down around the sternum. The collar is open, as is the well-traveled path to a posh and blessedly silent space upstairs. There is, quite literally, nothing at all on the agenda. The drinks are on the table. The other individual is opposite, all yours. Between that moment and the instant of unconsciousness when you fall into the sleep that immediately precedes the horrible moment of awakening the next morning, a yawning chasm of opportunity beckons. More than any corporate activity, this ceremony of the nightcap is perhaps the most frightening in its lack of structure, its terrible, fierce purity. It is very possible that nothing but friendly human interaction will happen. But everything, for a few moments, is possible. And that makes it special, and different.

Consider it for a moment. You are Harb. A lovely, powerful, well-dressed, mysterious woman toys with her beverage on the bar that stretches like an unmade bed before the two of you. Nobody is counting how many drinks have crossed its scarred mahogany surface in your direction. It's all but deserted. The bartender is giving you looks. It's time to take the party someplace else, if it's going to continue at all. Funny how you never noticed the little flecks of green in the bottom of her deep black eyes, the way the corners of her mouth turn slyly upward when she's thinking about something funny you just said. And what was it you just said? You can't remember! Oh, good. She can't remember either. And look! Her blouse, which began the day all crisp and bright white and frisky, has, throughout the course of countless assaults of heat, wind, conditioned air, a couple of spilled condiments maybe, lost all its starch, and the top button that concealed her clavicles from view is open now, and she is leaning forward to get a light from you, and you smell the collected experiences of the day on her, and how easy it would be just to lean into that and touch her cheek, and what

53

would happen then? Alcohol clouds the judgment, buddy. Fatigue clouds the judgment. Distance from home clouds the judgment. Who declared judgment to be the be-all and end-all anyhow! Whoever he was never found himself at a Ramada Inn someplace in middle Iowa while the snow is falling on the silent one-stoplight town. And the country music is playing low, and you're not a job description anymore, not a role that has to be fulfilled, you're just a little person at the edge of the great big universe, Charley, and wouldn't it be nice to have a kiss now, just a little kiss, and after that little kiss perhaps a big one, a big old wet one you could fall into and never come out of again?

I'm just speculating, of course. But these are perhaps the thoughts that might be going through a person's mind in just such a circumstance.

And yet, virtually all the time, in spite of this and that, we still go back to our rooms, read the hotel magazine, drop off to sleep. Frankly, and this is just my editorial comment here, you don't have to listen to it, I think that continual, daily renunciation of bad action represents a form of heroism in this sorry society in which we live. You won't read about it anywhere, this form of heroism. But it exists, unknown and unsung.

And Harb? Friends, if I may call you that, Harb was the greatest hero of them all, at least the greatest I have known, because, as I have noted, he often found himself seated stool-to-stool, knee-to-knee with a slightly tipsy Nefertiti, the only barrier between them their mutual discretion, together battling the fact that, at bottom, they truly, at that point in time, adored each other on virtually every level it is possible for two adults to love each other without touching.

For yes, indeed, it is true—and it must be made clear before any erroneous ideas are permitted to flower—that, after that first chaste kiss in the office at holiday time, CaroleAnne and Harb did not kiss again ever, not even in friendship. They did, however, enjoy ongoing, massive amounts of opportunity to reevaluate that status. And they always passed with flying colors. There are many places where two determined people can kiss, and even more locations where those with equal determination can avoid kissing, and in each of both locales, I must report, Harb and CaroleAnne resisted temptation. Which is not to say that the avoidance and ultimate rejection of oral intercourse eliminated the inappropriate feelings between them, if such they were. No human power can do that, although many have tried. And as anyone who has ever avoided kissing when a simple, affectionate exchange of that nature would be the most natural thing in the world will tell you, resistance is the ultimate aphrodesiac. I cannot relate what the effect months of such exemplary behavior produced on CaroleAnne, for her feelings, as it will become apparent, were a mystery to me and others as well. But Harb, I can tell you, was a Roman candle waiting to erupt into the sky. What wouldn't I give to experience that feeling again!

And didn't he pay for it!

8

Meanwhile, back at the ranch, calls continued to come in from Edgar. I was there for most of them.

CaroleAnne's extension would ring at least once a day, sometimes more, even when all her business associates knew she was on the road, and for some extended period, too. Each time it was sent to voice mail, it immediately came back. About half the time, the caller would merely hang up when the wrong voice answered. In another, say, 25 percent of these incidents, there would be a similar disconnect, but it would be preceded by an appalling spray of profanity, and the noise of termination was more brutal. I was on the receiving end of one of those, and I can tell you, it chilled me.

The remaining calls were more bizarre still. There would be a rather long, ruminative pause at the other end of the line, then a haughty, educated voice would say something like, "Good morning, this is Mr. Hornby speaking. I wonder if Ms. CaroleAnne Winter is about?" We would invariably tell him no, first because it was true, she was about Kansas City or Provo, Utah, or some remote Quality location like that, not about where we could see her here in Chicago, and second, we were under strict instructions from Harb to do so. We were only too happy to comply. None of us wanted to see CaroleAnne wearing those great big knockoff Ray-Bans again.

"Well, then," Edgar would say, "I wonder if you can leave her word that Mr. Hornby called and would like to speak with her. It's somewhat important." Then he would hang up.

About the tenth time this happened, I answered the department phone, for lack of anything better to do. The Human Resources implications of the Quality Process are interesting, but only to subordinates. Sometimes the view from forty thousand feet can get tedious, and I was bored. So I answered the phone myself. There's no rule against it.

At the end of the conversation, when Edgar got to the part about calling Mr. Hornby, I don't know what came over me, some impish impulse perhaps. "Is that Hornby with an *H*?" I said. The office happened to be rather busy at that moment, with people just coming back from lunch, and more than a few people heard me. I believe Blatt was the most amused, to the point of launching a fair amount of Diet Coke from her nostrils.

On the other end of the wire, however, things were not quite so noisy, or so jocular. There was a cavernous silence from the instrument, to the point where I thought he had hung up, as was his habit. There being no thunder, however, I said, "Hello? Mr. Hornby? Are you there?"

"I'm here," said a voice, and it was a completely different voice altogether, a low, dark voice, dripping with hatred and sarcasm. I don't know how its owner managed to get contempt, enmity, and a determination to do harm if thwarted into two little words, but he managed admirably. "I'm here," is what he said, and I knew that not only was he there but that he would not go away, not ever.

"I'll tell her," I said in return and prepared to end this pleasant conversation.

"You do that, fuckface," said the voice, still more quietly.

"Oh," I said, and as if as an afterthought, "was that fuckface with the traditional *F*, or with a *Ph*?" It wasn't a good joke, I admit that. It wasn't even really a joke at all. It was, to be most charitable, a quip, that's all. In my defense I will say that I was both angry and a little frightened. I heard him breathing for a while. Then he hung up. I didn't answer the phone myself after that for a couple of weeks. I was freaked, I admit it. I'm a lover, not a fighter.

A few days later, Harb and CaroleAnne were back at their stations, as if nothing had happened, and as far as any of us knew at that point, nothing had. It was only later that Harb told me of his continuing moral conundrum on the road, which at that point had been worked out as much as any of these problems ever truly get resolved. But as I said, he told me about all of that some time later. At that point, all seemed very businesslike, both on his end and also with CaroleAnne.

"How you doing?" I said to her when she first appeared back at her desk.

"Righteous." She seemed to be telling herself a little secret.

"In the biblical sense?"

"I ate a lot of peanuts," she said to me as if confiding a very great secret. "Everywhere you go," she continued, "there's peanuts. Peanuts and little breath mints. It's like, they think you eat a lot of peanuts so you need the breath mints. But that's stupid, because if you're eating peanuts then everybody else around you is eating them, too, and so you don't need the breath mints."

"The peanuts make you thirsty so you have to drink a lot," I said. You will notice that I ignored the non sequitur. It was truly the only way to maintain an ongoing discourse with CaroleAnne, and frankly I got a kick out of them.

"Yes," said CaroleAnne very thoughtfully. "That is true. We drank a lot of beer."

"Beer is good."

"We met about a million people." She was emptying a vast suit-case/briefcase back into her filing cabinets. Her filing, as always, was a thing of beauty to watch. So I watched it. "I didn't like the pillows," she added after a time.

"Yeah," I said. "They're generally bad. Too squishy or too bouncy."

"What's nice is to put your head down on your own pillow. I got home last night and there it was. I almost cried when I saw it. Then I went to sleep. And I slept very nicely, you know? None of the waking in the middle of the night, screaming. No terrible dreams. None of the voices."

"Hmm?" I inquired. Perhaps I should have pursued this line of questioning more aggressively, in retrospect.

"It's funny, you know." She paused in her filing for a moment. "I used to live in a place that I thought was going to be my home forever. Then it turned out not to be. Now I have a new home. What makes that my home? The fact that my pillow is there?"

I didn't know what to say to this, so I said nothing, an approach that's always worked for me quite well. She resumed her work, placing her materials an object at a time into each one's appropriate spot.

"Skeeter?" said Harb from within his den. He was unpacking, too.

"When you gonna stop calling me that?" she said as she rose to join him. But she was smiling.

So if perhaps there was a bit too much familiarity between them, who was there to notice? And even if we noticed, who was there to say anything about it?

Almost immediately upon their return, I told Harb about the onslaught of communications from Edgar. I suppose it was bothering me, and I wanted to get it off my chest. One reads about such people as Edgar in the newspaper, particularly if they have access to automatic weapons, making visits to establishments such as ours with murder in their hearts. It was not inconceivable that what we had here was a matter that should possibly be routed to corporate security. I didn't really know. I thought Harb might. At any rate I didn't want to take any action upon the issue on my own recognizance that might later be regretted by parties more immediate to the situation.

As I talked about CaroleAnne's demented spouse, Harb's face grew dark and stern. I don't mean to convey the wrong impression here. Harb in intense, deep, and gloomy cogitation did not quite conjure up the image of a Viking king plotting the conquest of Northumbria. He rather appeared to me as, say, a thoughtful, intelligent, and determined squirrel who had just been presented with too big a nut to carry. "Get me a phone number for this guy," he said.

I did so.

"Let's get him on the horn," said Harb. "At lunchtime. When Cici is out." This was yet another new diminutive, and I noted it.

I went into Harb's office at about twelve forty-five, right after

CaroleAnne had gone down to the park for her surreptitious midday smoke, and sat down. Harb dialed. After a few moments, he spoke. "Hello, may I speak with Mr. Hornby, please? This is Mr. Hornby? Well, hello, Mr. Hornby. It's a pleasure to speak with you at last. This is Mr. Harbert. Uh-huh. Of course. By all means."

There was a brief pause. "He's getting his inhaler, apparently," said Harb. He leaned back in his recliner and put his feet up on his desk. He appeared to be enjoying himself. "Yes," he said. "Well, it's about CaroleAnne . . . uh-huh . . . uh-huh . . . nope, she's not coming back . . . no, I don't think that's going to happen . . . no, Mr. Hornby, I am not, as you say, fucking her . . . no, no, sir. Look. If you hit her again, I'm going to come to your house with four armed men and cut you into tiny little pieces. I work for a very large multinational corporation and don't think we can't get a job like that done quietly and efficiently . . ." Harb shot me a wink here, and I almost swallowed my tongue. What a kidder he was!

"Uh-huh," he said. ". . . well, what was it you had in mind, Mr. Hornby? . . . Yes. I'm aware that Ms. Winter represented fully one half of your household income . . . no, no, I wasn't aware of that part of it. I'm sure you were quite a support to her in those early years. Uh-huh . . . Well. Gee. I'm sorry to hear that. That kind of thing must be pretty rare. Goodness gracious." Harb put his hand over the receiver of the telephone and whispered to me with an absolutely flat expression and intonation, "It seems that Mr. Hornby has had several major diagnoses rendered at area hospitals and it has been discovered that he is incapable of holding a steady job because he is . . . allergic to the workplace." He uncovered the mouthpiece and spoke again. "I wonder if I could contribute some-thing personally to your treatment. Something that would help you in your search for a pleasant climate in which you could complete your recovery. I find that dry air was always good for my allergies. How about a relocation to, like, Phoenix? How would that grab you?" Harb got up and walked to the window, his receiver at his ear. "Uh-huh," he said, and then, "Wow, that's a lot." He slowly rubbed one hand over his broad, wide forehead. "Oh, what the hell.

Four installments, once a quarter for the next year. After that, you're on your own. We never want to see you again, Mr. . . . Hornby. I can back up that polite observation with some real unpleasant muscle if you want to test me. We have corporate security guys here who used to work in the federal penal institution downstate. You may not be unacquainted with them. Uh-huh. Not to mention the effect it might have on CaroleAnne to hear from me that I have paid you to get this treatment for your . . . condition. Let me see if I have your address." He listened. He wrote. "Let me know when you're in your new location, Mr. Hornby. Beyond that, don't call us, 'kay? Have a good one. Uh-huh? Right. See ya." Harb hung up.

"Well," he said, "that's that."

How far That was from being That only time and the brutality of circumstances would reveal, although to be fair we didn't see Edgar again for quite a while. And by then it was all over, even, alas, the shouting.

9

Time passes oddly in a corporate environment. Hours very often seem like days, years, even. And yet days can whisk by like dreams, and weeks evaporate in the mouth like cotton candy. Suddenly, it was summer.

CaroleAnne took to wearing gray suits and did something with her hair that created an entirely different, more executive look. Beyond that, nothing changed in her except, perhaps, underneath, and we couldn't see that then.

Sometime in the mid–third quarter, when the differential between the temperature outside and the conditioned air inside our hermetically sealed office produced condensation on the windows, the economy, which had been veering upward incoherently for month after crazy month, year after year after year, spun out and downward, exploding into tiny incandescent pieces like the doomed space shuttle.

By late August, confidence in the ability of growth companies to pay back loans had fallen precipitously. The entire financial services business found itself sitting on a mountain of bad debt. We essentially closed up shop as far as the issuing of loans was concerned and began relentlessly focusing on squeezing repayment out of desperate, failing customers. We had become, almost overnight, little more than a high-profile, glossy, pretentious collection agency.

"The Quality Process generates no income," Harb observed many times. How right he was. "The process is built upon the principle of continuous improvement," the core white paper on the subject stated in its preamble. "Continuous improvement leads to superior positioning and customer satisfaction in the marketplace which, in turn, produces growth. Growth is our vision and our goal." Many an eye grew moist when that passage was read aloud for the first time by the Old Man.

In a flagging environment, however, when no one is growing revenue on the top line, doing everything possible just not to slip back into negative digits, squishy, cultural improvement efforts like Quality often appear superfluous to the initiated and uninitiated alike. Yesterday's prime directive may in this way become tomorrow's hula hoop.

That terrible autumn, Harb was at the top of a small, focused organizational chart that had an impact on hundreds of Quality coordinators, secretaries, mendicants, priests, oracles, converts, hypocrites, and true believers whose work produced nothing but better work in others. This was not a hierarchy whose existence could be justified in any but the most boomish of times. Harb knew it. We all knew it. But we kept on living, hour to hour, day to day, aware of the tickticktick of the inevitable corporate clock as it grew louder. We did not ask for whom it ticked.

I saw him very often during those days, sitting at his desk simply staring into space. Travel had abruptly been cut back to the point of nullity. No trip was smiled upon from corporate headquarters that had not been specifically requisitioned by the field. In short, if they didn't ask you to come, you didn't go, and since the field was required to pick up much of the tab when corporate folks came to town, the fact that Quality was no longer a mandatory activity handed down from Zeus sliced the number of invitations down to subzero.

Keep in mind, too, that the commissars of Quality had been relieved from all operating duties other than that attending the transformation of our culture and you will have some sense of the corner into which a guy like Harb had been painted by his role as standard-bearer of this time-dated fad. And what was true for him was true for his troops as well. In short, they had nothing to do. Paranoia walked the halls in big, bold strides, and we cleared a path before it.

During this period of forced indolence, those who were used to spending their lives away from home were suddenly forced to participate in their domestic environments at a level of intensity to which they were somewhat unaccustomed. This is a happy eventuality for those whose marital situation is basically solid. These kinds of mandated, extended shore leaves, however, tend to reveal the splits and cracks in the relationships of those less happily situated, bumps and other relational blemishes that are customarily concealed by the constant removal of the corporate spouse to regions unknown. Harb found himself at home by the good old hearth quite a bit is the point I'm making. And that, it turned out, was not a good thing entirely.

On any given evening, Harb would plant his fanny on the six fifty-two, his briefcase taking its place by his side in the hope that no fat commuter would dare displace it. He would sip on a double vodka with a splash of tonic and twist of lime, and when that was polished off he would slip into a light doze timed exactly to expire ninety seconds before his train hauled into the local station. He would then step into his car and drive the five minutes to his home.

At approximately seven thirty-seven, he would step into his kitchen, where Jean would generally be found doing one of two things, either cooking a meal on the stove or loading the contents of take-out containers onto plates. Either way, Harb kissed her hello, sometimes on the cheek, sometimes a small implant on the mouth, and would then hie himself off to a cabinet under the sink where the vodka was housed. He would construct himself a large alcoholic edifice and drink it standing while hearing the various news of the day from his wife, some of which he listened to.

At seven fifty-six, they would sit down to dinner either with the kids or not. Suburban children of a certain age have quite a bit to do and are often fed earlier and set loose to accomplish homework, attend lessons or tutoring of some sort, or simply honk away online until bedtime.

Between eight-seventeen and eight-thirty, dinner would be concluded. Harb would then go into the family's living room and join whatever entertainment was in progress. Sometimes Chas was playing a video game and Harb would crouch down in front of the PlayStation and watch, or even, on occasion, take part, if the game was easy or violent enough.

"My favorite is Grand Theft Auto," he told me one time. "You get to kill a lot of people and smash a bunch of cool cars into stuff."

"What do you see in that?" I asked him.

"It's a good way of relating to Chas on a level we both can understand," he said.

Sometimes Harb would just lie on the couch and watch television. The selection was always made by someone other than himself, which was fine because he was inherently interested in nothing. Kiki liked reality programming. Jean, when she was done in the kitchen, would come in and put on a DVD if nothing else was on. In this way an hour or so would pass. It was then nine-thirty. At that time, Harb would excuse himself, go upstairs, and fall asleep on his bed, fully clothed.

At eleven-seventeen, Jean would come upstairs, having fallen asleep in front of the news downstairs. The children were in their rooms, on-line. By eleven thirty-three, Harb was changed into what passed for his pajamas and was sleeping soundly.

At three-oh-seven, he would invariably awaken and stare up at the dark ceiling until sleep came to him again, usually between four forty-seven and five-twelve. He was often aware of his wife lying beside him in the bed, similarly awake. On rare occasions, they would acknowledge each other with a little conversation, but due to the nature of their wakefulness this was often on subjects that were bothering them both: unresolved issues with the children's classes, money concerns, professional tensions, hopes for that elusive house on the beach that never quite materialized, and other disappointments both transitory and permanent.

At six-fifteen A.M. precisely, Harb rose for the day, scraped his face, showered, dressed in one of his two-piece, three-button gray or blue suits, and made his way to the seven-twelve train. At the local station, he purchased a cup of coffee, which he drank on the train. He was in the office by eight-fifteen with a second cup of coffee and a corn muffin in front of him, ready to begin the brand-new day.

In this way, each day crept in its petty pace until the last syllable of recorded time. With a good expense account, it's tolerable.

So neither quality nor Quality was in total ascendance for my friend Harbert, not at home, not on the road. So it is somewhat ironic, if not typical of the world as it works, that we did, at that time, win a Malcolm Baldridge award, the most prestigious recognition of achievement in the Quality racket. Harb got a plaque, as did CaroleAnne. He put his on his credenza, behind a small cactus that he had been tending unto death for more than a decade. She hung hers on the wall outside her workstation, in full view of the entire office, and made quite a noisy fuss while she was about it. Why shouldn't she? She was proud of it! That's why they give these stupid things. Who could fault her?

The installation of this wooden tablet, incidentally, created something of a controversy. CaroleAnne was busy hammering in some nails upon which to hang the revered plaque. For some reason, she was having a bit of difficulty doing so, and the hammering went on for way too long not to be both intrusive and annoying.

Harb, in an uncharacteristic display of pique, came out of his office in a lather and indulged in what was, for him, a small explosion. In anyone else, it might have gone unnoticed. In Harb, however, it was unusual.

"What?" he said as he came out of his enclosure. "Are you killing a small animal out here or something?"

CaroleAnne's reaction was immediate and out of proportion to the remark, bordering on the insubordinate. "I beg your pardon!" she shouted. "Would you repeat that, please?"

"It sounded like you were nailing a raccoon to a tree," said Harb more quietly, almost apologetically.

"It most certainly did not!" CaroleAnne ejaculated in an extremity of dudgeon.

"Okay, okay! Jeez!" said Harb, exiting into his office.

"How could you say such a thing!" said CaroleAnne, and, furiously slamming her trophy up on the wall, she collected her purse and steamed off to the ladies' room. There was a vacuous silence. Then we all went back to work. Sometime later, CaroleAnne resumed her duties with her composure restored. She spent the rest of the day writing with great concentration in a small spiral-bound notebook.

It was not yet all thorns, however. At around this time, CaroleAnne was given another tasty raise in recognition of the fact that her cost of living had gone up, then not long after, another increase, because she was unhappy at her current level and was not really in line for a promotion in an office where jobs were being evaluated, not expanded. And still she kept up the pressure on Harb, who had less and less budget to work with. On several occasions, he issued a "bonus" drawn from his very own personal checking account.

This behavior calls for some comment, but I am at a loss to explain it. There is no room in business for personal checks. In fact, in a world where any of us could fly around the world, making copious recreational stops with nothing but our corporate Amex in our hands, a personal check is almost an offensive object. The only thing I can surmise is that Harb had taken CaroleAnne under his wing, and he meant to live up to that unspoken mutual contract.

Attrition began and, once begun, tore through our little group like dysentery through a luxury Mexican tourist resort. In June, Blatt was transferred to a small office on the second floor of the satellite annex down on Bush Street. Anyone aware of the geography of our metropolis knows that this was not intended to be a plum assignment and understands the message that was conveyed by it. Dick Podesky, after another series of farewell dinners, took his leave, although he continued to be under retainer at a very high fee as a consultant to the department. The place began to feel a little empty.

Harb was sadder than I had ever seen him, except, perhaps, for the day each year that the Chicago Cubs were statistically eliminated from the pennant race. We went to lunch quite often during those weeks. He talked a lot about sailing then, I recall. He had planned to get a small boat, something he had always wanted as a young man, and to moor it at the little club he belonged to on the suburban shore of the Lake Michigan. He frequently brought along catalogs in which sailboats and sailing gear were featured prominently. I noted, on one occasion, that in these boats he was scrutinizing there seemed to be room for one, two at most. "Yes," he said and went back to studying them.

"Does Jean like to be out on the water?" I asked him.

"Sure," he said, but his focus was on the page he was looking at. Then he added, "She's a photographer. She can photograph water." I thought then that as a response it was a tad odd, if not nonsensical, but I let it go. At a certain age, we all need to pursue a dream of one sort or another, and when we do we hope our spouse can come along. Most of the time, she will, certainly. And if she doesn't, sometimes we have to go anyway.

As things grew inexorably darker and more unappealingly businesslike in the air around us, CaroleAnne was changing too, although at first it was difficult to say how, precisely. One morning, she got off the elevator looking extremely upset, went into a roomy storage closet that afforded total privacy, and didn't come out for more than two hours. That was strange, but for some reason I could not then comprehend, we nervously noted the situation but did nothing about it. There was a sudden sense that we were all walking on a thin crust of ice with CaroleAnne that, if tested, would give, plunging the adventurer into an icy death.

At the same time, CaroleAnne developed a close friendship with Gretchen Kurtz, an eccentric administrative assistant on the thirty-fourth floor with a tower of strawberry blond hair and a super-abundance of neither kindness nor intelligence. Several times a day I would see CaroleAnne and Gretchen Kurtz together in the coffee enclave down the hall from our executive area, then they would disappear into Blatt's former office, reappearing perhaps half an hour later looking . . . how shall I put this? . . . defiant and triumphant. I was curious but didn't pry. I figured it would all come out in the wash, as it always does in close conditions such as ours.

Strangest of all was the following incident: One night when I was working late, I determined to take a little walk around the floor, just to stretch my legs. I heard rustling nearby, which is kind of frightening at that hour, when you believe that you are alone. It seemed to be coming from Blatt's empty office. I quietly approached and peeked my head into the space, which was supposed to be locked. On the floor, in what Buddhists call the classic lotus position, cross-legged and the heels of her feet resting lightly on her upper thighs, sat CaroleAnne, quite alone, still dressed impeccably for work in her new haute bourgeois style. Her eyes were closed. She was clearly praying, or at least speaking to someone who could not be seen. She ceased speaking and appeared to be listening to someone replying. She obviously was not aware of my approach and had no idea I had remained in the building. I decided to maintain that status and quietly tiptoed away. I sat in my office for a long, long time. Then I went home. I don't mind telling you, I was afraid . . . for Harb, for myself, for all of us. Nonsense, I told myself after a couple of drinks. You're overreacting. But I wasn't. Things were exactly as bad as I imagined them to be.

10

As quickly as it had begun, Quality abruptly ended. Not as a concept, mind you, where it still circulates through our system like a virus, percolating underneath but not visible to the naked eye since its remission. But as an organizing principle that guided our actions and our exercise of plastic day to day, it was history, and those who had gambled their slab in the corporate firmament on it, so recently the highest life-forms on the food chain, were now endangered species.

Staff was not simply laid off, it was lopped off. The corporation made an announcement: "By the end of the year more than fifteen thousand head count will be found, coming from each operating division." Many of those were found in staff functions, including Quality. Assignments, once blossoming in every corner of the nation, narrowed even more dramatically.

It was a tough time for all of us, but most dramatically for Harb. Meetings took place that he knew nothing of. Gatherings of important rabbinical entities were held, ones to which he should have been invited, and yet he was not. He was marginalized. This is not to say that Harb had suffered a career-killing injury. Many power forwards have to squat a couple of periods on the bench to find their way back into the lineup. In the meantime, however, Harb sat. Of course, while he sat he was also earning something north of half a million dollars a year. Some would say that his predicament, then, was not a serious one. But those would be mercenary people who do not understand what it means to work for more than just a simple living, to work for pride, for the adrenaline, for the joy.

CaroleAnne, for her part, was spending more and more time simply camping outside Harb's office for hours, the telephone silent to her right, the computer sporting the ubiquitous sign of office rot—solitaire. She was quite lonely, as were many of us back then, but CaroleAnne's loneliness manifested itself somewhat strangely, and the bizarre nature of interpersonal discourse with her grew with time. You must remember that CaroleAnne was a highly functioning, polished, seasoned corporate player, intelligent, sensitive, and well-spoken. So when the truly abnormal stuff started kicking in, there was kind of a wicked head snap to it. Who was this person?

Like this. Suddenly she would stop you as you were hurrying by in an obvious swivet, or heading to the rest room, or dashing out for lunch, or simply marching, head down, thinking, and engage you in what I can only describe as a metaphysical subject—the impermanence of life, for instance or, still more disconcertingly, the inevitability of sin. She would fasten on you with those big brown eyes of hers, all rapt and gooey, and not let you go until your bladder was ready to burst or your lunch date was seriously annoyed by your tardiness. But you couldn't just blow her off, because . . . well, I don't know why. You couldn't just blow her off, that's all. It was too scary even to try. You didn't want to go there.

At times, she fell into what appeared to be a trance after she had terminated one of these manic talky sessions. The lucky recipient of the sermon would be gone, but those remaining behind were treated to the sight of CaroleAnne, radiant, her lustrous dark hair shining, eyes lightly closed and fluttering. I asked her once, after witnessing just such a spectacle of fervor, what was up with her.

"I need to achieve serenity," she said, peering speculatively into me, as those do who have a great and mighty message to impart and are waiting only for the slightest encouragement to do so. I was loath to serve that function. But I felt like I had to know more.

"We all need that," I said respectfully. "But we don't all necessarily fall into a state of semiconsciousness in a public place."

"True," she said. She seemed to give the matter some thought. "For the best part of our lives we are encouraged to keep the spiritual side of our natures hidden. It embarrasses people. But some of us reach a point where we can't keep it hidden. Like a songbird in a dark cave, the soul still has the urge to sing. And it will sing."

"Yes," I said. I was seized with a terrible nervousness and a desire to be away. Instead of leaving, however, I said, "I was wondering if you had finished the quarterly head count report." She had. Of course she had.

I never discussed philosophical matters with CaroleAnne again. Not that we had a dearth of conversation. She was chatty. I am a listener. So as the days grew into months, and the work dried and shriveled, I spent a lot of quality time with her. And it was from this vantage point that I began to perceive the gradual decomposition and growing irrationality of her everyday life and mind.

She began to wear more jewelry. Much of it was quasi-religious in nature, with ankhs and reversed crucifixes and other symbols of questionable nature in evidence. Her stories got longer and ever more sincere in their circumlocutory ramblings. And then there was that spiral-bound notebook, which was now bloated and demented looking, pregnant with her squirrelly observations.

"I'm getting out of here," she would say with some regularity. Then she would launch into a detailed description of the newest of her business ventures that were sure to pluck her from this admittedly depressing milieu. Many were quite fantastical.

"I met this very interesting person," she said to me one time as I tried to be somewhat on time for a twelve-thirty lunch.

"Yes?" I said hopefully.

"He's a real-estate philanthropist."

"Hmm?"

"He's going to be buying up a bunch of row houses on the South Side and turning them into utopian communities."

"Ah," I said. "Really." I've always been curious about utopian communities. In every century there have been those who attempted to form them, to live in happiness, comfort, amity, and tremendous, somewhat unconventional sexual activity. There is nothing to indicate that these individuals were any more confused or unhappy than we are. Some may perhaps have even been happier. So I don't reject the entire notion out of hand. Harb on his boat. Me on my porch with a Bud. There is a utopia for each of us somewhere, I am convinced of that. Each of us must try to reach it in his own way. Those who don't try are a little sad, I think.

"Each investor is putting up ten to twelve million dollars," said CaroleAnne. I kind of woke up at that.

"How do you figure in this situation?"

"I'm a partner."

"And . . . you're obtaining the investment capital from . . . what?" I could feel the road we were traveling on veering imperceptibly into the swamp.

"I don't need capital," said CaroleAnne. "I'm contributing my expertise."

"What expertise?" This was still plausible, if only barely. The woman did have prodigious professional abilities, after all. In an era where a make-believe Internet concept was still worth several hundred million dollars, why shouldn't a perfect personal assistant be worth some small percentage of that?

"As an architect," said CaroleAnne.

"Are you an architect?" I wasn't being rude. I really wanted to know.

"I have an architectural background," she said earnestly. "Several thousand years ago, I helped to design the Temple of Dendur in the Nile Valley."

"Then they're lucky to get you on this project," I said and departed.

Suddenly, we were really terrified. Could it be this marvelous woman was . . . a nut? Impossible. We were all under tremendous stress. This madness, if you could call it that, was the stress talking. Perhaps she needed a bit of counseling. But she was our coworker, almost our friend. There was no reason for alarm. Someone would have to speak with her, surely. But who would that someone be?

It should have been me, I admit that now. I have certainly directed dozens of peers and fellow employees to our Referral Assistance Program. I made no such suggestion to CaroleAnne, however. At this moment, I am at a loss to explain this lapse of function. Maybe I sensed where a substantive confrontation would lead, but no, I'm just kidding myself. I had it within my power, at some point, to alter the course of this thing. And I did not do it.

11

And now Harb was filled with an immense, incontrovertible yearning—to be away from the former subject of his great affection. It was as if he woke up one morning and discovered that CaroleAnne was not the person he had taken her to be. In most ways, she wasn't. The core of the person we had known was still there, but it was now wrapped in a cocoon of incandescent strangeness. And strangeness of any kind is anathema in a setting where the highest good is the ability to perform as one is expected to do.

It happens all the time. He had done a lot for the woman, no doubt about it, and no question, he didn't want to hurt her. But the job had changed. Life had moved on. It was time to grow into new vistas and all that. And at a certain level, you know . . . a guy can fire anybody he wants to, right? It's what separates the business family from every other kind.

Perhaps most dispositive, CaroleAnne had ceased to work well as an assistant to Harb. He didn't need his travel arranged . . . he had no travel. He didn't need reports processed . . . he wasn't writing any. And slowly, inexorably, the tone between the two had grown increasingly fractious, to the point where they now spoke almost never and Harb spent a good part of his day behind a closed door while she apparently fumed and fussed over unknown matters at her workstation. When they did talk, there was a frosty bickering quality to the discourse that was truly grating.

"She's driving me bonkers," he said to me one afternoon early the following April as we were taking a seasonable walk to the cigar store. This was not a regular occurrence, since neither Harb nor myself smoked more than perhaps six or seven cigars a year and then only when there was an occasion for it. Smoking in general was more than frowned upon at the office—it was scowled at. So smokers were condemned to stand outside in all kinds of weather to indulge their habits. It was hard to enjoy an expensive and delicious stogie in the spirit the Lord intended while crouching against the wind with a ragtag assembly of secretaries, shoeshine men, and addicted executives. Cigarettes were conceivable, they took only a minute, but who wanted to go back to those?

At any rate, we were walking, possibly because the weather was nice and perhaps because Harb wanted to get out of the office for this little conversation. "Absolutely around the bend," he said, almost to himself. "She's . . . crazy, you know," he added, as if he was changing the subject. I looked to see if he was kidding in some way. I couldn't tell. An enigmatic little grimace was teasing the corner of his lip. It was impossible for me to tell what it meant without opening his skull and looking inside. "Totally charming and incredibly sexy and beautiful," he went on. "But, you know . . . completely bent. For a long time I thought, eccentric, but then I changed my mind. Didn't make me feel any different about her. Everybody has their things, you know."

"Yeah," I said. "But she's not, like, insane, right?"

"Certifiable," said Harb. "But . . . lovable. I'm gonna need your help, my friend." We were crossing Rush Street at that point and a UPS truck was bearing down on us at a high rate of speed. Instead of dodging out of the way, as the aggressive, hateful driver expected he would, Harb simply stopped walking and turned to face the truck, which seemed at that moment to be picking up speed. Preferring to watch this little event from the sidelines, I ran for the curb. Harb stood his ground. The light was in his favor. The crosswalk was his. I could see from the safety of the sidewalk that Harb's eyebrows were raised ever so slightly, as if he was curious himself to see how this whole situation would work out. And then, with a great screech of brakes, the truck slid to a halt precisely as the light changed to Don't Walk for Harb, who did not take this opportunity to move out of the way at all, but instead continued his vigil in the middle of the crosswalk, staring coolly at the driver of the truck fuming less than two feet away through the windshield. "Move out of the way!" the driver screamed so loudly I could hear him from the not inconsiderable distance. Harb shook his head sadly but politely. After a few moments, the light again changed, to red for the driver of the truck and green for Harb, and Harb, kind of scuffing his shoe on the pavement a little to show he wasn't in any hurry, moved on to my side of the street.

"That was great," he said as we continued down the street to the cigar store. Then, "I think it's you who's going to have to do something about it." We pretended to know enough about cigars to choose a good one.

You see, Harb suffered from a common affliction of senior management: He couldn't bring himself to fire anybody personally. In spite of all the terrible things he was called upon to do in his role as arbiter of the fate of thousands, in spite of the inexorable, everyday brutality that role required, Harb wanted to be a good person. There was no reason anybody needed to suffer, right? So Harb moved what was left of his heaven and earth and found a plum assignment for CaroleAnne, one that came from the Old Man's office itself: executive assistant to the general counsel, all the way up on the tippity-top floor! What a job!

"She's gonna love this," said Harb.

I'm sure it won't surprise anyone to learn that CaroleAnne refused this peerless opportunity. Like many of us, she had a destiny to fulfill, and nothing could dissuade her from it, no matter how dark and rotten it might be.

"My place is here with you and the guys, Harb," is what she said to him when he triumphantly offered it to her. She had listened carefully to the proposal, first to him and then, it seemed, to an internal voice that she was consulting. This did not seem overwhelmingly odd at the time. We all discuss matters with the man or woman inside us, particularly crucial issues such as this one. "You've been too good to me," she said to him after a time, and rather coldly, I thought, under the circumstances.

"This would be good for you, Cici," he said. I hadn't heard him use that endearment in quite some time. He, too, seemed to be bordering on the peevish.

"I understand you want to get rid of me, Robert," she said quietly. "But I'm not going." Then she just sat there. In a few moments, a couple of big, juicy tears popped from her eyeballs and began making their way down her cheeks. In years past, this might have occasioned something soft and comforting from someone in the vicinity, but I believe that all of us, including Harb, had grown somewhat used to her tears at this point, and so they were less effective than they formerly had been.

"I need you to go, CaroleAnne," Harb said. He was moved as well but disguised his distress in a torrential fit of sneezing. And so they sat that way for a long interlude, CaroleAnne snuffling, Harb exploding from his nasal region. Then they both calmed their systems, and she departed from his office, and nothing had changed.

Thus they did not resolve the issue, and the deep, emotionally charged situation languished for several months.

It was at this juncture that CaroleAnne's visits with Gretchen Kurtz to Blatt's former office, which had been taking place for some time now and become the subject of intense office interest, speculation, and public hilarity, took on some added color. Where before they had been silent, mysterious affairs, it was now possible, in the recent quietude of our head count–deprived office area, to hear rather nonbusinesslike sounds emanating from the enclosure. The pattern, once it became apparent to us, was generally the same every day. First came the sound of the door closing, then a fair amount of mumbling and, incredibly, the smell of incense. After that, for a period of time that was somewhat elastic, stretching from perhaps five minutes to more than fifteen, there was what I can only describe as chanting, and the sound of chimes, I think. The effect was not what you would describe as religious. It was . . . spiritual. After a while, the door would fly open, and CaroleAnne and Gretchen Kurtz would emerge with some kind of attitude it was hard to pinpoint. They didn't seem unhappy, though.

Attempts to inform CaroleAnne of the singular inappropriateness of this behavior met with a stony glare and a threatening sequence of remarks that seemed to pertain to core American concepts like freedom to congregate. When, on my final attempt to rein this thing in, she gravitated over to a brief, trembly lecture on cultural tolerance, I realized we were entering a region where no Human Resources professionals go without an attorney, and I dropped it, the more shame to me.

The fact that I was temporarily stymied, however, did not mean that I was beaten. It was clear to me that the need to help CaroleAnne transition to her next job iteration was more extreme than ever, and I meant to effect the solution as quickly as I possibly could.

12

It's not easy to kill a person, as anyone who has seriously attempted the task can tell you. He cries. He bleeds. And even when he does not emit any horrible fluids, he tends to scream as you are doing violence to his person. Truncating another's life is perhaps the most intimate act one human being can visit on another and, except for a few extremely sick individuals, among the least pleasurable.

It is almost equally difficult to kill a career. There are many senior officers who never, not once, have been capable of firing a single living soul. That is to their credit. Interestingly, it is often these sensitive types who are most likely to require periodic executions from their subordinates. That is not quite so admirable. "Fire him!" they will say of one poor individual or another. And yet, if put in that position, they could not. Oh, well.

Of course, when it came to CaroleAnne, a woman of matchless corporate record, nearing forty, of an indeterminate race, there was no question about it: She could never be fired. Perhaps, in a massive liquidation she could possibly be swept out with the other dispensable protoplasm, but not as an individual, no. She was safer than a Supreme Court justice. As a longtime secretary to senior management, she was part of the permanent government of the place and knew too much to be allowed to roam free. But she didn't need to be near Harb, and her weirdness was now, as I have said, transcendent.

Because she would not accept the general counsel job under any circumstances, CaroleAnne was therefore assigned to serve the executive vice president of Finance who worked in a part of the Castle referred to as the Tower, the pompous, semimedieval home of a robber baron just short of Carnegie status. I'm afraid Harb assigned me to tell her about her new opportunity. I understood.

So CaroleAnne was offered the Finance job, and I personally thought that would be the end of the matter. Once again, I was mistaken. There is no way to end an inexorable process before it comes to its inevitable conclusion. You might as well try to cheat death. You can plot and scheme. You can wriggle and twist and try to spend your way out of it. Eventually, what is meant to happen will happen.

I have to admit that I never had the foresight or, if you prefer, the deep-seated pessimism, to guess that CaroleAnne would summon up the sheer guts and blind desperation to pull the ultimate power move in any company—refusing to accept reassignment. It's a bold ploy few employ, but it's quite effective. The determined Bartlebys who simply decline to accept the status assigned them, who come in each day to their disputed positions and do a marginal job and *will not get lost*, have a tremendous amount of psychic force. Most of the time, common sense ultimately prevails and the hapless individuals bow to the pressure of the disconsolate and incredulous humanity around them, accepting the fate the social unit has decreed for them. Not CaroleAnne. She hung in there, day after day. She would not go away. And then one morning, in some kind of manipulative stratagem or other, CaroleAnne came into Harb's office, sat down, wept, as was her obvious pattern, we could see that now, and offered to resign. And—God, it pains me to write these words, even as I know I must—Harb, in a tragic, final act of prodigious compassion and stupidity—Lord, give me strength for what I must tell you—Harb declined to accept her resignation.

"I had a clear moment," said CaroleAnne, leaning forward in her chair and playing with the long string of rather liturgical beads she was sporting at the time. "I'm just a fucked-up person. I'm screwing with you guys and you've been pretty good to me, or at least you sorta meant to be. Anyhow, I quit. It's the right thing to do and I quit. Work me out some nice package and I'll get out of here. Okay, Harb?" She did sniff a tiny bit right then, but I was kind of sporting a slightly runny nose myself from my position near the fax machine, just out of sight.

"Nah, Ceese," I heard Harb say. "You gotta take that Finance job. We can't be together anymore. We just get on each other's nerves too much. You can't argue with that. But you can't go out there in the cold in the middle of a recession like this without another job. You just can't. And this Finance thing is a good position."

"Yeah," she said. "I know I know. Let's not go all over that again." Then there was one of those silences I had come to detest. Finally, she added, "Maybe I should think about the Finance job."

"You should!" said Harb, the big nimrod. "Take a couple of days and think about it, Cici. I'd feel a lot better about it if you did."

"Okay, Harb." She got to her feet and stood before him on the other side of his blotter. I could hear them looking at each other. "I just want to say that I appreciate a lot of what you tried to do for me."

"I didn't do anything for you, Ceese," said Harb. "We've been friends."

"Yeah," said CaroleAnne. "Uh-huh."

"At least go see Fred Tell about it," Harb said, and I practically ran into the room, waving my arms and screaming. I didn't, though. Perhaps I should have. "He'll tell you more about it than you've been willing to hear so far," he added, "and if you don't like it then maybe there are some other opportunities we can look at."

"Uh-huh," said CaroleAnne. I could once again feel her looking at him, and I could swear I felt that it was Harb who was first to pull his eyes away.

At that point I felt a small poof of scent coming from my idiot friend's office door and knew CaroleAnne would be emerging in just a moment. So I made myself scarce.

I returned to his den a few minutes later to find him sitting stock-still in his recliner, which was far from reclined. Both of his feet were planted on the floor and his hands were folded in front of him. He was staring, unseeing, into something very dark indeed.

"What did I just do?" he said to the air in front of him.

"I don't know, man," I said to him. "You're the big business genius."

Then we sat there for a long while, after which we put on our coats and went out for a drink. That whole evening, I think Harb might have said maybe thirty words. Maybe fewer. He just kept on demolishing those martinis and digging through those bar nuts. Every now and then, he'd look at me and shake his head back and forth for a while. I found the best response to this was to nod sagely, so I did that. He said, "Well, fuck me," several times. At the end of the night, he said, "See ya around the ranch," and went home.

13

It was late afternoon the day CaroleAnne came to my office for the meeting that began the next phase of this history.

She seemed very distracted and agitated, incapable of remaining in her seat. The sun was setting outside my wall of plate glass windows, so it must have been sometime in the rag end of fall. The lights were coming on all over the city, and my office was at its coziest. In the old days, I would have lit a cigarette and offered her one, but since that option is no longer available, I asked if she wanted a beverage of some sort, to give her a chance to compose herself. She accepted a bottle of water. During the discussion that followed, she did not open the bottle but did, throughout the time we were together, entirely strip it of its label. It was odd, later, to see the completely full, naked bottle of water without its label. It looked like a found object, more a piece of evidence than a thing that could be utilized for a purpose. Awareness of these kinds of little details pops into our minds at the strangest moments under stress, working to distance us from unpleasant events as they are transpiring and, in the end, clarifies, purifies what is happening, the actions, feelings, thoughts, and issues that are really and truly important. I don't know why. Perhaps God gives us the ability, when experience becomes too direct and painful, to remove ourselves in this fashion. Or perhaps there is no God at all, that's just the way things are. Maybe the way things are is God.

In our conversation, CaroleAnne made several points, which I will lay out with some brevity. They were, in generally chronological order, these:

- She was unhappy in her current position, which had once provided her with challenge and pleasure but was now stagnant and pointless.
- She had performed admirably during the long time she had been with us, and had more than earned the many promotions and raises she had received.
- Her pay over the years was good for a person of support stature, but in essence she had been an executive of the company for many years and should probably have been compensated as such, not as a common assistant.
- That was all right, that was water under the bridge, it was too late to complain about all the injustices that had been done to her during the years of her employment, and anyway she was not going to use this opportunity simply to complain, she was not that kind of person, her mother had raised her to be a better person than that, etc., etc., and so on and so forth.
- Whether anyone around the office knew it or not, she was an extraordinary individual with a very special relationship with God (!) who needed fresh challenges to succeed, and she had, in fact, been held back by a variety of factors, none of which were her fault or responsibility. On the contrary . . .

It suddenly felt to me like all the air had been sucked out of the office, and something shifted in CaroleAnne's center of gravity, as if a vast weight was settling in her midsection, one that would be denied no longer. I knew what she was going to say just before she said it. And I could not stop it, no matter how desperately I might have wanted to. Mine was simply to sit and listen to it, let it hit me like a tidal wave, one that would not pass by or break, not ever, until anyone and everyone in the vicinity was utterly and thoroughly drowned.

Before I knew it, CaroleAnne had spewed out the following thoughts, which seemed not to flow from her prior discussion but to arise from a font of emotion unrelated to the mostly rational flow of discourse that had preceded it:

- She had, since her arrival at the company, been the victim of an organized campaign of sexual harassment, particularly focused on thwarting her naturally pious bent with cynical innuendo.
- All of the employees of our company with whom she had contact were a part of this conspiracy of harassment: Each and every one was obsessed with degenerate thoughts of sexual congress and all were attempting to drag her down into the gutter with them.
- Harb was, among the ongoing horror of this unfair treatment, the worst of the worst. As a person in a position of trust he should be held most accountable.
- She wanted an internal investigation reaching to the highest levels of the corporation.
- She had felt this way since the day she began on the job but was speaking now only because God had finally succeeded in convincing her to do so.

On this last point, she was quite clear: God had spoken to her several times in the last weeks and, after begging her for some time and finding her recalcitrant, had given her a direct order—and several visions accompanying those instructions. It was now his will that she was carrying out, not her own, she was his instrument and could not be turned aside, unfortunately, because she liked us all as people, especially Harb.

I took copious notes and immediately initiated an internal investigation. It was the only thing to do, and I went about it in my customary businesslike fashion. But inside, I wept. I wept for us all, but mostly for Harb. Good God, I thought. What will become of him? It was a rhetorical question, of course. I knew.

I went to see Harb the very next morning and laid out the situation for him. We had a highly performing employee of good standing in the corporation for several years claiming that the entire organization, and he in particular, had created a hostile working environment and driven her to the brink of mental and physical collapse. The charge was sexual harassment, with a portion of cultural insensitivity on the side, and even though no allegations of specific or inappropriate intimacy or rude behavior seemed to be forthcoming, the implications of the charge alone were horrifying.

We sat together for a while. There was little to say. Harb was in his chair, feet up on the desk in his characteristic attitude of repose, but I knew that inside him there was no repose, only turmoil. A very small twitch was worrying the little pouch of skin immediately beneath his left eye. This was never a good sign.

"I gave the woman my car," he said after a time. "I suppose that could be taken several ways."

I was fuming. I wanted to buck him up, to stick up for him with himself, but that was not my role. I was there to handle this thing honestly and without any prejudice in the deepest sense of the term, for everyone's sake. A fake inquest that could later be discredited would be in no one's interest. So my job was to be impartial, and I fully intended to be. But I was also Harb's friend and knew him to be innocent of everything except loyalty and love. And where love is around, there is always a fair amount of stupidity to be found also, I guess.

I was conflicted. Perhaps I should have recused myself at that point and given the case to somebody more removed who would have railroaded him immediately for the greater comfort of all, but I had no intention of doing so then, and even now, at this point, with so much of the river having run past the road, I am still quite glad that I did not. In my hands, and mine alone, lay the power to see that justice, and not procedure, was done.

"I sort of don't know what to do here, Harb," I said. But we both knew what needed to be done. I wanted him to articulate it.

"You have to conduct a complete investigation," he said as easily as anything in the world. "You have to talk to everybody, including CaroleAnne, Blatt, Dick. You have to get out on the road and talk to all the people we visited. You have to find out what happened and what didn't. Then you have to write a full report. It's the only course of action that has any hope of getting me off the hook."

"I suppose we could settle it quietly right away," I said. I was nauseated with myself to hear me say it. But it was an option and I wanted to offer it to him.

"No, no," said Harb. It was quiet in his office and even under the circumstances snug and comfy. Outside his window I could see a cab run a red light at the corner below. A policeman impassively watched him streak by. "I don't want that kind of thing on my record," he said. "Frankly, I don't want CaroleAnne to get a fucking dime. Now if you'll excuse me, I think I'd better talk to a lawyer, huh?"

I left. About a week later, performance review time came around again, as it always does, and CaroleAnne received a very nice raise. In these situations the appearance of retribution must be avoided at all cost.

14

We conducted a first-class inquiry, I must say, not that I'm tooting my own horn, but there you have it. I will describe some of the material that came out during the process during my full and final report, but the upshot of the thing was that Harb was cleared by a massive body of testimony of utterly everything but perhaps some excessive favoring of the complainant, for which a letter of an unfavorable nature was placed by the Old Man in his personnel file. This stung him deeply, and he was never the same man after that.

A host of previously unknown facts, opinions, and attitudes came out about CaroleAnne, though, that were both fascinating and appalling. Chief among these was CaroleAnne's deposition itself, which was later played out for the dispassionate observers who decided where civil justice lay in the situation, if any was indeed to be found. I will spare you the details of her brief at this juncture.

As we read this lengthy and bewildering document and prepared for trial, CaroleAnne stayed on at her desk, as was her right. The babbling, lunatic prayer meetings now were taking place daily. Comment and joking about the matter had ceased. When CaroleAnne entered an area, conversation stopped entirely. Business environments are all about order, about the leaching out of personal material, the pursuit of emotionless objectives, the pleasure of operating in a known universe. In her person and behavior, CaroleAnne was in the deepest possible sense not businesslike.

Given CaroleAnne's evident madness, which had been well concealed from all, it would have made sense that the charges of sexually inappropriate behavior she leveled at Harb would be dismissed out of hand. And so they were, in our hearts, particularly after the inquest was past. But nothing of this nature is dismissed out of hand officially, not in these advanced days in which we live. The people who know the most about it are those who are the least informed, and they talk, they talk, they talk.

The details of what Harb had done to benefit CaroleAnne over the years thus seeped into the local grapevine, and through the executive corps via their secretaries, and thence to the wives of those executives, and so the story of Harb's intense devotion to CaroleAnne was at last made known, in a completely different color and tone, in the one location where it could do the most harm: at Harb's house, where, quite naturally, it was not well understood.

"This is great," he said to me one evening as we were waiting for the town car that would take us downtown for dinner. "It isn't that Jean believes I had an affair with Circe." He had started calling her that. "She's just completely disgusted that I've made such a public spectacle of myself. She hates that everybody is talking about us. It's humiliating to her."

"So, what . . ." I said. I was a little miffed at Jean right then. "She views this in terms of the inconvenience to herself?"

"Yeah, well . . ." said Harb. "I do look like a dork. And I'm done, Fred. I'm just . . . done around here, you know."

"No, man," I said. "Not while there's breath in my body."

"I almost believe you, Fred," said Harb, and the car came.

And so, battered both at the office and at home, Harb continued to go from one to the other, a diminished, grayed-out shadow of himself, forced to pass his nemesis each day as he traveled between his two worlds.

After my report was published and circulated throughout selected senior management, Harb was welcomed back with full honors into the top ranks, or so it was made to seem. At the same time, he had no real assignment, but that was as much due to the death of Quality as it was to any political fallout from his great embarrassment. For one as talented and beloved as Harb, a focused task would surely come.

And yet, it did not.

What is it like to live in such undeath? At first, it is perplexing. Are you not the same individual who was the object of such veneration just a few days ago? What could possibly have changed in such short order? Then, after the confusion, comes the shame, the sense that there is something unclean, unwanted, negligible about yourself, and the conviction, underneath it all, that this was true all along, that you have, in fact, been fooling people all this time, that your position was the product of some lucky mistake that was made in your favor that has now been rectified. Then comes the grief, the overwhelming feelings of loss, sadness, and regret. The world is over! How nice it was while it lasted. And it will not come again. Where did it all go? How unfair is the scimitar of fate! Almost at the end now comes the rage. It is in this healthy phase that people sue their corporations for a variety of transgressions both imagined and real. I knew a man once who was fired the day after he purchased a three-bedroom apartment in the most expensive part of the city. He had been advised to do so by the boss who fired him the very next day. For months, armed with his key card, he roamed the hallways, skinny, unwashed, red-eyed, little drops of spittle on his three-day growth of beard. We finally had to reprogram the system to keep him out and still, to this day, he appears in the hallways and anterooms, haunting us like a malevolent spirit unable to go to its next destination. In the end, at last, is a form of acceptance, or at least the peace that comes with the knowledge that life must be lived and there is nothing to be done. But Harb was far, far from that last and most blessed state of mind. He was just a soul suspended in time and space, awaiting what most surely was destined to come. And sure enough, it did.

Three months after my report was issued, the Equal Employment Opportunity Commission denied CaroleAnne any relief in their finding on the subject. The next day she quit and sued the company for $150 million.

book
two

The Trial

15

It took seven months for the matter to come to trial in federal court. During that time, things quite literally stood still. Nothing happened, much as nothing occurs in the heart of a dark and towering thunderhead quietly preparing to dump a load of hail on the windshield of your car one summer's day. One minute, it's scenery. The next, it's big frozen balls the size of your fist.

When it arrived, the trial itself whipped by at lightning speed, taking something under four days. As the salient testimony is presented before you in the next segment of our narrative, I'm sure you will enjoy the opportunity to pass upon the facts of the matter, which you may judge differently from the way the jury saw fit to do. I leave that up to you. Without spoiling whatever suspense I hope you feel at this point about the outcome of this travesty, I will say this: People hate big companies, no matter how many individuals we give jobs to, no matter how many pensions we pay out every day. And who's to say they're not right? No matter how serious the enterprise, all we are in a corporation is a gathering of human beings. That immediately imposes certain limitations.

Very little got any better for anybody during this time, but misfortune seemed to single out my foolish friend Harbert both during the formal and less-structured proceedings, on the job and on his suburban beat. Harb's marriage, for instance, was pretty typical for one of some duration, probably no better than yours or mine. You can never tell until you're tested. The Harbert edifice was built on certain unspoken agreements. As anyone who has been married will attest, when even minor breaches to those agreements are forced into the open, the entire substructure of the tower can begin to teeter like an ancient house undermined by earthquake, where one tiny fissure may reduce the entire edifice to rubble.

And one can only imagine the pressure that was brought to bear on the Harbert union during the months preceding the trial. Like all of us, Jean Harbert thought she knew her spouse. All of a sudden, she had doubt cast on that subject. That caused her to pause. And once one pauses, well then, anything is possible.

The first thing that goes is the routine. Previously, Jean's routine was relatively unvaried from day to day. She would awake at six-fifteen with Harb, roused by the incessant beeping of the digital alarm, which was positioned across the room from her side of the bed so she would neither smash it to bits nor hit the snooze alarm until noontime. Once roused in this fashion, she would leap completely naked from the bed and, with the greatest possible dispatch, shower and dress in her invariable costume: black jeans, extra-large T-shirt in whatever color served her mood, and sneakers. She then went downstairs, as Harb continued to minister to himself, to make the lunches required by her two children. While down in the kitchen, she would also feed the Harbert cat, whose name, I am sorry to report, was Filbert, a great gray and brown monster with yellow eyes and a stomach the size of a cantaloupe. Although he would never admit to it in the slightest, Harb loved the animal immoderately, possibly because it smelled rather bad and behaved quite antisocially. Jean loved it too, but less sentimentally, as befit the partner who was forced to be aware on a daily basis of the creature's hair balls, smells, and other attractive secretions.

As I have noted, Harb would be downstairs between six forty-three and six fifty-eight, completely ready for work except for his shirt stays, which Jean would insert carefully in his collar. If they were on decent terms at that moment, Harb would kiss her on the cheek. He would then go to the table and sit for a few moments, since his normal train did not leave until seven-twelve, and they were only five minutes from the station. During that ten-minute

96

period, Jean would continue to work at the assembling of lunch while Harb paged through the paper, looking for news about his company and nothing else, and at the same time watch her with nothing in particular on his mind. After many years of marriage, he still found her quite interesting, a fact that in itself gave him a great deal of pleasure and no little surprise. Twenty years is a long time.

I have described Harb already, and kindness dictates, I think, that I refrain from doing so again. He was what he was, that's all, which made it all the more surprising that he had managed to snare an individual of Jean's stature. I use the word *stature* quite deliberately and literally. If Jean was anything under six feet in height, it was not an amount that mattered. Tall, then, and not particularly willowy, either, and . . . well, meaty is the only term I can think of to convey the correct impression. She was big all over, but not fat, no. Just large. My wife and I were once at a party with the Harberts. It was a party given to celebrate the launch of some society magazine or other; we were involved as potential advertisers, I believe. I will add, parenthetically, that my wife, whose name is Sally, is rather petite, not tiny by any means, but a small handful. I am used to squiring that size woman from place to place, in other words, accustomed to the size of her upper arm when I help her into a cab, for instance, the feel of her taut, compact rib cage against my hand when we are dancing. That night, my wife was somewhere, who knows where, perhaps cadging a cigarette on the roof of the building, secure in the misplaced assumption that I do not know she does so. There was a band, and it was playing a romantic tune, and I became aware of Jean Harbert at my side.

"Let's danch," she said.

It was a rather slow song, so I was called upon to put my arm around the somewhat inebriated Mrs. Harbert, who I suddenly realized was almost as tall as I am, and I am six foot one and a little more. As I said, I don't believe Jean came all the way to the impossible seventy-two inches that marks a woman a true Amazon, but she was darned close. Her blond hair, far too yellow for the illusion of authenticity, was sort of cemented to her head with one of those thick masks or gels or whatever they are that make the wearer appear as if she is wearing a stylish bathing cap and also smell very nice. Mrs. Harbert, on that occasion, was not perhaps as slender as she has since become, after her most recent enthusiasm for Pilates, but I don't mean to imply that there was anything adipose or excessive about her person. She was large, true, but in a way that excited in me, I will admit for this record, an unseemly level of interest. I suppose I had been drinking as well. I remember placing my arm around her waist, and being aware, suddenly, of how the line of her hip rose, ample and inviting, under my hand. Her eyes, as we danced, changed from light blue to a smoky sea green and back again. Her face was all angles—high, ruddy cheekbones, a well-defined jaw that perhaps imparted more character than is generally accepted as the standard for traditional good looks, a tall forehead under the aforementioned helmet and, I noticed for the first time from up close, the most remarkable skin, at once both translucent and luminescent. She pressed against me, and she was very soft, and I did not pull away.

"Thanks for the danch," she said when it was over. We never spoke of it again. But I always liked her after that.

After seeing Harb and the children off to school, Jean would find herself alone in the quiet house. She would play with the cat for a while, I believe. Read the paper, with coffee. This was all part of the general procrastination that put off the moment when she would be called upon to go down to the basement and begin the portion of her day dedicated to her work.

I wish I could tell you that Jean's photography was purely artistic, but it was not. She took pictures of children, for the most part, and also for the local newspaper. Some of the work she did purely for herself, but this stuff she never showed to anyone, until recently, when a small display of her digital suburban images attracted some attention in a tiny gallery on the South Side. She came up from her darkroom at one P.M. or so for a peanut butter and jelly sandwich and a glass of milk, which was her lunch of choice day after day, year after year, from the time she hit her thirty-fourth birthday and gave up meat. Then it was back down again until two, give or take, when it was time to clean up and begin preparations for the reentry of the two children, both of whom would be needing snacks, rides, and exhortations involving homework. In the late afternoon, with everyone ensconced at his or her desk and the house quiet once more, she began preparations for dinner, generally made phone calls pertaining to billing for her services, dealt with the vagaries of plumbers, roofers, driveway repairmen, chimney sweeps, and all the other vendors that keep a house in fair repair. By seven thirty-seven Harb was home, and the two indulged in the form of parallel play known as the long-term marriage. At sometime after eleven P.M., as we have ascertained, she fell asleep next to her husband.

A happy life, all in all. What is somewhat ironic about its rigor, repetition, and structure, however, is that Jean, more than her colossal square peg of a husband, was a child of the utopian generation that believed in free love, intoxicants, and art as a means of perpetual growth and happiness. I saw a picture of her once, taken when she was in her youth. The discrepancy between that picture and her bourgeois life with Harb was most poignant. Me, I never had outlandish hopes for the future, or for that matter, for my own life as it could be lived. I got my first internship in business when I was a freshman at Penn and never once looked back at a life outside the castle. And not that Jean and Harb did not have happiness, of a sort. But it is fair to say that neither Harb at his financial services job nor Jean wiping snot off the faces of reluctant second graders posing for their class picture were scaling the Olympian heights they had envisioned in their youth when both dreamed of forging something new in their respective worlds of art and commerce.

It is my understanding that the dawn of Harb's trial broke much like any other. Jean was downstairs making sandwiches. The cat lurked at her feet, weaving in and out, waiting for falling debris.

Harb lay there for a long while in his bed, wondering if there was a way a man could kill himself without feeling any pain. Deciding that there was not, he rose to face the beginning of the rest of his life.

16

UNITED STATES DISTRICT COURT NORTHERN DISTRICT OF ILLINOIS

CaroleAnne L. Winter, Plaintiff, v. Civ. Global Fiduciary Trust Company, Defendant

Monday, November 18, 10:00 A.M.

The court's opening remarks to the jury

THE COURT: Hi. I'm the judge. My name is Lerner.[1] Now that you have been sworn, I will give you some preliminary instructions.

Your job is to ascertain the facts. My job is to explain the law. Get it? You do facts. I do law. Incidentally, it doesn't matter if you agree with the law or not. It's the law and you've got to make your decisions based on it. Okay? All right.

Along the way, you may see me yawn. Eat an egg. Read *TV Guide*. Nothing I do is intended to flip you a wink or give you an inkling. And while it may also appear at times that my head has lolled onto my chest and I am drooling very slightly onto my robe, I am not sleeping. I am just listening in my own very special way.[2]

There's a lot of stuff I could tell you about evidence. Some is circumstantial and of less value than that which is direct . . . but ultimately, folks, the most important thing you have to do is decide who is telling the truth and who is lying. So listen for the truth, because if you got that, you got everything. I know, most people think

---

1. Short, fat, some sixty years of age with a big head of silvery gray hair. Lerner gave to the proceedings an abiding air of mock seriousness.
2. Lerner slept continually during the trial, awakening periodically to make his presence known.

that if you've got your health, you have everything, but in this case, it's about listening, not health.[3]

Here are my rules. They're simple. First, don't discuss the case. Second, don't discuss the case. And third, and most important, don't discuss the case. Not with each other. Not with your family at home. Not with your pals at a bar after work. I find you do, I will dismiss you and take away your dessert.

We'll begin at nine forty-five every day and end no later than five o'clock. Be on time or I will be very annoyed. First up is the attorney for the plaintiff.

3. At this point several jurors began to titter, after which the entire jury box seemed to relax and get into the swing of things. One woman took out a nail file and got to work. The other happily extracted a Chap Stick and assaulted her lips with goo. A large man in a denim work shirt in the second row took off his watch and began winding it, an activity he continued from that moment until the end of the trial.

17

Harb missed the judge's opening remarks and a bit of what followed on that first morning of the trial. Not that he wasn't interested. Of course he was. He was detained, however, by matters at home.

It began, as most important incidents in family life, in the kitchen. Jean was munching on an English muffin. Having at last hauled his carcass from bed and completed the best part of his preparatory ablutions, Harb came in with his shirt stays in hand and sat in the chair at the head of their kitchen table.

"Here," he said. He handed her the shirt stays.

"This is all so degrading and atrocious," said Jean.

Harb said nothing. They had been over this many times, or some version of it. There is a school of thought, I'm sure not completely without merit, that when one member of a couple loses his ability to tolerate verbatim repetition of key discussions, the marriage is in jeopardy. Several years ago, my wife entered into a fugue state in which she could discuss nothing but the failings of our corporate health coverage. I had, of course, complained about her behavior for a time, since there was nothing I could personally do about this corporate policy that had an impact on thousands of people, but because I work in the Human Resources department, she chose to believe otherwise. Several times I tried rising to my feet in a towering rage and impolitely requesting her to cease discourse on the subject, although I did not perhaps use those exact words. This had a most adverse effect. So finally I simply sat there, not taking any part so as to prolong the episode, and endured. Once, I actually put my head down on the dining room table and wept. It did no good. My wife has a tremendous ability to be outraged at the common injustices that society visits on its members, and her dudgeon was roused beyond endurance at that point. I have certain issues that push my buttons, too.

At long last, she simply ceased perseverating on this subject and moved on to new ones, predominantly the issue of which colleges we should be looking at for our kids, both of whom are now in their teens. That subject is still raging in our home, and I am now at the point of participation in this matter that I was on the question of insurance. I'm not saying it's not an important issue. I just can't stand to talk about it anymore.

"Pathetic situation," said Jean. She was clearly looking to stick the tip of her knife into just the right spot in the oyster.

"Yes," said Harb. But on this occasion, under the considerable stress of the impending public humiliation he was sure the trial would produce, he said a few things more. And that, my friends, made all the difference. "Part of it is my own fault, I guess," he muttered as he bent down to tie his wing tip.

"In what way?" said Jean. A very slender pair of gleaming, metallic antennae emerged silently from the back of her head and pointed slightly forward. Perhaps Harb could not see them—you know, I am sure, how unobservant spouses can be about each other after years of cohabitation—but there they were, and fully extended, too. In all the discussions the Harberts had heretofore conducted on the subject of the sexual harassment suit, Harb had admitted to no culpability whatsoever. This, on the opening day of his public humiliation, was the first whisper that Jean had picked up, and it had the stench of reality about it.

"Oh, I don't know," said Harb with thoroughly bogus indifference. He had immediately, if somewhat belatedly, ascertained a change in his wife's tone and was aware that he had stepped off the path and into the woods. He could not go back, for that way was utterly obscured by brambles and bushes laden with poisoned berries, but any move forward would have to be done with the greatest of care, for the road ahead was strewn with mines.

It would be unfair of me to imply that Harb was completely

dismayed by the prospect of having a substantial exchange of limited duration on this difficult and terrifying issue. There would be much talk and perhaps even some press over the days of the trial. He didn't want Jean totally in the dark about matters as they had allegedly transpired. He knew what she might hear. It wouldn't hurt to put a bit of English on it beforehand. Jean, unfortunately, was large, generally dedicated to her own course, and somewhat hard to spin.

"Because a lot of stuff may happen over the course of several years," Harb muttered vaguely, "that can be misinterpreted by an obviously disturbed and demented person, which is what CaroleAnne turned out to be."

"Go on," said Jean. She was sketching on the edge of a bit of newspaper, meticulously building an edifice of parallel lines at a variety of angles with a small fountain pen she favored for doing her accounts. Every now and then, she took a bit of coffee.

"Well, like, for instance . . ." Harb stared at his shoes for a while. "Oh, Jeanie. For God's sake. I don't know." He put his face in his hand.

Jean did not move. "Maybe you'd better leave it alone, Robert," she said after a time.

"Like, for a long time there was an accelerated succession of raises, which could give the appearance of favoritism of one sort or another. There were the personal bonuses that were paid out over a period of years out of, you know . . ." Here Harb's voice dropped precipitously off the cliff of silence. ". . . my own pocket," he concluded.

"Oh, for Christ's sake!" said Jean. Without any particular warning she threw the pen across the room, where its point exploded on the wall, leaving an ugly Rorschach hanging on the lemon and white wallpaper of the kitchen. Then, quite inexplicably for one of her anal disposition, she did not move but simply stood there huffing and puffing for long, critical minutes in which the ink could possibly have been expunged before drying. So the stain is there still, as far as I know.

"What else is there?" she said into the void.

"I'm not going to talk about this if you're going to start with that kind of stuff!" Harb looked up defiantly at his wife. Little hot patches of red illuminated her cheeks and her eyes were tiny, wet stones glowing in the middle of the spinning vortex of her face. He looked away, knowing there would at this time be no understanding or forgiveness there. And still he pressed on.

"The Nissan," he said.

"You sold it."

"No."

Somewhere out beyond the house, a dog was barking. The blare of the horn that called the volunteer fire department the next town over went off a few miles away, bleating its call to arms every few seconds. Harb listened and wondered whether he would be in a position to hear these sounds in just that way ever again.

"What happened to the Nissan?" said Jean very quietly. The car had been a bone of some contention a few years back. Harb had suddenly and inexplicably indicated a desire to be rid of what his wife considered a perfectly serviceable train station vehicle. They had discussed it for a few months, during which time Jean was shocked that the topic did not go away, then argued about it for some weeks more, as it became clear that a set of new wheels represented something powerful to Harb. Finally, amazed at the sheer force of this particular obsession and the attention span it seemed to have generated in her customarily fragmented husband, she relented, and Harb got his midlife crisis car. The Nissan disappeared, for no financial gain, she was told. Now this.

"Gave her the Nissan," said Harb.

"Uh-huh," said Jean.

"Wasn't worth anything." This sounded unconvincing, even to Harb. "She has . . . had . . . nothing," he sort of choked out. "Her life . . . her life was falling apart. Fucked-up dude beating her up all the time. I felt like, you know, I could make a difference. I'm sorry I didn't tell you, but if I had told you, you would have made some kind of a huge deal out of the whole thing and taken the magic completely out of it. So I just did it." There was a silence you could drive a herd of cattle through, then Harb completed his soufflé of self-destruction. "All day every day for more than twenty years I do what I want and everybody listens to what I say, except . . . here," he blurted out. "And on this one occasion, Jean, on this one occasion I presumed to act in an executive manner as it pertained to an issue at home. I didn't wish to be questioned. I didn't want to go through the wringer on it and I still don't. Forgive me." He rose with dramatic decisiveness and then, realizing he had nowhere yet to go, sat down again.

"Well, I could be wrong, but that doesn't sound like much of an apology . . . to . . . *me!*" said Jean. She stood up. "On the contrary, it sounds like a bunch of belligerent bullshit self-justification. Mostly, it appears like evidence across the board of what a jury might find an inappropriate level of affection between you and this crazy woman."

"I liked her. I valued her contribution. She was . . . a friend." And then, as if this were not enough, he stupidly added, "We got loaded a lot on the road."

"Wait a minute," said Jean.

"Nothing happened." Harb arranged his face for maximum credibility, was aware of doing so, which upset him. Why should he have to consciously compose his features? He was telling the truth, goddamn it! Right? Except . . . there was something . . .

"No, no," said Jean. She turned abruptly and with a sequence of herky-jerky movements got herself to the sink, where she began washing her breakfast dishes. Water pounded. Steam blew.

"I can see how somebody inherently as loony as CaroleAnne, particularly about quasi-religious subjects, could possibly feel in her distorted imagination . . ." Harb was trying to be soothing but succeeded in producing instead a tone both pompous and analytical, as if he were an expert guest on MSNBC.

"Did you, like, get all slobbery with each other at the bars and stuff and, you know . . . what . . ." The pace of the washing was increasing exponentially. A certain amount of pot banging was going on, too. "Did . . . like . . . people see you and stuff?"

"Not at all! I mean . . . no!" said Harb, which seemed as an answer to be both too much and not enough. This was going all wrong. She was reading into him. But there was nothing! And yet . . . This was a terrible mistake, to go all loose and runny like this at the last minute. He had to get out of there before things got unmanageable.

Jean seemed to agree. "Get out of here," she said into the soapy water. She had fished out a carving knife she had used to cut the bagels for the kids earlier that morning and was looking at it. It was long and serrated and very, very sharp. "I can't talk to you, Harb. I see the whole thing. You didn't have an affair with the woman. You're not that honest. God, what is the next week going to be like?" She stared into the frothing sink for a few seconds and then exploded. "There are going to be court reporters there! You work for a huge corporation! There's sex! And business! And oh, I just can't take it. I can't!" She started to cry.

Harb felt bad, but there seemed to be little he could do to improve the situation. So he rose and put on his coat. He was aware that Jean was capable of doing something impulsive with the knife, particularly when she was in this state of emotion. People did kill their spouses and for just such excellent reasons. Not long ago, a Texas woman ran over her husband with their Mercedes three times outside of a hotel where he was meeting his mistress. He died. Newspapers said there was a lot of sympathy for the woman. This case wasn't as bad . . . if it happened to him, possibly there might be a little sympathy for him as well, at long last. On the other hand, it occurred to him that it was just possible that whatever was happening now was not worth dying for. In his narrow little chest, something stirred. Harb stood.

He looked around him. He saw his wife at the sink. He longed to comfort her but could not. He had been the source of her pain, and who was he now to presume to diminish it? He saw the cat, sitting in a patch of sunlight, chasing a dust mote with her paw. He longed to go over and pick her up, but did not, since to do so would almost certainly produce nothing but unpleasant wriggling and possibly even a scratched face. The cat was capable of great shows of affection, but only if permitted to offer them unsolicited. He saw their kitchen glowing in the early morning sunshine. They had spent so much money on the kitchen. Now what had all that money produced? A kitchen, that was all. He saw the various papers stuck to the refrigerator. Report cards. Postcards. Christmas cards. Artwork from the kids, years old. Coupons. He saw his wife again. She was weeping less and just staring into the water. There was nothing to say. He picked up his cell phone from the kitchen table. Patted his pockets to make sure all his billfolds, keys, pagers, and pertinent papers were in order.

"I'm sorry, peanut," he said. It just . . . popped out of him. He hadn't known he was going to say it. It sounded so stupid once it was hanging there in the heavy air of the room. Of course he was sorry. And was she still his peanut? Not at the moment, anyhow.

"I know, Harb." She looked exhausted. The knife was still in her hand but was no longer being used to provide emphasis. She did not look him in the face. "You better go now. You should be in court. An innocent man would be in court."

18

Monday, November 18, 10:32 A.M.

Opening remarks of Bruce Morgenstern, attorney for the plaintiff

----

MR. MORGENSTERN: Hello, ladies and gentlemen of the jury, my name is Bruce Morgenstern, and I represent CaroleAnne Winter.[4]

CaroleAnne Winter was a former employee of the Global Fiduciary Trust Company here in Chicago. She was working there since 1997. What I intend to prove is that during her tenure at that august and serious institution, one that is responsible for actions that impact upon the lives of millions of people daily, CaroleAnne Winter, a very decent, intelligent, hardworking, fine, upstanding, God-fearing kind of woman, that CaroleAnne Winter was the victim of a continuous onslaught of sexually insulting behavior that no human being, let alone one who is deeply spiritual, should be forced to reckon with. Today she faces her tormenters, the power of that gigantic corporation arrayed against her. And who will speak for her? That is my assignment.[5]

4. I have to state at the outset that I immediately loathed this greasy, stupid fellow, as tall and lanky as a lamppost but also graced with a noticeable paunch that his atrocious posture did nothing to ameliorate. His blocky head, long and angular with a bulbous chin at the end of a weak, jowly jaw, was topped by an unruly shock of mud-brown, wiry hair that refused to stay appropriately arranged on his scalp. I don't mean to imply that it was false, for no toupee would ever be so poorly fashioned. I am willing to admit to the possibility that my aversion to this learned counsel was based on his adversarial role in the proceedings, but having admitted that I reject it entirely. I believe that the judge, the jury, and all onlookers in the courtroom took an instantaneous dislike to Mr. Morgenstern's personal style and means of communication – pompous, falsely humble, verbose to the point of madness . . . he was a fool that any rational person of taste and substance would have eluded if the chance was provided, and we were compelled to remain in his presence, enduring him at close quarters, for the entire length of the trial. Wherever he is now, I hope he has a blister on the bottom of his foot.

5. I'm going to cut Mr. Morgenstern's comments down radically. Believe me, as bloviated as they seem here, they were literally ten times as bad in the real-time world of the courtroom.

We will further show that this continuous assault upon her began right at the start of her employment and was based on the pervasive atmosphere of depraved sexuality that ran through that office. They should have known better, ladies and gentlemen of the jury. But they did not. And it is for this lack of common decency that they should be punished in the name of all that is right and proper.

You will also hear testimony that CaroleAnne Winter is a very religious person. And that at lunchtime she would hold prayer meetings at her place of employment. Did this adhere to the policies of the company? Perhaps not. Was it appropriate for her coworkers to use these spiritual interfaces with the Divine as the butt of jokes, often lewd and lascivious ones? Again, as jurors, you will decide.

The defendant will call a psychiatrist and try to convince you that this woman is insane. You will hear her speak and hear how she suffered. And in the end, because you are reasonable and fair people, I know you will find that Global Fiduciary Trust was guilty of gross misconduct against this woman.

I thank you for your attention, your minds, and your hearts.[6]

---

6. The fellow really made me want to barf.

19

Now imagine, if you will, Harb in his car. He is driving, and by that I mean that he is sitting quite still. He would be making better progress if he was, in fact, walking. And he is not a fast walker.

This is by no means the fault of his car. After he gave his elderly Nissan to CaroleAnne, Harb, as we have noted, went out and got himself a Z3 roadster. Anyone who has seen the vehicle knows it is a tiny car, a useless car in snow and ice, a foolish car for men trying to distract the world from their bald heads and tiny penises. Still, I rode in the car a couple of times, and I can tell you: It rocked. Harb could pass anything God had chosen to put on the road that day. I saw him vie with a Ferrari once on an open stretch on Lake Shore Drive late at night. We were tooling along minding our own business, and this limp little fellow blew by us at what must have been eighty in a fifty-five-mile-per-hour zone. It was clear to both of us that this idiot could not be allowed to dominate the road unchallenged. Harb looked at me for a long moment, a smile of enormous proportions threatening to explode around the edge of his mouth. Then he gave the Z3 as much gas as it would take. We went from sixty to ninety immediately and caught up with that idiot in less than five seconds. In perhaps less than ten seconds, he flipped the other guy the bird as politely as he possibly could, then pulled away at last. I was laughing quite hard by that time, not due to anything Harb was doing but because our adversary had taken this interlude with exactly the kind of blustery ill temper for which we might have hoped and was righteously pissed off. But like most fat, bald men who drive Ferraris, he was incapable of conducting his superb vehicle to its true potential, too frightened to do what was necessary to kick our butts.

The Ferrari's lights disappeared in our rearview mirror. Harb was grinning like a death's-head, his hands clenched to the wheel, his eyes bugging out of his skull. "Ease it off, Bob," I said. There was no indication that he heard me. But I felt the car pull back a tad. "The mark of a great champion is knowing when the battle is won," I added. This was something I picked up in one of those moronic business books they make us read. It seemed an appropriate comment. He gave no indication that he had heard me. But once again I felt the car ease down a bit. We were now going perhaps seventy-five, a proper speed for late-at-night drivers who know the route upon which they must travel each and every day.

"Okay," said Harb, after a time. Once again, the Z3's mighty engine torqued down its impressive roar.

"What the fuck is the matter with me?" said Harb.

"You're sorta crazy these days, Bobby," I said.

No further comment was required and none was offered. Harb dropped me off at my suburb not long thereafter. I considered getting myself one of those cars for a few weeks after that but decided against it. I didn't want to end up the weenie behind the wheel of a transcendent machine of which I was not worthy.

Anyway, I'm not Harb. And I know it.

Now picture that very same Harbert festering in traffic on the way to the trial at which we have already sat in attendance. He is listening to the radio in this car that is tuned to take off for the moon. Now it is standing stock-still. In the next lane is a gigantic SUV whose hubcaps are at Harb's eye level. His car phone rang.

"Yes," he said. He sounded quite grouchy, because serious players in business find it best to project an irritable temperament until the situation decrees otherwise.

"Harb! My man!" It was Nevsky, the high controller of the corporation and perhaps the most adroit politician in the nest.

"Yes, Bill," said Harb. He had the sensation that a gigantic halberd was about to descend on the naked skin on the back of his neck and was determined, when it fell, not to whine about it. This is often a terrible strategy. Nobility in the doomed tends to make things easier on the executioner.

"Harb!" the connection was scratchy. Harb said nothing. He waited. "What we want here . . ." There was a pause. Nevsky was having trouble.

"What is it, Bill?" said Harb. He fished a small cigar butt out of the ashtray and punched in the lighter.

"Well, we were talking to Ned, and . . ."

"We, Bill? Which is the we we're talking about here?"

The traffic suddenly opened up inexplicably, as it does, and the flow started moving down the highway without impediment.

"Well, me, Harb . . . and of course the guys on five . . ." That would mean the accounting department, which worked for Finance, which was Schlink. Harb felt a large bubble of bile rise from the depth of his system and coat the back of his throat. He suddenly knew what this was about. A small trembling membrane broke within him, and he wanted to cry. This was about his job. Most important, this was about his expense account, the entity that ties all executives to the bosom of the corporation. What would life be like without it? He could not bear to consider the question. And yet, it was now clear, he must.

"Go ahead, fuckface," said Harb.

"What was that?"

"I said you're breaking up on me."

". . . looking at the level of expenditures at the corporate center . . ." was what came through the digital pipe.

Harb thought about it. "Tell the Old Man," he said after time, "that I find it very disappointing that he personally wants to fuck with me on this level. Tell him that I don't believe it's he who is raising this question with me. Tell him if he wants to talk to me about my personal expenses I will discuss it with him and only him, because it is him I report to, not you, or Schlink, or Karpovski, or anyfuckingbody else. Did you get that loud and clear, Bill? Am I breaking up on you?"

"No, Harb, no no," said Nevsky. He sounded scared, even over that insufficient conduit. "I get you. And I hope you didn't take this the wrong way in any way."

"Not at all," said Harb. "I understand you completely."

He pressed the disconnect button and settled back behind the wheel. The traffic was moving nicely now, and the feeling of mastery that always accompanied the unfettered motion of his vehicle descended upon Harb.

There was no question that if Finance was going after his expenses, his time on this earth was not to be measured in years, or even months, but had now entered the arena in which hours were an appropriate yardstick. When the boys went after that, it was clearly open season on you, because no one's use of corporate expenses was above reproach. The unspoken agreement with any senior officer was the inviolable nature of his or her discretionary expenditures. All executives had business friends they lunched, weird presents they bought for former associates, Palmtops, laptops, and other gizmos of uncertain corporate utility. "O! reason not the need," cried Lear. It was the ultimate howl of the executive divorced from his unquestioned expense account.

Harb shot by a Mercedes convertible, and a peculiar sense of peace descended upon him. He speed-dialed his cell phone one more time and cranked the Z3 up to seventy.

"Louise?" he said, and for some reason he felt lighter than he had in a long, long time. "I'm going to be staying in town for a while."

20

Opening remarks of Greg Biddle, attorney, Global Fiduciary Trust Corporation

----

MR. BIDDLE: Good morning. My name is Greg Biddle, and it is my honor, ladies and gentlemen, to defend the people and the honor of Global Fiduciary Trust Corporation.[7]

Global Fiduciary Trust. My, my, that's a faceless concept. But is it really? I think not. Because in addition to being a big, impersonal corporation, Global is also people, ladies and gentlemen. People like you and me. Flesh-and-blood people. And you will meet many of those people. Men and women with husbands and wives at home and children out on the playground and dogs to walk before bedtime. The people of Global. You will meet them. And then you will see that a great injustice is being done here. Because it is not the honor of a big, cold corporation that is being assailed here. It is the honor of the people who work there. It is for them I now speak.

Let's cut to it. If those terrible things alleged by Mr. Morgenstern happened to Ms. Winter, there is no question that my client is made up of terrible people and you should find for the plaintiff. But you know what? They didn't happen. Nope. Not any of them. Not one. Because Ms. Winter, ladies and gentlemen, is a very disturbed woman whose mind is filled with very bizarre stuff. That's what this case

7. I liked Biddle, our out-of-house counsel. He was a bit of a wimp, but he had a firm command of the law and liked a joke now and then. Unbeknownst to the gallery, he suffered from crippling stage fright before every contest. Then he went out there and performed like a Trojan. Unlike many fighting men who sport prominent jawbones, Biddle had no chin whatsoever. Other than that, he was okay to look at.

is about. What it's like to put your trust in somebody, and think you know her, and then suddenly realize that the person you have been working closely with every day for years is not the person you know, but is, in some very fundamental way, a deluded and dangerous person. A monster. Harsh, you may say. But think about it, ladies and gentlemen: Monsters are not always ugly. Monsters are not always hateful. And it is quite common for a monster to generate our sympathy. I urge you to resist that impulse and place your sympathy in the right location—with the people who have been victimized by this terrible transformation from friend and colleague into an unknowable force of evil.

You will hear from associates. You will hear from a psychiatrist. And you will hear from CaroleAnne Winter herself. And at the end of the day, I am sure you will find that the tragedy of CaroleAnne Winter lies not in what was done to her but what she has done to herself and to those who once called her a friend. Thank you.

THE COURT: We will break for lunch. Oh, by the way, did I mention this? Don't discuss the case.[8]

(Luncheon recess)

---

8. I'm sure this judge thought himself to be one of the funniest guys on the planet, but he was already beginning to get on my nerves.

21

Harb stood in the back of the room and regarded the pomp and majesty of the scene before him. There wasn't any.

The room was large, with a high ceiling and room enough in the gallery to accommodate at least a hundred onlookers. There was nowhere near that number now. Perhaps sixteen, certainly no more than twenty, dotted the worn wooden benches that squatted behind an equally tired railing that functioned to separate the audience from the proceedings. There was no one he recognized in the house, except for me, sitting on an aisle, and of course CaroleAnne, who was perched on the edge of her chair in the space reserved for the plaintiff.

He entered the room just as Mr. Biddle was finishing his serviceable remarks. No eyes turned to note his entrance. Except for two. CaroleAnne's head immediately swiveled on its well-oiled neck support system and took in the object of her legal crusade. If you expect me to report that a look of pure hatred and wronged female dignity suffused her features, you will be disappointed. If, on the other hand, you are hoping for a long regard reeking of pity and shared humanity, you will once again be deprived of satisfaction. If, finally, you were expecting a querulous, adoring gaze, a tremble of the lip, a little cry, a small elevation from the seat, a slight opening of the mouth, a sudden, sad remembrance of the pertinent actuality of the situation, a soft, slow easing back into the cold, harsh reality of the courtroom . . . well, then. You are far more prescient than I. For that is indeed the reaction Harb's appearance produced in the wronged plaintiff. She appeared nothing less than fully ecstatic at last to behold his marvelous visage. And then she recalled what had in fact brought them together at this time and place. And a terrible tristesse flowed over and through her.

Harb, for his part, simply stood there. He reviewed the onlookers. He regarded the jury. He took a long, assessing gaze at the judge, which I admit I found appropriate, given the somewhat idiosyncratic mien with which that gentleman had already graced us. And finally, he looked at CaroleAnne, who was right then oozing her silent, metaphysical greeting at him. Nothing. Not anger, which would, I think, have been appropriate. Not hatred. Not amusement, for the ridiculousness of the situation. Just . . . not anything. He stood at the back of the room exactly as Biddle was concluding his remarks. The jury filed into their enclosure offstage, like kids ready for a lunch prepared especially for their field trip. The judge gathered up his pompous, breezy self and hied off to his chamber. There was a bit of chaos in those who remained, then they dispersed. For a terrible moment, I thought perhaps that CaroleAnne was going to say something to Harb, and that he would have to answer. But she thought better of it and crept down the center aisle in the company of her long, bony, flatulent attorney. And then we were alone.

"Harb," I said. There was so much I wanted to say to him. About friendship, and loyalty, and what I would do to stanch his pain if I could. But goddamn it to hell, I could say nothing.

"It's all right, Fred," said Harb. He was looking straight ahead, as if inhaling the entirety of the room. "Let's go get some Chinese food."

So we did. It was greasy. It was good. We were back on time for CaroleAnne's testimony.

22

Direct examination of CaroleAnne Winter, plaintiff, by Bruce Morgenstern

----

MR. MORGENSTERN: Good afternoon, everyone. Good afternoon, Ms. Winter.

MS. WINTER: Good afternoon.[9]

Q: Where do you live?

THE COURT: Counsel, is there any reason you are speaking in such a loud tone of voice? Is the witness deaf in any way?

MR. MORGENSTERN: No, your honor.

THE COURT: Then keep it down, okay?

MR. MORGENSTERN: Thank you, Your Honor.

A: I live at Two Toledo Place, Chicago, Illinois.

Q: How long have you lived there?

A: Several years.

Q: Prior to that?

A: Before that with my husband, who abused me.

Q: Where was that?

A: In Toledo, Ohio, and in Denver, and for a while in Oakland, California. Then I came here.

Q: Tell us about yourself. Did you go to school?

A: I have a high school diploma. I went to secretarial

---

9. CaroleAnne was dressed very conservatively in a blue pinstriped suit and white shirt, with a tasteful, understated scarf around her neck.

school as well. And I have tried to keep up with my reading.

Q: Where did you graduate high school?

A: Baton Rouge, Louisiana.

Q: After secretary school, did you get a job?

A: I was a temp, and I worked for Consolidated, and for an employment agency named Manpower, and so on. My first real job was with Forbst, on the receptionist desk.

Q: How long did that last?

A: Just short of two years.

Q: After that?

A: I worked in St. Louis for a large beverage concern for about three months. Then I worked for Microsoft in Seattle, but the hours were horrendous. I think they try to flush out people with any hope for a private life there. Then I worked in the motion picture industry in Southern California, but that was too alternately boring and hectic, so I quit.

Q: Go on.

A: I worked at an HMO as a senior secretary, and also for a satellite entertainment business, where I ended up performing executive functions under the guise of secretarial status. Then I came to Chicago.[10]

Q: When did you get to Global?

A: Shortly after I got here.

Q: Who was your boss?

A: I was hired by Robert Harbert.

Q: Can you describe your duties?

A: Just secretary-type stuff, word processing, filing, ordering supplies, handling personnel matters like promotions, job transfers, salary increases, things of that nature. I liked it.

Q: How big was the department?

10. Why didn't we pick up on this amazing pattern of establishment and flight? I blame myself for this failure of procedural analysis.

A: It was enormous. We had Pittsburgh offices and offices in Cleveland and Kansas City. We loaned, like, fifty billion dollars out at any one time. And everybody reported to Harb. I mean, on paper they reported to Mr. Podesky, but by that point it was really Mr. Harbert who carried the weight.[11]

Q: And what kind of a boss was Mr. Harbert?

A: He was nice. Of course, he was very smart, with a good sense of humor. From the start, though, I found him to be overly . . . personal.

Q: Did you bring this quality to his attention?

A: Not at that time, no. We were secretary and boss. He was satisfied with my work and I was satisfied working for him.

Q: Did there come a time when you perceived a change in your relationship with Mr. Harbert?

A: Yes. One morning, about three months after I had joined the company, Mr. Harbert called me into his office. I remember I was wearing a very nice red blouse and skirt combination, with a pink scarf at my neck.

Q: Go on.

A: I suppose it showed off my body, but up until that point, I was not at all self-conscious. And I walked into Mr. Harbert's office and he stopped talking to Mr. Tell, and I saw that his eyes went over me from top to bottom. Hungry eyes, is what they were. It made me feel very creepy.[12]

Q: Go on.

A: And then there was the matter of his prying into my personal life, as I've said. I'm sure he meant well, but the effect on me was quite negative. I'd come in in the

11. I should mention at this time that Podesky was finally in the throes of senescence and was too infirm to attend these proceedings.
12. CaroleAnne entered Harb's close personal space dressed as she said, in a silk thing that wrapped around her body and revealed down to just short of nipple height a pair of generous, optimistic breasts of a luminescent, golden hue. It was red, this article of clothing, and the skirt she was wearing was black leather and ended approximately three inches below her pudenda. I could barely catch my breath, and I was not halfway as smitten with the woman as was my poor besotted friend.

morning, and he'd start on me about what I did the night before. His prying, and the way he looked at me, I began to feel uncomfortable. And that didn't stop.

A couple of weeks after the whole thing with the red shirt, Mr. Harbert called me into his office supposedly to do something secretarial, but I felt it was just because he wanted to be with me. And he started in on his personal questions. This time he wanted to know where my people come from, so I told him Louisiana, and he started quizzing me. Like, whether that's near Texas, and honestly, I don't know a lot about geography, and I could tell that he suspected me of lying to cover up my past. And this hurt me.

Q: Did you ever raise this problem with him?

A: I tried. I told him that his constant references to my personal life were unwelcome.

Q: What kind of references were those?

A: Well, "You look nice today," things of that nature.

Q: I see. "You look nice today."

A: Yes.

Q: Go on.

23

"I was living at that time in Deerfield, Illinois," said CaroleAnne, her eyes clouding over with the darkness of the memory. "In order to get to work on time I had to get to the train very early, get up very early."

I will note the fact that at this juncture I personally was rising at the ungodly hour of five forty-five each day, which gave me just time enough to do a half hour on the stationary bicycle and still get into the office by eight, the absolute limit of tardiness for the Total Quality executive. Still, it was hard not to feel sorry for CaroleAnne, pulling herself out of bed in the dim light before morning next to her skunk of a work-allergic husband.

"I was living with my husband, Edgar, then," she went on with a touch of stone in her demeanor, "and several of his family, and some of their friends, and it was a chaotic lifestyle, and I didn't get a lot of sleep at that time what with the yelling and partying going on all night long. And when I would come in a little bit late now and then, Mr. Harbert said it wasn't a problem, but I could tell that he and Mr. Podesky would share jokes about my being late and have a good little laugh over it."

"You actually heard them laughing at you?"

Yes, my friends, here was what we would all come to recognize as vintage Morgenstern, the attorney for the plaintiff honing in like an eagle on the exact question most likely to undermine his own client. Then, and later, I found myself wondering why there are so many court shows on television. The actual experience is torture, the perfect mixture of boredom and aggravation.

"No, it was more subtle than that. And that's what hurt," said CaroleAnne.

"Of course you were hurt," said Morgenstern sententiously. "Which of us would not have been?"

"Counsel," growled Lerner as if from the depths of a deep coma, "let's keep the personal observations to a minimum."

Morgenstern was crestfallen. "I'm sorry, Your Honor," he said with quiet humility.

"Then we had a whole problem about how I was supposed to address . . ." here she took a significant pause, considering. Then she said quite clearly, "Dick."

"That would be Mr. Podesky?"

"Well," said CaroleAnne, "it was ridiculous. Everybody in the office was on a first-name basis. And I'm a naturally friendly and upbeat person, you know, and so every morning I would come in and say, 'Good Morning, Harb,' 'Good Morning, Fred,' 'Good Morning, Dick.' And I could see something was wrong with Dick, but I couldn't tell what. And then Harb told me that Dick didn't want me calling him Dick." She really seemed to be enjoying this opportunity to call Dick Dick, and I didn't blame her.

"He didn't want you to call him Dick," said Morgenstern without expression.

"Those were his words, but the way he said it made it very clear what he was talking about. Particularly when he said that if I wanted to call Dick Dick it would probably be okay to do so in private. That left very little to the imagination."

"How did you react to this blatantly suggestive remark?" said Morgenstern. Biddle rose but did not speak.

"Cut it out, Mr. Morgenstern," belched the judge.

"Well," said CaroleAnne. "I refused to let it make me feel degraded, but I recognized that that was its intent."

Poor Podesky. Dick is a heavy name to carry, unless you're a very substantial guy indeed. And Dick wasn't.

"And then?"

"Well, Harb too was, you know, getting more and more personal." CaroleAnne shivered a little, a small tremblor that ran from the top of her head to the base of her spine. "And his comments and jokes to other people about me increased. It became even worse if we wore casual clothing to work on, like, Fridays. One day I wore jeans and sort of a polo shirt. I can't tell you that anything specific happened on that day in particular, but after that his attention appeared to me on many occasions to be nonprofessional, that's all I can say. I don't think I was imagining it."

Nah. She wasn't. She was great looking, and sometimes it's hard even for a Human Resources professional not to notice. Those without our training are even more susceptible, I imagine.

CaroleAnne's visage was smote with a sudden shadow. "And one day, I remember, he came by my desk for a chat, and I had a cold and was taking a little cup of DayCare. It's by Vicks. Very good cold medicine."

"Thank you for that testimonial," said Lerner.

"Okay, okay," said CaroleAnne, and blushed. "Anyhow, Mr. Harbert saw me taking this medicine and he said something like, 'Give me a couple of those and we can have a party.'" She shook her head at the unpleasant memory. "I thought that was very . . . inappropriate."

"And . . ." Morgenstern took a weighty pause to wind up this punch, "when did he start telling you that you should get a divorce?"

Biddle erupted from his seat. "Your Honor," he said. "This is a jury trial. It's very hard to recuperate from outright falsehoods being trotted past the court by Mr. Morgenstern."

"Sustained. The jury will disregard the question. Rephrase it, Counsel."

"Thank you, Your Honor," said Morgenstern as if he had just won a great victory. "Did Mr. Harbert ever discuss your marital situation with you?"

"Yes," said CaroleAnne. She had gone very hushed all of a sudden. I felt sick.

"Shortly after I arrived at the company," said CaroleAnne.

At that point I got up very quietly and moved from my position up front by the railing to the very, very back of the courtroom, behind the last row of seats, where I stood, pacing slightly, for the rest of her horrendous testimony that day. Now it was going to be said that Harb had interfered with CaroleAnne's marriage in a way that was unprofessional and inappropriate. What's a manager to do? Stand by and watch from a distance while a person you have affection for is pounded like a piece of veal?

"What kind of observations did Mr. Harbert make about your marriage?" Morgenstern appeared saddened at the necessity to delve into this kind of seamy material but determined to do his duty nonetheless.

"He teased me about sleeping in late," said CaroleAnne with what I am bound to report was a sexy little pout.

"Go on."

"I feel like I have already described the type of things they would say," CaroleAnne murmured vaguely, a little resentfully, suddenly at a loss. She seemed to be having some difficulty.

"Did he ever tell you that you should leave your husband?"

"Oh, yes," said CaroleAnne. "Many times."

Morgenstern let that hang in the air for a little while.

"And he helped you to find a new apartment, isn't that right, to help you leave your husband."

"Yes, that's right." Hectic patches of color had appeared on CaroleAnne's cheeks.

"But honestly . . . you wouldn't have just left your husband because Mr. Harbert told you so?"

"No. That's probably true. I'm just not certain, though," said CaroleAnne. And she genuinely did seem uncertain. "The whole office sort of conspired, although I'm sure they wouldn't see it that way, to make me feel bad about myself," said CaroleAnne.

"Really."

"Yeah. It was subtle, of course. What I've said. Hints, insinuations, innuendos, looks, you know, snickering. One time somebody put out a rumor that I was pregnant, and supposedly people could tell because my skin was glowing. Stuff like that. I'm not sure whether it was Harb or one of his subordinates who got that one going. Perhaps they all thought it was a joke. They all played a lot of pranks and teasing with each other. I just can't really take it, maybe that's it."

"I guess the jury will have to decide whether that should be part of anyone's job description," said Morgenstern, visibly moved. "Look," he said, railing. "I'm finding it hard to believe that anybody would want to spread such a shocking thing."

"And then came the rumor that I had had an abortion," she said darkly, "which is really terrible. I remember once or twice Mr. Harbert didn't actually *say* that he thought I had had an abortion, but he made jokes about it, because I was hammering a nail into the wall behind my desk and he came out of his office and watched me for a while, and then he said, 'Did you kill it?' or something like that, and I mean, there was no real response to that, you know what I mean?"

An icy hand of dread had plunged itself through my tie and into my chest. I looked at the placid, affable CaroleAnne and knew I was staring into the face of madness.

"I think we do," said Morgenstern, with a drippy smile at the jury. "Who else seemed to think you were pregnant?"

"Well," said CaroleAnne thoughtfully, "one of the people that came to my mind that I think I heard it from first was a lady named Rose that worked in national accounts."

Rose? The woman who hands out the paychecks?

"She was the one who came by my desk when Harb gave me flowers for secretarial day, and she said, 'Everything around here is blossoming!' And she let me know she wasn't talking about the flowers, if you know what I'm talking about."

There was a brooding silence. Then CaroleAnne, in a whole new tone entirely, said, "And then there was the whole thing that happened with this guy . . . Buddy Keaveney."

Good gracious. I haven't even mentioned Buddy Keaveney to you because he was so unimportant, a bit player left over from the Podesky years.

"Who was he?" asked Morgenstern. I could tell this was a new one on him, too, but he was game for a go at it.

"He was a consultant," said CaroleAnne, as if this explained everything.

"I see," said Morgenstern. "Okay." He looked down at his notes for a few moments, flummoxed. "Did Mr. Keaveney play a part in the overly sexual atmosphere of your office?" he said at last.

"Sustained," said the judge, although no objection had been offered. "I am going to start saying 'Sustained' every time I feel like it," he continued into his third chin, "even if Mr. Biddle has become too dispirited to object every time Mr. Morgenstern oversteps. It's easier for me because I don't have to pop up like a jack-in-the-box every time."

"We had planned a trip to this place called Morgantown, West Virginia," CaroleAnne went on, a little nonplussed. "Don't ask me why anybody would want to go there. There's nothing there, believe me. Wow. Anyhow, I went on the trip. At dinner on the final night of the seminar, I was sitting beside this Buddy Keaveney fellow, and Harb was sitting on the other side of me—it was a horseshoe table. During the entire time every time I looked up Harb was staring at me in the face, and it was making me feel very uncomfortable. And that consultant was Buddy Keaveney, as I have previously testified."

"Go on," said Morgenstern, confident and pleased at the direction in which they now were going, even though I am convinced he had no idea what it was.

"While we were leaving the dinner I saw Mr. Harbert talking with Mr. Keaveney at an almost empty table. I was then waiting to get a ride from Mr. Keaveney back to the hotel, and I had gone to get my wrap . . . and when I returned I overheard this comment." She paused, with evident distaste.

"What was the nature of this comment?" Morgenstern was riding the curl now, excited about the possibility that this could this be the wave that would carry them all the way to the beach.

"Pie," said CaroleAnne.

"Pie?"

"That's right," she continued quite sardonically. "As I was leaving to take a taxicab with the consultant fellow, Harb walked us to the door and then said to him, 'I guess you've had enough cake and now you want some pie.'"

"What was your perception as to what that comment about cake and pie meant?" said Morgenstern, now chopping valiantly through the jungle with the machete of his legal acumen.

"I had my ideas, so I confronted him about it."

"And what did he say?"

"He said they were talking about pie," said CaroleAnne with exquisite irony, "but it was not about pie. It had to do with Buddy Keaveney having sex with somebody other than his wife."

There was another quite sizable gap in the proceedings. Mr. Morgenstern consulted his notes for some time, then sauntered over to the jury box, which he leaned on insouciantly for a while. Some additional silence ensued as he regarded CaroleAnne. Then he spoke.

"Since you've filed the claim, things have gone from bad to worse, is that a fair statement?"

"Yes. The first to show me what life was going to be like was of course Mr. Podesky. He called me trash."

"He called you trash?" said Morgenstern with huge faux outrage.

"Yes," said CaroleAnne. "Julianne Blatt was being moved to another office, and there was a bunch of books outside her area and some other supplies, and he came very close to my desk and said to her in a very sarcastic tone, 'What are you doing with this trash up here, don't you know we have a basement in the building?' That sent chills down my spine, because I had been called trash in the elevators. Everyone had been ridiculing me now because it was out in the open that I had filed a claim against Mr. Harbert."

"You must have suffered a great deal," said Morgenstern, giving her a look drenched with empathy.

"Yes," said CaroleAnne, as if remembering a very important matter that had just now occurred to her. "You can't imagine how badly I've suffered because of all of this. I can't eat. I can't sleep. I can't ever . . . trust people again."

"Particularly Mr. Harbert," said Morgenstern.

"Yes. Especially him. I remember . . . I remember now early on that I had gained weight and I was not able to fit in my regular clothes, and a friend of mine had given me some that were a bit more flashy but they fit me. So I had on this particular dress with this flare back and Mr. Harbert seemed to be paying me an unnecessary amount of attention, and when I left the building that afternoon, I was surprised . . . I was sitting out in the park and was getting ready to have a cigarette before I took the train home and I found Mr. Harbert staring down at me from just a few feet away. I was shocked because he didn't really say anything to me whatsoever, but yet when I looked up, there he was. He takes the train home, and even though I have no right to say it was out of his way, in my opinion, where he was in that particular part, it wasn't going directly toward the train station. But I found it very disturbing."

"And since you filed the suit?" said Morgenstern. "Have the nature of his attentions changed?"

"Yes," said CaroleAnne sadly, "I suppose so. The other day I heard him tell Fred Tell, 'Well, at least she has taken the For Sale sign down.'"

I remembered. We were talking about real estate values in Harb's town. The conversation had nothing to do with CaroleAnne.

"I knew what that meant," the witness continued. "Everybody around there seemed to think I was a whore. But I never expected it of Harb."

"And you perceived," snapped Morgenstern, "that the For Sale sign meant that you were flaunting your sexuality?"

"You don't have to be a rocket scientist," said CaroleAnne.

A horrible, wracking sigh, almost a groan, really, came from the corner of the courtroom where Harb was sitting and ascended to the top of the very high ceiling. Harb! I had forgotten he was there.

So my friend watched this travesty, and he was bewildered. He sat in the courtroom and listened to what CaroleAnne was saying, and it bore no resemblance to his remembrance of the reality as he thought it had come to pass. They had a friendship, and now it was gone. It had not been beautiful after all. It had been an abomination, ugly, twisted, deluded. What a disappointment. He had thought otherwise. And yet, if that is how she had perceived the intercourse between them, who was he to assert that all had been different? Harb considered. He had made jokes at her expense, which had injured her? How he disgusted himself. Of course he had humiliated her. He made jokes at everyone's expense, including his own, mostly, in fact, his own, right? He certainly hoped so. But more than one fellow officer had told him that his need to trivialize and ridicule corporate life would get the better of him one of these days. And so it had. What an amazing boob he had been!

Why shouldn't he be punished?

24

THE COURT: Could we move it along, please?

MR. MORGENSTERN: Ms. Winter, would you describe yourself as a religious person?

MS. WINTER: Yes, sir.

Q: Did you ever engage in any religious activities at the office?

A: Yes, sir. I'm not sure now, in retrospect, if it was an appropriate use of company space . . . but I felt the need to pray before my noontime meal, and I found a very nice woman who felt the same way, and so we would pray in a little unoccupied office. I hope that was all right . . . We spent half our lunch hour praying and the other half, you know, having lunch.

Q: How frequently did these half-hour prayer sessions take place?

A: As often as we could, sometimes daily.

Q: Did anybody ever make any comments to you about these prayer meetings?

A: The comments weren't about prayer meetings, they were about meetings.

Q: What was the first time you remember hearing a comments about meetings?

THE COURT: Does this have anything to do with the case at hand here?

MR. MORGENSTERN: Yes, Your Honor.

THE COURT: There is no complaint about religious discrimination.

MR. MORGENSTERN: No. But we are talking about the notion

of meetings, Your Honor. And how her lunchtime activities frequently became the butt of abusive behavior.

THE COURT: All right.

A: I remember reading the memo that Mr. Harbert had sent to his boss, and he had mentioned something about while the staff was out of town there would be meetings with hundreds of employees in the home office, and the reason I was able to pick that out was that Mr. Harbert had constantly been telling people that I was like Union Station, that there were always people around my desk, and by people he meant men, you know. It could be somebody fixing my computer and he would hear a male voice and he would come tearing out of his office and stare the person down and then look at me. It was the body language again, the eyes, the feeling that he gives you like you're doing something wrong, like I am making some type of illicit date on the job while all this guy was doing was replacing my toner cartridge.

THE COURT: Wait, wait. Was there a question in here someplace?

Q: The question was essentially when for the first time did Mr. Harbert start this campaign of ridiculing "meetings" in your presence, comments that you took to be aimed directly at you?

A: It was after Gretchen and I would go into this empty office and have prayer meetings. He was calling it meetings, but later on he referred to it as sexual encounters.

Q: Did anybody else in the department refer within your earshot to your meetings?

A: People would look at me and make reference to them, like, "I understand the meetings have been cut down or cut out or there are no more meetings," things of that nature. Out of the clear blue sky I would get on the elevator and they are making fun about the whole subject of meetings. They thought I was stupid. But I got their meaning clear enough.

Q: Did there come a time when something was posted near or around your work area that dealt with this issue of meetings?

134

A: Mr. Harbert would put up some type of joke or sign or remark that related to me. It was something to harass me further and make me feel bad. So this particular day I found this on the wall, and I thought it was particularly interesting since they kept denying that they had ever alluded to me holding meetings about sexual encounters.

THE COURT: That wasn't the question put to you. I wish you would listen to the question.

A: What was the question?

COURT REPORTER: Did there come a time when something was posted near or around your work areas that dealt with this issue of meetings?

THE COURT: You can answer that question yes and see what the next question is.

A: Yes.

Q: I show you what has been marked Plaintiff's Exhibit M. Is that a copy of the poster?

A: This is.

Q: Could you just read that into the record.

A: It reads: "Are you lonely? Hold a meeting. You can see people draw organizational charts, feel important and impress your colleagues, eat bagels, all on company time. Meetings, the practical alternative to work."

Q: When did you first see this poster?

A: It was after I had heard myself being referred to as bagels.

Q: Bagels?[13]

A: I know it sounds incredible. But you people have no idea what a frivolous and amoral place a big corporation can be. These people lend money for a living! What did our Lord say about that?

Q: I'm sure every member of the jury has heard their fill about corporate malfeasance. I wonder if some of them even have lost jobs and destroyed pensions to show for it.

THE COURT: Sustained sustained sustained.

13. Here even Morgenstern seemed at a loss about how to go on. So he just stood there and looked inquisitively at his client until she spoke again.

135

Q: I'm sorry, Your Honor. Sometimes my passions on the subject get the better of me. CaroleAnne, who referred to you as "bagels"?

A: Well, I guess the first time was from Dick Podesky.

Q: Can you describe that remark?

A: He had been out sick and he is known for being extremely healthy, but he bounced back real fast and I came in to welcome him back. I knew it was his stomach and I said something like, "Gee, Dick, you must have a cast-iron stomach." He looked at me and he said, "Yeah, but I have a hole inside . . . like a bagel." I was able to draw a reasonable conclusion from that.[14]

Q: What did you perceive the term *bagel* to mean?

A: I understood it to have a sexual meaning.

Q: With respect to all the incidents that you have described, can you describe whether they had any effect on you personally?

THE COURT: She's done so every time you asked her, for goodness sake.

Q: After you left Global, was there an emotional effect upon you?

A: Oh, yes. I suffered very much, like I said. I was very depressed for a couple of weeks, doing a lot of crying, hurting, wondering in my mind how I could have handled things better.

Q: Did you ever seek any psychological, psychiatric, or social work treatment with respect to the treatment that you have testified—with respect to the environment that you testified to?

A: No. I really believe in the—

THE COURT: That is enough. The answer is no.

Q: Did you ever seek any kind of counseling, whether from a layperson, clergy, or other—

A: I spoke to my pastor about it a number of different times, but when I first was laid off from Global, I wasn't

14. A reference, presumably, that did not include the consideration that Dick was talking about his bleeding ulcer.

affiliated with a church because I moved from the community where I was going to church to Chicago, you know, and . . .

Q: Did you undergo any kind of course of treatment with respect to the pain and suffering that you endured?

THE COURT: Where?

MR. MORGENSTERN: Anywhere.

THE COURT: She said she didn't see anybody on a professional basis, Counsellor. I think that covers it, don't you?

Q: Let me ask you this. What was your mental condition by the time you departed from Global?

A: When I was finally permitted by God to leave that place, I found that I was not capable of working. I was an emotional wreck. I was having some strong, strong inferiority feelings. I felt very small and very unworthy. I don't think I could even use the computer for anything but mindless Web surfing.

Q: After you left, did you obtain employment elsewhere?

A: I tried. But for a long time, I could not. Finally I moved to Cedar City, Utah, for a summer and secured a job as a maître d' in a Mormon steak house. Boy, can those folks eat. Three kinds of starch at one meal.

Q: How long was that after your departure?

A: At least six months.

Q: You couldn't work because of your emotional state for those six months?

A: I was unable to work both spiritually and physically. I could barely function on the lowest human level. I would start crying at the least little thing, and I couldn't stop talking about it. I was at the lowest point a human being can be. I never want to be in that place again. And I think the people who put me in that place should be held accountable for it, the way we are all held accountable for our actions in the mind of God. Why should they not?

MR. BIDDLE: Your Honor.

THE COURT: The jury will disregard the content of this outburst.

MS. WINTER: No, I didn't handle everything perfectly. Maybe a lot of people would have just shrugged it off. I know people do. But that's not the way I see it. This was a mean, mean corporation that was sexually as well as morally and financially perverted. And there has to be some justice in the world and I hope you guys will see that and help little people like us show them a lesson.[15]

Q: Apart from what you have testified to already, informed the court and told the jury, were there any other incidents . . .

THE COURT: Good Lord. Do you know how many times you have asked that question?

MR. MORGENSTERN: I do, Your Honor.

THE COURT: Then do you have any additional—or should I say different—questions?

MR. MORGENSTERN: Probably not, but I want to make sure.

THE COURT: Take your time.

MR. MORGENSTERN: Thank you. I have no further questions.[16]

THE COURT: We will break for the day. Tomorrow is an off day and we're closed. Wednesday, then. And remember, don't discuss the case.

15. This last portion was directed at the jury, which in truth seemed transfixed. I know I was. This was a potentially successful strategy that CaroleAnne had stumbled on. Even I hate dirty rotten businessmen and I guess I'm sort of one of them.

16. I am leaving out the part where CaroleAnne contended that she and Gretchen Kurtz were thought to be lesbians engaged in homosexual sex, based on a statement Blatt made about some rabbits in the window of a nearby department store.

25

The courtroom cleared, and Harb continued to mull things. First, it was obvious that he couldn't go home right now. He could physically return to his house in the comfortable suburb in which he had constructed his bourgeois life, certainly, but the home that he had built would not be there. It would be a cold and lifeless edifice that would greet him, with no smell of meat cooking in the oven, no potato or rice dish simmering on the stove, no salad being tossed on the countertop. His wife would be roaming in the upstairs hallways, muttering imprecations. His children would be sequestered behind closed doors, acutely tuned to the dark vibrations. All was lost.

Where was he to go? He turned and regarded the jury box, now empty of its inscrutable freight. What could these people possibly know of the complex matrix of need, love, hope, ambition, despair, and work that bound an organization together? And yet, was it not obvious, even to this untutored crew, that CaroleAnne was grossly delusional in some way? Perhaps not yet.

He walked out into the hallway of the courthouse, which, unlike the actual courtroom was very grand, with a lot of marble and institutional signage. He felt like having something to eat, but there was nobody he could have it with. In the hurry after court adjourned, I found myself in discourse with several corporate attorneys who wished to convey certain odious instructions from ultrasenior management. I cannot now remember the point of their various briefs to me; all I am certain of is that by the time I was able to extricate myself from their meaningless burble, Harb had vaporized. This upset me, because I was physically aware of a vast, incredibly heavy cloud of despair and confusion that had been emanating from his corner of the gallery. Now he was gone, and there was nothing I could do but go back to the office and finish out the rest of the day in a pretty fair sized funk myself.

As it turned out, Harb was standing not all that far off on the avenue that ran in front of the courthouse. He considered going back to the office as I felt the need to do, it being only the middle of the afternoon with plenty of working hours still available, but that seemed inadvisable for some reason. Perhaps it was because there was no work left for him to do.

So he stood there. After twenty minutes or so, he awoke to the world around him and determined with what was left of his formerly organized personality that simply standing in the middle of the downtown area with no particular destination in mind was no longer feasible. The one thing a person of any standing is not permitted to do in society is stand still in a public place for an inappropriate amount of time. The more rural the location, a park, perhaps, or some bucolic roadway in the middle of a verdant forest, the easier it is to sustain this immobility. But the individual who does not move when those about him are on the roll is almost immediately targeted by the two bookends of society—the police and those who seek to evade them. So Harb stood there and was eventually approached by both. First came one of the miscreants who feed on other people's marginality.

"Hello," said a neatly dressed young man with a fifties-style crew cut and a small fan of literature in his hand. "Would you care to hear about our program of free personality testing?"

"Get the fuck away from me," said Harb. This was admittedly a hostile reply to the relatively commonplace approach of an intrusive Scientologist, but it did show that Harb was still capable of responding in a focused manner to certain urban stimuli. It did not succeed in warding off the applicant for his attention, however.

"You seem to have quite a bit of free-floating hostility there, my friend," said the man. He was smiling, but his eyes were not friendly, and he was so close Harb could smell his breath. It smelled like fine cheese. And while this smell is fine for cheese, it is not an appealing aroma for a human being. In this context, in fact, it was a rather potent weapon.

"Here," said Harb. He reached into his pocket and pulled out a roll of bills. He gave the sparklingly friendly fellow a five.

"I don't want your money," said the Scientologist.

"Then what do you want?" said Harb.

"I want you to take this and read it. It helped me a lot and I'm sure it would do the same for you."

"If I take this and promise to read it, will you go away?"

"Yes," said the Scientologist. "Believe me, you need it."

"I need something," said Harb. He took the little booklet.

"There's a phone number in it. Use it."

"If this stuff helped you so much, how come you're doing this in the middle of what's supposed to be a working day?"

The Scientologist thought about that for a moment and then made a visible decision to level with his new, potential convert. "I need to bring new members in to pay for the teaching," he said. "But it's a fair trade for a whole new take on life, take my word for it."

"I guess I'll have to," said Harb.

The guy left, jaywalking across the avenue in front of the courthouse and zeroing in on another stationary citizen on the opposite corner.

Harb walked over to a garbage receptacle a few yards away and tossed the pamphlet into it. Then he just stood there, staring into the depths of the garbage can for a while. There was a mountain of what seemed to be fast-food packaging in it, the remainders of lunch for a group of hungry tourists, perhaps. On the top of the pile, as fresh and crisp as the day it was minted, was the ubiquitous, solitary child's sneaker that shows up with amazing regularity in all kinds of places—tossed across a telephone wire over a busy intersection, on the median strip of a rural highway in the middle of nowhere, always single and relatively new.

"What's up, bud?" It was a policeman looking at Harb with a mixture of wariness and a small amount of sympathy, which was afforded to this particular vagrant only because he was obviously clad in apparel that had only recently resided in the window of Brooks Brothers. Also, he was standing outside a courthouse. Bad things happen to even the most substantial people in a courthouse, as this policeman was well aware.

"Nothing," said Harb. It was the truth. Indeed, nothing was happening at that time. Things had happened, true, and would happen in the future. But at that moment? Nothing.

"Got a place to go or what?" said the police officer.

"I have a number of possible alternatives," said Harb. "None of them are altogether attractive at this juncture."

"I get ya, buddy," said the cop. He stood for a few moments next to this questionable character, unsure of how to proceed.

"Wanna cigar?" said Harb to the police officer, rather abruptly.

"Hmm?" The officer squinted at Harb.

"These are Robustos from Honduras," said Harb, pulling two from his jacket pocket. "They're not Cuban, but they're quite good."

"Okay," said the cop. He took the cigar but not before some thought. Was this a bribe? It was clearly an object of value. This was not some White Owl in evidence here. It was a first-class smoke. And yet it was certainly being offered with no possible suggestion of recompense. The man was not under any threat of arrest. In fact, there was something eminently respectable about him. Likable, even. Actually, this was a person, for some reason, the cop sort of felt like having a smoke with. He took the cigar.

"I'm afraid I have no cutter," said Harb. He looked excessively crestfallen about the situation.

"Come on," said the cop and laughed. "We'll bite the ends off, like men."

"Like men indeed," said Harb, a horrible and crooked grin distorting his face.

They bit the cigars and grimaced. Then they lit them, drew in, and looked at the passing scene for a while.

"Well, I fucked up," said Harb after expelling a balloon full of smoke.

"I figured," said the cop.

"I don't suppose it's any kind of unusual story or something to you. You've probably seen everything."

"Not everything."

They smoked for a while.

"You didn't kill anybody," the cop finally said.

"No," said Harb. "I didn't do anything except get all fucked up with this woman. Except I didn't know I was doing it until it was too late, and then I'd done it."

"I hope it was worth it."

"Well," said Harb. "It wasn't."

They smoked. A cigar is not simply a quick injection of nicotine. It is a steeping of the system in an alien resin. The smoke rises in the stomach and the brain, and time stands relatively still, and yet there is more cigar, and one keeps drawing in and puffing out and, inevitably, slowing down. And thinking, thinking.

"You fuck her?" said the policeman.

"Nah," said Harb. "I shoulda."

"Maybe not. Maybe it was the wrong thing. And you didn't."

"Frankly, you know, I never really considered it," said Harb. "I just wanted to suck her face."

"You didn't?"

"Nah," said Harb. "I shoulda."

"Yeah," said the cop. "You shoulda."

They smoked more. A concerned expression had crept over the face of Harb's companion. "You gotta go someplace eventually," he said. "You can't just stand here."

"Why not?" said Harb. He sounded interested. "I mean, I have a right to stand wherever I want for as long as I want, don't I? Isn't that like an American right or something?"

"I guess," said the cop. He was standing a little off to one side now, just sort of staring into the upper levels of the stratosphere. It was clear from his lack of definitive response that he was unsatisfied with Harb's approach to the matter and that he considered the entire situation to be in need of eventual resolution of some kind.

In the face of this commitment to order, Harb could do nothing but relent, eventually. But the question remained: Where was he to go? His car was back at the office, not very close at hand. He had elected to park it there and take a speedy Town Car to the court, to avoid parking issues in that congested municipal sector, so he couldn't just mount his steed and fly off to parts unknown. Louise had reserved a hotel room for him at his request, but for some reason the idea of going there was odious to him. It felt like the ultimate admission that all was lost.

"If you had to go someplace and you didn't want to go anyplace, where would you go, Officer . . ." He searched the policeman's face.

"Allerton," said the policeman. He stuck out his hand sideways, as if as an afterthought. "Lieutenant."

"Harbert," said Harb. He considered giving his title along with his name, so the lieutenant could place him in the sociological strata, but decided against it. In what sense could he currently be defined by his role of executive vice president? He was one in name only now. "So where would you go?" he said at last, turning, childlike and inquisitive, to his new friend.

"Well . . ." The lieutenant turned it around in his mind. "You got money?"

"Oh, yeah," said Harb.

"Well, that's good!" said the cop, and although nothing was inherently amusing in this remark, they both had a substantial laugh. "I guess I would go have a drink or two in the nicest place I could think of. Sort of . . . you know . . . treat myself. Maybe have a bite to eat at the bar, watch a little TV." The cop was now looking outright wistful at the prospect.

"I have just the place," said Harb. "Thanks." He stood there for a while longer, smoking. Allerton did the same. They had each simultaneously achieved that midcigar conviction of universal well-being that virtually nothing can puncture. Sadly, this blessed state can continue for a maximum period of perhaps ten minutes, and certainly no longer than fifteen, after which one is merely a nicotine addict sucking down the overly potent end of an odious weed designed to deliver untold medical indignities to one's system. This moment, in which the true nature of the vice is revealed in all its hot, soggy, ugly clarity, is always signified by the need on the part of the smoker to remove the cigar to arm's length and gaze appraisingly at it. Shortly thereafter, the experience inevitably ends with the casting away of the object, a deep breath or two, and a total-body shake that would be canine were it not so thoroughly human.

"You want to come with me, Lieutenant?" Harb said, almost as an afterthought.

"I'd love to, Mr. Harbert. But I just got on duty and I'm not a corporate executive." He smiled.

"Yes," said Harb, sadly. "The corporate life is a good one, while it lasts." He stuck out his hand once more, gave the policeman's a firm double pump, and without further word, as if parting from a loved one at an airport or train station where an embarrassing display of emotion is forestalled only by the speed of one's departure, he turned and strode into the future with a crisp and manly step.

He went to the office.

26

It had been a few days since our hero had been in the gigantic office building that housed his corporation, and everything looked both immeasurably bigger and incalculably more tiny than he had remembered it.

Lester, the security man who had sat for twenty years before a phalanx of monitors at the entry to the corporation, sat there still. But he greeted Harb with a slightly different visage than he had employed in the past. Lester had been with the company for a good long time and knew all the players. It was clear to him that Harbert was in the process of being reevaluated. This did not necessarily mean that he could not in some way come back into prominence, and even if he did not it was not Lester's way to denigrate any of the former executives who came by his station. Everybody, eventually, did come by his station in reduced circumstances. So it was not for him to judge, nor did he do so. But there was a different pitch to his greeting.

"Mr. Harbert," he said, without the mix of excessive grandiosity and flippancy that was his trademark style with successful executives. On this occasion, he was genuinely friendly and looked Harb in the eye, man to man. That just about said it all as far as Harb was concerned, but in his new condition he found he did not resent it, and that, too, made him very sad.

He had never really noticed the elevator before, viewing it simply as a transient location of no inherent status whose purpose was to convey its occupants from one place to another. He recalled being filled, in the past, with an irrational resentment toward those who stopped what he thought of as "his" elevator on its way to its destination, either up in the corporate aerie or down to ground level. Now it was all one. Up? Down? Who cared? He considered the nexus between his job and his suburban existence. That double reality had defined a certain person who seemed to be there no longer. Who needed that person, except for the money he brought in? His children were well on their way to being grown. They spent more time with their friends, or up in their rooms on-line, than with him. On weekends, the four of them no longer went on family excursions. He had tried to enforce some such in years past, with mandatory museum visitations and healthful country hikes, but had, after a time, been hooted down not only by the kids but by Jean as well. He was living in the past, he was told. It was time to move on, not cling to the activities that once rendered all of them such mutual pleasure. Very well, then.

The elevator climbed for a long time, then gave a slight *ding* and coughed to a halt on the floor that had housed his office for many years. The doors slid open. In the waiting area outside the elevator bank was a gaggle of executives, deep in discourse. It was impossible to tell whether they were waiting for a conveyance or had just arrived from the earth below and were too immersed in their conversation to postpone it until they got themselves into a meeting room. They were between here and there and happy to remain that way.

He did not recognize any of them. Were they from out of town? It did not seem so. They appeared quite comfortable in this location, using it as a part of their everyday existence, not one alien way station en route to another.

No, now that he noticed, there was one he did slightly seem to know. Burbage? Cruddup? Northridge? Something like that. When he had known him a little, the fellow was quite junior and as timorous as a field mouse in a house of cats. Now he seemed taller somehow and far more self-assured. It had been a while since Harb had been in the mainstream around there. Had he missed the ascendancy of a new protoplayer?

An older man was talking. He was one of those people who used to be thin, with a lean face, high forehead capped with a gleaming white widow's peak, and long, slender arms and legs, but his midsection had seen too much of expense account living and was so round that pregnancy would have been a possibility were it not for his gender. His face was rosy, with that flush of satisfaction that comes with wine at lunch and the right to drink it. The group was leaning in and listening to him, so Harb deduced that this must be the one with the best title. The guy he knew a little—what was his damn name? Burbury? Furnival?—was the only one not leaning inward. He was standing at his full height at a very small remove from the group, listening with one hand on his chin and the other in the pocket of his slacks. Had he seen this attitude of repose in an article in *Gentleman's Quarterly*? It wasn't easy assuming a credible executive aspect when one still retained a strong memory of one's real self in all its gangly, unpolished authenticity.

"If we convert the bonds using the same core assumptions we developed on the Grandy thing, we can dump out of the highest exposure and coalesce around several fixed-attribute resolutions that will enable almost limitless value creation," said the thin man with the fat stomach.

"It's possible," said the young fellow whose name Harb could not remember. "If we apply some torque and spin it."

What were they talking about? Had he come to the right place? Was this English, or some new tongue that had been invented since his departure from the heart of the organism? He walked by the group very carefully, heading for the glass doors that separated the elevator bank from the inner lobby of the floor.

"Hello, Mr. Harbert." It was the man Harb could not recall. He felt he should know him now most certainly, since the guy knew his name.

"Yes," said Harb. "Hello . . ."

"Pogue," said the man.

"Pogue?" said Harb.

"Yes, sir," said the man. "You hired me a few years ago. I never really had a chance to thank you and I wanted to now that . . . I had a chance."

"Well, then," said Harb, smoothing the top of his head with one hand and straightening himself up. He felt moisture on his hand and looked at his palm. There was a small speck of blood on it. Had he nicked himself some place?

"Anyhow," said Pogue. "See ya."

"No," said Harb, "you won't."

Pogue stuck out his hand, and without thinking, Harb took the younger man's paw in his own. Pogue didn't seem to feel anything amiss.

"Bye, Harb," said Pogue.

"Bye, Pogue," said Harb. He wished he could pass along some wisdom to the young man and for one last time fulfill his role as a senior manager guiding those on their way up the ladder. "Don't let your understanding of the system spoil things for you," he said. "A lot of great stuff can happen anyhow."

"Yeah," said Pogue, regarding him gravely. "I plan to have a lot of fun."

"Oxnard is coming along with the Bortz thing nicely," said the man with the stomach.

"Validation from the Vegas focus groups is the next vector we need to explore yesterday," said another in the circle.

"Deep-six the process implementation and go for internal boundaries that allow exponential EBITDA growth on an insignificant operating base," said Harb to the group in the most helpful voice imaginable.

". . . er, thanks," said the man with the stomach. "We will."

Harb pushed into the inner lobby. It seemed strange to him. Had there always been a grandfather clock over there in the corner? Certainly not. And yet he knew it had always been in exactly that spot, as long as he had been an employee of the corporation. That glass case over there in the corner, was that new? No, it had been there, loaded from top to bottom with statuettes and Lucite tombstones of awards done, deals won. There was a picture of him, smiling in front of a group of fifty beaming people. All of them looked so happy! They must have been the Quality Conference at

Sea Island in 1998. They had all loved each other so much that week. Look. In the corner of the picture was a small, unsmiling person shoved off to one side, a clipboard in her hand. CaroleAnne had worked hard to pull off that meeting, and it had gone very well. Did she feel like an outcast even then? Why had he not noticed that she was the only one not smiling in their bright and jovial group? He should have noticed. Now he was being punished for the sin of not noticing. What difference did it make, really? It would all balance out in the end. And that end was coming.

"Hey, Harb," I said. I had been told of his arrival by Moe, the very slow guy who delivers envelopes from the mailroom, none of which ever have anything of value in them, or why would they let Moe carry them?

"Mr. Harbert in the lobby by the clock," was what Moe told me. Why nobody else told me I have no idea. Certainly someone else must have seen Harb.

"Hello, Fred," said Harb. "I was just noticing the lobby out here pretty much for the first time."

"It's nothing special," I said. There was a large, semisolid object stuck in the back of my throat and I couldn't get it out. I could barely force words around it, and my eyes were playing tricks on me, too. I was having a hard time not putting my arm around my friend and hugging him to my chest. "I been sort of waiting for you, buddy," I told him, and it was true. I knew he would come. Harb was a gentleman and he knew that I had a job to do, a job that was mine because nobody else had the decency, honesty, and courage to do it, and so it was given to me because in most cases I am the organizational stand-in for those virtues.

"Can I go to my office and sit for a while?" said Harb. It wasn't a complaint or a cry of need or anything like that at all. He just wanted to know whether the space was still open to him.

"Of course, man," said I, glad to be able to grant him this simple request. It was still his office, thank God. In recent days, I had fought back an attempt by several senior staff members to pack up his stuff and leave it in a box by the door, change the locks, and otherwise eradicate all trace of his presence. There are always people in corporations who want to handle a career death in their midst like that, may they rot in their leather recliners.

"Thanks, Fred. I was worried that Armando and Leaky would make a move to hose me out of the place before I had a chance to do it my own way." Of course, he was right. Those were precisely the two midlevel managers who had tried to Stalinize his work area. I had seen Leaky in there only yesterday, looking hungrily around the space, measuring it with his eyes for its next executive occupant.

"Get out of here, Gary," I had said to him. "I'll let you know when it's vacant."

"We're turning this entire area over to MIS," he replied. "It's got to be scrubbed and painted by the end of the month."

"I'm telling you to get out of here, Gar," I said. He looked at me and could see I meant it.

"Jeez," he said and went to the door. "Mr. Armando isn't going to like this at all," he said with what he thought was menace.

"You have him give me a call if he feels like it," I said. Armando is the vice president of Office Services, six grade levels down on the food chain from me and eight from the title Harb still held as an officer of the corporation. Leaky was his number two and slated for great things in the Office Services hierarchy, until now, that is.

"All right," said Leaky, and left. I made a mental note to destroy his career before the end of the year. And I did it, too. It's not difficult. A word here. A wink there. Pretty soon, the guy is toast. It felt good to do it, I'm not sorry I did it, and I was glad when I heard that he had gone to AOL, where he probably belongs.

At any rate, Harb's office that afternoon was still his to enjoy, if that is the right word under the circumstances. It was perhaps the only site in the building where his presence would not have attracted unwelcome notice. So we headed there.

The corridor we had traveled together so often was sad and dingy. I was officed on a different and much more grandiose floor by then. Virtually all of the others were also gone. It was dead quiet. Only

151

Louise was there, playing solitaire and answering telephones. She was scheduled to take an early package as soon as the Harbert matter was cleared up. And that was what I was assigned to do today.

"Hi, Harb," said Louise. Her lower lip was doing something funny. I felt bad for her. Louise was never very good at maintaining the professional shell. In the past, I had viewed this as a career-limiting liability, and perhaps it was. Now, however, I appreciated her trembling lip a lot.

"Hi, Louise," Harb said, very calm, very tender. He took her hand in his. "I want to thank you for all you've done for . . . how many years has it been?"

"Eight," said Louise. She was gulping a little now, and while I appreciated her humanity, I didn't want to allow things to get too emotional at this juncture.

"Louise," I said, "how about you go down to Starbucks and get us all some real coffee. Here." I handed her a ten-dollar bill, which is nearly what it costs these days to get three tall boys and a couple of nonfat muffins.

"Yes. I will," said Louise. She leaned up and planted a small, dry kiss on Harb's stubbly, weathered cheek. "I'll be back in a few minutes," she said and, gathering her purse and a little scarf for her hair, fled down the hallway to the elevators.

"Come on in, Fred," said Harb. I could tell he was going to make it easy on me. And he did.

We sat in companionable silence for a while. He was playing with one of the bobble-head dolls he kept on his desk.

"What kind of package are we talking about?" he said at last.

"You know the drill," I told him. The corporation had in its wisdom tried to strip Harb of his executive severance extension, but I had told them that I would not deliver this news and would force them to do it themselves. This leverage alone made it possible for me to carry that particular point. "Two weeks for every year and an extra two weeks for your status. That comes to a month for every year, which in your case would be about twenty-two months. We'll extend it to two years, full salary and benefits."

"Bonus?"

"First year at target, next year at fifty per cent of what you would have been able to expect had you been here."

"Options?"

"Vested for the next ten years."

"That's good. That's not too bad at all."

"It's pretty standard. For somebody with your years of service who has done . . . nothing wrong . . ." For some reason, I couldn't go on and had to blow my nose for a while. It was quite embarrassing. Harb was not weeping like a little girl, why should I? We were grown men. This was business, not personal. Crying is such a grossly intimate activity. I tried to stop it at once and did a relatively decent job of it.

"Don't feel bad, Fred," said Harb, who was staring at the various trinkets he had accumulated at that spot after years and years of executive living. "It's gonna be okay."

"For Christ's sake, Harb, don't fucking comfort me."

"Sorry. I won't, then," he said. There was a large cardboard box that had been on the floor near his credenza for God knows how long, one of those objects that had been brought in one day for a specific purpose and never left. Harb stretched out his foot and brought it within arm's reach. He then hauled it close, opened it, and slowly began to place the toys and trinkets of his career into it, looking at each one with a sense of wonder and evaluation. Some, I noticed, he tossed into the circular metal can that rested beneath his desk. I just sat there, watching, collecting what remained of myself for what I had left to do. There wasn't much, but it was the hardest part.

"I can't believe what I kept," he said after a time. He was looking at a paperweight with a tiny sign on it. "Quality Rocks," said the sign, with the small postscript underneath, *Hilton Head, 1998*. "Look at all this silly stuff. Really."

"I guess it didn't seem silly at the time," I said.

"No, but it was a delusion. It's all silly. All of it but the friendship, I guess."

"Don't say that." But I knew that it was true.

"Don't you have one more thing you need from me, buddy?" He had a plastic barrel in his hands, which he twisted open. A profusion of small, red plastic monkeys popped out. "Barrel of monkeys," said Harb.

I pulled the single piece of paper from my jacket pocket. It was Harb's release form, the document that verified that, in exchange for Harb's severance, we were buying his agreement not to compete with the company for a period of time and, perhaps more important, his promise not to talk to the press about us or to sue us for ruining his life the way we most clearly had, in my opinion.

"You know," he said quite idly, perusing the sheet as if it was a menu of tasty tidbits from which he had the privilege to choose his supper, "I suppose I could hit you up for even more than what you've offered, which, while it is fair, is relatively standard. I've suffered a lot. My career is over. Nothing whatever has been proved against me. I'm well over forty years of age, which puts me in a protected class. Why shouldn't I take the company to court and make you guys settle with me for a hefty sum? I'm just asking. Like, I'm actually pretty curious why nobody, including me, thinks I'm going to do that."

"You could," I said. I almost hoped he would.

"There would be something sort of right about it, wouldn't there," he continued thoughtfully. "Why should only bad and crazy people be able to cynically manipulate the system?"

He smoothed out the document on the desk. In a variety of containers on his desk were a profusion of pens and other writing implements. As long as I'd known Harb, he'd had a massive collection of pencils and pens of all kinds and descriptions. None of them ever worked, to my knowledge. "Have you got a pen that works, Fred?" he said without a trace of irony. I gave him my Mont Blanc, which never fails me.

"Thanks," he said, and signed.

We remained there for a while, and I witnessed something very strange. As Harb sat in his chair, he appeared to shrink into it, as

154

would a child in a large armchair that belonged to the adults in the family. The contents of the office seemed, as he took them one by one and placed them into the cardboard box, to detach themselves from him, to become less part of him. After approximately twenty minutes, he seemed to have completed something, although the room was still very cluttered with the detritus of a twenty-year career.

"This is impossible," he said, looking around him. "How am I going to clear this out?"

"Take it a step at a time. Nobody's kicking you out of here."

"Okay." Louise came in with some coffee and what looked like fat-free cake of some sort. You can always tell when it's fat-free. It looks not like food itself but like an illustration of food. I took a bite into something heavy, sweet, and sandy and chewed it for a while. Harb was drinking coffee.

"I'll be out here," said Louise.

"You'll stick around for a couple of weeks more, right, Louise?" said Harb. "I'm gonna need you to sort things out."

"I'm here until you . . . aren't, Harb," she said. I could see she had been brimming with tears but doing her best to contain them for our sake.

"Good," said Harb. "I just realized while I was sitting here that I have more drawers in this room than I can deal with. There are the six drawers in my desk, which are filled to the top with photos and files and magazines I thought it was important to keep at some point, and check stubs and pocket change . . ."

"We'll take care of it, Harb," said Louise.

"And then there's the credenza." He looked over at the towering combination of shelves and drawers that took up almost an entire wall from the floor to the ceiling. Books and CDs and clippings and I don't know what all . . . He looked hopelessly at Louise.

"You'll bring them all home." She walked to the gigantic piece of furniture and opened a few of the doors. The enclosure within was comically filled with a profusion of what can only be described as junk. I saw the differential from a car engine in there, polished to a bright shine, with some inscription on it. Everything we own,

I sometimes think, has some message or brand identification on it. "Good God," Louise said.

"I'm not sure where I'll be sending all of this," Harb said without apparent emotion. "Why don't you box all of it except the dust and dirt and hold the boxes here for me until I decide what I'm going to do with them."

"Okay," said Louise. I could tell she wanted to ask why she was not being told to send them to Harbert's home in Glencoe. But she thought better of it, and Harb said nothing. There was a somewhat shamefaced silence then for a while.

"Thanks, Louise," said Harb.

"Okay," said Louise again and went out. I heard crying at her desk. We sat.

And then, with the cold light of the sun shining through his office windows, a sun that gave illumination, to be sure, but no heat whatsoever at that time of year, the enormous pressure of events as they had befallen our friend Harbert finally broke through the top of his skull, and a powerful bolt of dark energy flew out of the top of his head, escaping vertically upward in a great, black beam and rocketing off into the void of space that encircles the planet in a blanket of empty space, gas, and stars. I want you to imagine our friend sitting there in his leather chair. We are standing above him and looking down on the top of his cranium, and in the place where his bald spot used to be, why, there is nothing. No skull, no hair. And his poor old brain is right there for all of us to see, and it is surprisingly not gray at all, this overworked organ; it is a glowing red ball, throbbing and twisting within its confines. And as the cool air hits that writhing brain of Harb's, we can almost see steam rising, then dissipating, and the color of Harb's brain changing from red to pink, then pink to a lighter, healthier rose, and then, after a few minutes in which we can almost feel his eyes coming off their hinges, back to gray, gray with a subtle, paler white sneaking around the edges of its folds.

And then, from the place where the black light had just gone, way up in the highest realms of the cosmos, there came a very low, sustained chime of some sort, it's very difficult to describe even by the man who experienced it, I am sure, and this chime was accompanied by a glow that was predominantly golden in color, with a bit of bright white that surpasses understanding tossed in around the periphery, and this golden presence parked itself in an area about ten feet above Harb's head, then resolved itself into a short, powerful burst of energy that smote our friend like a blast of water from a fireman's hose, pouring into the trepanned opening in the back of his head and knocking him into the very back of his chair like a rag doll.

"Oho," said Harb, who was at that moment unaware of where he was and, possibly of greater importance, who or what he was. "I get it."

Harb's eradication of his internal persona was complete, but as I can testify, he lived through it. His job, what was it? It was nothing. The twitching about of an infinitely tiny organic body in meaningless, Brownian motion, nothing more. What was his office, the little box where he had conducted his professional life? Not a prison, because he had felt free there, and full of power, but something very much like a prison. What did he need of such a demeaning space? And what of his power, which had given him such freedom? What was it? Nothing. Less than nothing. He had given orders. He had felt so large, so very large. And what was he? A little squeak on the surface of a tetherball one hundred trillion light-years across.

He was infinitely small. Yet he was also infinitely large. This idea filled him with strength and a sudden feeling of intense well-being. What had he lost? Everything. So what? Why be disappointed that the myth of permanence, of status, of substance, had faded like perspiration on the side of a can of soda? His life, up until that point, had been heavy on structure and control, with alternating spasms of impulse either accommodated or denied. Now the future lay before him, pristine and undisturbed by landmarks, an unbroken tundra of despair.

Yet he did not feel despair. He had things to do. He had duty. What was that duty? Simply that he must do when there seemed to be doing that needed to be done. He must sit when sitting was possible. He must accomplish his duty when duty presented itself at the proper time. And whatever happened, in all circumstances, he must absolutely refuse to rejoin his self. For in that self was desire, and in that desire was pain. And he had had enough of pain.

A gigantic wave of elation swept over him and with it he laughed out loud so that even I smiled. Here, then, was a happy man!

"Fred?" he said after a time. "Have you seen my keys?'

27

Wednesday, November 20, 10:00 A.M.

Cross-examination by Mr. Biddle

THE COURT: Will the plaintiff take the stand.

(CarolAnne Winter, resumed)

THE COURT: You are still under oath.

MR. BIDDLE: Good morning, Ms. Winter.

MS. WINTER: Good morning.

Q: You were first employed by Global in May of 1997, is that right?

A: That's right.

Q: From the outset, you claim you were subjected to a continual barrage of insults, comments, and communications generated by your supervisors, is that correct?

A: That's right.

Q: You began working for Mr. Harbert as a temporary secretary, is that correct?

A: That's right.

Q: He spoke with you about becoming a permanent employee working with him?

A: That's right.

Q: And you agreed that you would do that?

A: That's right.

Q: During your employment, did you receive performance evaluations from Mr. Harbert?

A: Oh, yes.

Q: Did you receive salary increases?

A: Yes, I did.

Q: Those were put in for you by Mr. Harbert?

A: They were.

Q: You received your first salary increase about six months after you started?

A: I believe so.

Q: And another one six months later?

A: I believe so.

Q: Then you received a thirty-five percent increase or so the following year?

A: Yes.

Q: And then they stopped for about a year?

A: I believe that is right.

Q: Do you recall why that was?

A: As far as I can remember, it was because I had reached the maximum of my salary range.

Q: Did you in fact receive additional moneys that year?

A: Yes, I did.

Q: How did that happen?

A: At Mr. Harbert's request, I was given a one-time, lump-sum payment in lieu of a salary increase.

Q: Would you agree with me that over-the-maximum increases like that were unusual?

A: That I have no knowledge of.

Q: I see. May I remind you that in your deposition you did state that such an action was highly unusual.

A: I remember testifying to that even though I had no knowledge of it.[17]

Q: I see. And each year thereafter, you received like salary increases.

A: If you say so.

Q: And the performance reviews you received. What grade did you receive on those?

A: Outstanding.

Q: Was that the case through your career?

A: Consistently.

Q: Let me show you Exhibit D in evidence and ask if you recog-

---

17. I thought she was doing well. She appeared truculent, proud of her position, feisty. A little woman up against a plump, slick corporate attorney.

nize that as your performance evaluation for this past year.

A: It is.

Q: And that was an outstanding evaluation?

A: It is.

Q: And that was after the time that you had made your claim concerning Mr. Harbert?

A: That is right.

Q: Did you have occasion sometime in 1998, I believe, to receive an additional cash award from Global?

A: I did.

Q: What were the circumstances?

A: The circumstances were in the area of doing work that exceeded my responsibilites, doing an outstanding job.

Q: That was in connection with your help with the meetings the Quality unit was conducting, is that correct?

A: That is right.

Q: Did Mr. Harbert give to you gifts or tokens of appreciation on other occasions?

A: Frequently.

Q: On what occasions?

A: Secretary's Day, birthdays, Christmas.

Q: What did he give you?

A: Flowers on Secretary's Day, and a hundred-dollar check.

Q: Were the checks from the company or from Mr. Harbert himself?

A: They were from Mr. Harbert.

Q: Did there come a time when Mr. Harbert learned that you needed a car?

A: Yes. In fact, he did.

Q: What happened there?

A: Mr. Harbert gave me his old automobile.

Q: He did! I see. It was old. Did it work?

A: Yes. It worked very well, considering.

28

The knowledge that Harb had in fact given his present tormenter a fully functional automobile sat oddly on the populace in the courtroom. The jurors squinted a couple of times virtually in unison, in evident shock and light consternation, then one by one turned their eyes on Harb, who remained fixed in his seat, with furrowed brow. Well it might furrow. The car, which had seemed so extravagant a kindness back then, now seemed in some way tainted, inappropriate. Even I didn't know what to make of it. I kind of think Biddle was a moron to bring it up.

Morgenstern, who had been taking notes at his table, glanced up smugly, looked as if he was about to say something, thought better of it, offered an oily smile to the jury, and returned to his doodlings.

"So Ms. Winter," said Biddle, "you acknowledge that he treated you very nicely as to matters such as these?"

"As to matters such as those, yes," said CaroleAnne, staunch, courageous, not giving an inch to the opposition.

"And Mr. Harbert also gave you significant assistance when you needed to move to a new apartment, did he not? Securing that apartment for you, providing money to use for the deposit or for moving expenses?"

"That is right." What we were seeing, at least what I hope someone other than me was seeing, was a full display of CaroleAnne's meanness and lack of gratitude. The car. The apartment. A pattern was certainly clear, all right. Was it a pattern for which the giver should be punished? CaroleAnne's face suddenly grew sharp and savvy, like a cat that had discovered a new vantage point from which to attack its prey. "But the apartment was not the direct doing of Mr. Harbert," she said. "That was through the Employee Assistance Program."

"Un-huh," said Biddle. "And to whom does Employee Assistance report?"

CaroleAnne's reply was unintelligible. I caught the phrase "several important managers."

"I beg your pardon?" said Biddle.

"I suppose it reports to Mr. Harbert in a rather circuitous fashion," CaroleAnne conceded graciously.

"So Mr. Harbert did what he could to make a new life for you possible, giving you means of transportation and enabling you to move away from a situation in which you were suffering abuse, is that correct?"

"Yes and no," said CaroleAnne.

"Okay," said Biddle. Then he just stood there and looked at CaroleAnne for a while. This was a smart thing to do. In the silence, the witness twitched several times and succeeded in looking at once self-righteous and vaguely guilty.

"Never mind," Biddle said at last. "The first time you went to the EAP[18] it was about your husband, is that right?"

"It was among the subjects I discussed," CaroleAnne sniffed.

"Isn't it a fact that your husband was becoming increasingly hostile?"

"No."

Biddle looked confused and disappointed. "I again call your attention to your earlier deposition testimony, at page sixty-five," he said, "where you state, 'I went to EAP because my husband had become increasingly hostile and bitter toward me.' Is that your testimony?"

"If you have it right there, why are you asking me about it?" said CaroleAnne, very testy.

"The fact is, throughout your years at Global, you visited the EAP offices eighteen times, did you not? For a variety of reasons

18. Employee Assistance Program.

163

ranging from marital problems to issues pertaining to housing, family matters, other random issues . . ."

"If you say so."

"Well, I do. I do say so. Eighteen times," said Biddle, paging through a large sheaf of papers he was carrying in one hand. "And your meeting with EAP in February—your eighteenth visit—was the first time you ever brought to anyone's attention that you were having problems at work."

"No, that is not correct," said CaroleAnne.

"Well, once again, I will draw your attention to your own deposition, which was taken under oath." Biddle did not seem angry, but he would not be denied.

"Oh, all right. All right," said CaroleAnne. "It's scary to tell EAP anything real. They report to the guy who pays your salary, for goodness sake. Is it any wonder there's a small breakdown in trust there?"

"Ms. Winter, are you aware that the files of Global's Employee Assistance Program, which are in evidence as Exhibit L, reflect no comments concerning your work situation prior to February of this year?"

"I was harboring these feelings for a long time. In February, I got up the courage to talk about it."

"Uh-huh," said Biddle. "Or maybe you just made the whole thing up recently."

Morgenstern leaped to his feet. "Your Honor!" he shouted.

"Sustained," said the judge, who appeared to be reading something in his lap.

"As of the time of your first meeting with Mr. Tell, had you disclosed to him or to anyone else in Human Resources that you were having problems with Mr. Harbert?"

"Friends in Human Resources?" said CaroleAnne thoughtfully. ". . . Yes."

In other words, no. Just to make clear Mr. Biddle's point, if it is not sufficiently obvious, at no time in her many years at Global did CaroleAnne Winter raise her ostensible problems with anyone in

Employee Assistance or in Human Resources on the whole, even though she interfaced continually with our department. This is not to say that her mind was not a raging inferno of sincere and honest paranoia, just that without an X-ray machine or resident psychiatrist on location dedicated to reading her innermost thoughts, there was no way that anybody near her could possibly have gleaned the depth and power of her persistent delusions. To the aforementioned "friends in Human Resources" she had simply indulged in the constant activity of all people who labor within any organization, no matter how small or large that might be: bitching about her bosses.

"Okay," said Biddle. "When you met with Mr. Tell, and told him about the rumors that employees were spreading, did he ask you to consider making a formal complaint?"

"I guess so."

"And you decided to do so?"

"Not immediately. I didn't want to get anybody into trouble."

"Oh. Then you subsequently submitted to him the two-hundred-and-four page document you have marked as Exhibit Y?"

"Yes."

"This is it?" Biddle handed her the tome that was her voluminous beef against the company. CaroleAnne held it in her lap, stroking its cover for a moment.

"Uh-huh," she said, staring at it.

"I guess you worked out your problem about getting people into trouble pretty well," said Biddle.

"Goodness gracious, Your Honor!" cried Morgenstern. "Is this kind of callous abuse to continue even beyond the term of this poor woman's employment?"

"Overruled," said the judge. "Ms. Winter brought up the issue of her goodwill toward all her fellow creatures."

But Morgenstern had won his point, I think. I made a mental note to remind Biddle that we needed to be a whole lot nicer than the other guys. We were, after all, bad.

"Your complaint is very long, Ms. Winter," said Biddle, paging through it. "But let's just take one specific allegation as illustrative of the quality of all the rest. In your charge, you refer to your receipt of the ten-thousand-dollar incentive award, right?"

"I do." CaroleAnne didn't know which way this was going, but she didn't like it.

"You regarded that award to you as . . . deceitful, is that correct?"

"Yeah, I said that. It was deceitful."

"Why is that?"

"I was the main coordinator for every single meeting for every location, and I had in each primary city a contact person. So if I was at the top of the pyramid, then there would be secretaries from whom I would get assistance in the local offices. It was an enormous amount of work. I was working extra hours, coming in early, staying late, working through my lunch hour. I volunteered to come in on a Saturday, things of that nature. Now, that project lasted for however long it lasted, and the incentive, the award was not offered, no thanks was given, no recognition." Her face was a mask of child-like pain.

No, I thought, as I watched her assume the role of victim to herself. Other than the twelve aforementioned raises, the car, the new apartment, the cash bonuses, the time off on Fridays and Mondays, the promotions in grade, the paid vacations before they were required by policy, the easy attitude toward tardiness and absenteeism, other than that, there was no recognition for CaroleAnne whatsoever.

"The point is this," CaroleAnne went on grimly. "There was this young lady who initiated one meeting, I think it was in Pittsburgh. I had forgotten about my role in the setting up of that meeting, except for the day that I had heard she received a two-hundred-and-fifty-dollar gift certificate and roses for planning the particular assembly. I was happy for her. But it struck me as extremely wrong that I got not even a thank you, nothing for planning the entire department's initial phase of the Quality program. It wasn't that I didn't want her to have the award, it was just what about the fact that the main focus was planned by me exclusively,

166

coordinated by me exclusively, and I didn't get a rose or anything. It was painful, yes, and she is young and blond, yes, and she is a secretary, yes, and she and I were on a friendly basis, yes. And it hurt."

I must add that, based on subsequent analysis, neither Harb, nor myself, nor Dick Podesky, Shelly McVeigh, or Julianne Blatt has the slightest recollection of any such person, in Pittsburgh or anywhere else. There is, quite simply, no such person, I believe, but it is possible that CaroleAnne heard of such an incident of local recognition for work well done. That was a part of the Quality Process and would not have surprised me.

CaroleAnne was once again very upset, close to tears. Biddle asked, very gently, "And so you subsequently received a cash award for ten thousand dollars. Which you found deceitful. What was deceitful—please let me finish—what was deceitful about it?"

"Because," said CaroleAnne, a little hitch in the back of her throat, "because the memo that alerted me that an award was coming was written not by Robert Harbert but by Julianne Blatt for Mr. Harbert's signature. That was very impersonal. And you know, it was after I was on the phone with the secretary in Pittsburgh and Harb heard the conversation, and heard my surprise. Then a couple days later I get this memo that I was going to be given this big incentive? You have to say that's pretty suspicious."

It is interesting how many times employees react to generosity from senior management with disappointment and resentment. I once gave a valued subordinate a raise from seventy-five thousand to ninety-five thousand dollars per year, and saw her face fall because, as she related when I with some annoyance pulled it out of her, she was hoping to be in the six-figure range by the time she was thirty. She was then twenty-eight.

"Now," said Biddle. I saw something focus in his eye that gave me a little thrill and I knew we were about to get down to it. "We're almost through."

"Yeah," said CaroleAnne. "They told me that was when I had to watch out for you."

The judge was hit by a fit of coughing and everyone took a respecful pause.

"You have claimed that you were called names that were sexually offensive, is that correct?" Biddle was now standing very close to the jury, with his back to them, looking at the witness from their point of view.

"It was offensive," said CaroleAnne. "The names were not always blatant. They were hinted and implied. But the feeling and impact were real."

"You testified that you were called trash."

"Yes."

"Who did you say called you that?"

"Mr. Podesky on one occasion, Mr. Tell on another. And some others I don't remember the names of, but just passing them in the hall after the rumor mill had spread, yes."

Biddle looked sharply at her and shot back, "Mr. Tell? Really?" I must say I was gratified that Biddle stuck up for me here. I didn't get where I am today by calling employees rude names.

"What else were you called by those you claim were sexually offensive?"

"Scum, garbage, Grand Canyon. I was watched a lot and whispered about."

"Grand Canyon. That's an unusual insult. Do you recall who called you that?

"Julianne Blatt, and she was talking to Patty DelFonzo. Of course, they didn't look in my face and say Grand Canyon. They would cross their words as if they were talking about something else."

Yes, I remembered. Blatt had gone to the Grand Canyon. She was talking about her trip to just about everybody. In my mind's eye I saw CaroleAnne sitting there at her desk, a seething, bubbling cauldron of hatred and insanity, and the skin rose on the back of my neck as if someone had just walked over my grave.

I looked over at the jurors. They appeared quite somnolent, although there was one of them, a stocky, middle-aged man in a pinstriped blue business suit, who throughout the trial seemed to be evolving into a state of increasing agitation. I thought I sympathized. What could Morgenstern possibly have been thinking to allow an individual of this type onto the jury? Plaintiff's only hope was to assemble a group who cared nothing for the facts and were hell-bent only on punishing a large corporation for the imagined wrongs that they themselves had suffered in their lives. Several appeared to fit that description, but this individual seemed caught in the center of a successful business life and possibly to be a manager of some sort in the world outside the courtroom. There was no way, I dared to hope, that such a fellow would not recognize the insanity of the stuff to which he was now being subjected.

"Can you give some other examples, please." Biddle was now leaning against the jury box, enjoying himself.

"Well," said CaroleAnne in a chatty, informative tone, "they would also walk by my desk and say 'ho ho ho,' and I knew what they were talking about."

"When was that?"

"At Christmastime," said CaroleAnne calmly.

"Oh. One last thing," said Biddle. "I understand that you believe Mr. Podesky made a code word reference to a lawyer that you had consulted?"

"Yes!" said CaroleAnne with evident pleasure.

"What was that name, please?"

"A Jewish synagogue."

At this juncture, I looked over and saw Harb, who had been watching rather impassively, rub his face with great energy for several seconds. He then rose quietly and exited the courtroom in the back.

"You heard a conversation where Mr. Podesky referred to a Jewish synagogue and you inferred that was a reference to a lawyer you were consulting in your suit against the company?"

"No, no," said CaroleAnne. "I need to clarify. I heard him say, 'And what about her lawyer the Jewish synagogue,' in other words, he used the word *lawyer* and then *Jewish synagogue* and it was all about me. See?"

"Sure," said Biddle. "He didn't refer to you by name in that conversation, did he?"

"Oh," said CaroleAnne, "they very rarely did."

29

MR. BIDDLE: Okay, now. To conclude. Do you recall testifying that Global tampered or spoke with the ministers of
your church?

MS. WINTER: They found out about my claim, yes, and then
their sermons were suddenly directed toward people who try
to extract money fraudulently from companies and schemes
and things of that nature, yeah. I know it sounds crazy,
but do you have any idea how much money Global gives to
philanthropic activities sponsored by the church?

THE COURT: I am confused. The ministers made these speeches?

MS. WINTER: Yes. The sermon coming from the pulpit was
relating directly to some of the accusations that I filed,
that it was fraud, that it was wrong, that type of stuff.

THE COURT: I see. The sermons were delivered directly to
you?

MS. WINTER: Small portions of them . . . but yes. I can
see by your face that you don't believe me, but it's true.
Look, I found it pretty unbelievable, too.

THE COURT: Not at all. I just wanted to understand you
correctly. Mr. Biddle?

MR. BIDDLE: You believe that Global was listening in on
your conversations, correct?

A: Excuse me, but I think the idea that a huge company
with the greatest technology in the world couldn't be
listening in on little old me is pretty far-fetched.

Q: According to your deposition, you were confirmed in your
belief in part by a vision you had on that subject. Is
that correct?

A: It's true. I'm certainly not ashamed of it.

Q: What was that vision?

A: Well, I had a vision of a listening device that was supposedly located over my desk.

Q: You had a number of visions concerning your employment with Global, is that correct?

A: At given times, yes.

Q: And late last year, did you have a vision regarding Mr. Harbert's name?

A: I did.

Q: Would you please describe that.

A: I had a vision of simply seeing the name Harbert written on the wall.

Q: What did you take that vision to mean?

A: I understood the vision to mean, based on the word of God, that the handwriting is on the wall. I had to look up that portion of Scripture to find out what that implied.[19]

Q: Miss Winter, the meaning of the vision and of those remarks in church were revealed to you by the Holy Spirit, is that correct?

A: Could you repeat that?

Q: Am I correct that you learned about many of the various statements against you because they were revealed to you by the Holy Spirit?

A: It's called discernment of the spirit, yes.

Q: And you had a vision concerning Mr. Harbert, did you not?

A: That was after I left Global, I believe.

Q: Would you describe that vision for us.

A: It's a bit bizarre, but it did happen. I was awake fully. I had my eyes open at the time, but when I felt the presence of the Holy Spirit I closed them, and I saw

---

19. Harb at this time reentered the courtroom and took a seat not far from me in the rear of the gallery. He seemed intent on something in his hand and I looked over to see what it was he was doing. In his lap was a Nintendo Color Game Boy, and he was working away at it, mercifully without sound, his brow furrowed and his lips moving.

a vision of a person walking toward me clothed in a garment that was loose fitting, not trousers or pants. It was, not white, maybe like an eggshell or off-white. As that individual walked toward me, I started to see blood in the genital area.

Q: And what did you see in the back?

A: After I recognized that it was in fact blood and where it was located, that individual turned, and in the back the garment was between the buttocks.

Q: And could you tell the jury how you describe that?

A: You know. A wedgie.

Q: A wedgie?

A: That's what we called it where I grew up.

Q: Me too.[20] And that individual with the wedgie was Mr. Harbert?

A: I believed that it was.

Q: What did you discern from this vision?

A: I believed that he would be exposed as having emotionally and mentally raped me, and that he would leave in shame.

MR. BIDDLE: I have no further questions. Thank you.

Redirect examination by Mr. Morgenstern

THE COURT: Redirect is limited to only matters of confusion. Which should leave considerable latitude.

MR. MORGENSTERN: Thank you, Your Honor. Good morning, Ms. Winter. Good morning, members of the jury.[21]

Ms. Winter. You described visions that you had. Can you give an explanation of your faith?

---

20. At this juncture the entire courtroom erupted in silent, surreptitious giggling. The members of the jury were particularly afflicted, appearing to be intensely fraught with inappropriate mirth, hiding their faces and finding matters of ostensible interest in the ceiling and floor much as would a class of children forced to appear serious in church after the occurrence of something publicly ridiculous. The only one who was not laughing was Harb, who had ceased his game while the recitation of this anecdote was underway. As the tittering in the room reached its apex, I saw one gigantic, salty tear pop out of his eye and make its slow, sorry way down his ruddy cheek.
21. For some reason, Morgenstern seemed even more happy and smug than ever.

A: It is one of the gifts of the Holy Spirit, which comes from God who is God, and the spirit realm that you would not be able to see with your natural eyes. You see it with an inner eye.

Q: Would you describe these as hallucinations?

A: Certainly not.

Q: Can you describe what your emotional response was to these visions?

A: I was in awe. Tranquility always comes when the presence of God is manifested, and peace, and it was sustained for a while.

THE COURT: Do you see God in these visions?

MS. WINTER: I have seen the face of Jesus.

THE COURT: What color is he? *(Witness laughs)*[22]

MS. WINTER: When he appeared to me the first time he was an olive kind of color.

THE COURT: Does God speak to you?

MS. WINTER: Yes, he does. Not always, you know. You can't be greedy. But sometimes, yes, very softly, if I listen hard, I can hear him.

THE COURT: What language does he use?

MS. WINTER: English. He would speak to anyone in their own language. He is God.

THE COURT: What has God told you?

MS. WINTER: The first time I heard the Lord speak to me was in Cairo, Illinois, where I was a prayer warrior working for a local radio station. He said don't tell anybody your problems but God alone. They will not understand. And I was floored.

THE COURT: Could you describe him to us so we have a picture of God.

MS. WINTER: He looks very much like the pictures people paint of him. I believe he appeared to me that way so I

22. CaroleAnne laughed in surprise, and in fact there was nobody in the room who was not surprised by the question. I saw the jury peering at the fat little man in the black robe, looking to see if he was in earnest or was having some fun at the expense of the plaintiff.

wouldn't be frightened and would recognize who he is.

THE COURT: But we have all seen different pictures of him. Which are you discussing?

MS. WINTER: He looked like humanity. He looked like love with a face to it.

MR. MORGENSTERN: I have no further questions.

THE COURT: Thank you. Be back here in fifteen minutes. Recessed. The witness is excused.

30

There was a hushed silence in the courtroom as CaroleAnne's testimony reached its awesome conclusion. I looked over at the jurors, who were goggling pretty good. There were six of them. Two had religious signs of varying persuasions around their necks, and one of them was wearing a yarmulke. Come to think of it, the skinny woman in the last row was sporting a very serious kerchief. That could mean anything as far as I was concerned. Would any of those have a problem with a woman who spoke directly to God? What if they all spoke to God, too? Why had we let this thing get to this ragtag bunch of civilians?

I took a second and sucked it up a little. It was far, far from over. Harb, that decent soldier, had yet to testify. My turn was coming. In fact, we had yet to introduce a single witness.

I'll be honest. At that point the entire jury looked to me like a bunch of religious moralists who hate big corporations. A few were standing, dumbstruck, like wildebeests squinting in the equational sunshine, but the majority were sitting stock-still in their box, stunned and blinking. The fellow in the blue pinstriped suit seemed to be on the verge of something, it was hard to figure out what, precisely. He looked as if he might laugh but also as if he would like very much to yell at someone. His eyes were wide with disbelief, and he was gazing intently at CaroleAnne as she demurely exited the witness box and approached her attorney with a sense of quiet resignation and a job well done.

She made her quiet way up to her bushy, inept attorney, who was then rummaging through a large file as if he had recently concluded a successful presentation before the Supreme Court.

Arriving at the table where he was hard at work, she squeezed the top of his biceps in her tiny hand and brought her face close to his. He greeted her with what appeared to be benign affection, and he too was grinning as if they had both just won the Derby.

"Thank you so much," she said to him.

"We're on our way," her attorney answered softly, suffused with modesty and pleasure. He took her other hand and squeezed it with appropriate solemnity.

The six sober men and women belonging to that august group had now moved slowly, without speaking, out of their corral and into the room assigned for their repose during breaks in the activity. They were gone. I had got nothing from their general aspect, except a general impression that they wanted to be anywhere else. I couldn't blame them.

I looked in the back to see if I could catch my poor friend's eye, but his seat was empty. Where could he have gone in such a hurry? Only one place, I speculated, the site to which all men repair before contests of great moment, as such this was, for my friend was next on the docket to testify. It did not take an oracle to ascertain that he was in no mental or emotional condition to face the ordeal with equanimity. This would have been a challenge for any man, but for Harb it was especially daunting, for my friend hated public speaking, and in this case there was no possible upside to which he might look forward except the upside where his head was going to be kicked.

On the other hand, CaroleAnne's testimony could not possibly have gone better from our perspective. She had shown herself to be an utter and complete lunatic who certainly was capable of hallucinating the entire contents of her Pandora's box of complaints. If the jury was at all sentient, how could they possibly find otherwise?

And yet.

The men's room was huge, a square box in tile and porcelain designed to allow a full weight of male humanity to discharge its duty in the briefest amount of time imaginable before court would once again draw it back to a higher calling. At the far end of the room, in a separate enclosure, some dozen stalls awaited; closer in to the left and right a host of vertical receptacles beckoned for the less seriously inclined. As one entered, in a small anteroom preceding this grand display, five sinks were lined up on the right, and at the very last one of these, bent over regarding the drain plug with evident interest, was my friend Harbert. He was throwing up.

I stood and looked at this gentleman, who had so recently been a prince of the realm in the only kingdom that has mattered to me in the last twenty years or so, the only one likely to do so during the rest of my working life. And I was sad.

"Harb, man," I said, more to announce my presence in the room than for any other decent purpose. I didn't want him to feel I was sneaking up on him.

"Fred," he said. "I feel so sick, man. I wonder if you could testify in my place."

"I would if I could."

"It's funny," he said, standing up and staring at himself in the mirror that lined the wall before him. "You would think that a metaphysical experience like the one I had the other day would prepare you for contests such as these." He wet his hand and smoothed it through his hair. "Perspective isn't worth much," he added. "You always lose it when you need it the most."

"I guess so." I took a sink down the row somewhat, to give him a little excess barfing room, if he still needed it. "I don't think CaroleAnne's testimony helped her any," I said.

"Who could have known the woman was so desperately ill?" Harb said and turned to face me. His face was the color of milk that had slightly turned in the carton, thin, white, a little chunky around the edges. "I thought she was such a wonderful person, and, well . . . she wasn't, not inside. I feel like such a schmuck. I deserve whatever is coming to me." He turned and contemplated the sink again, but just for a short time, and then decided against it. Then he said something that sounded like, "Oh," and leaned back against the tiled wall and closed his eyes.

"Hold it together, Harb," I said. "The jury has to see a rational, thoughtful, mature business manager who is above suspicion, not a grieving, self-doubting pile of jelly on the way to a nervous breakdown." Perhaps that was a little tough, but Harb was going to have to get down to business in a couple of minutes, and I wanted to treat him like a businessman, and for him to react as one.

"I'll be all right."

He washed his face. I waited and said nothing. He straightened his tie and looked at himself in the mirror again. And then something came over him almost like a veil, or a mask. It began with his eyes and radiated outward, first to the rest of his demeanor, then to his spine, then over his entire body, and Harb, the Harb I always knew and admired, was with me again. "I can put the face on one more time," he said.

We went back into the courtroom together.

book
three

Harb

31

Direct examination of Mr. Harbert by Mr. Morgenstern

MR. MORGENSTERN: I would request the court that I treat him as an adverse witness.

MR. HARBERT: By all means!

THE COURT: Mr. Harbert, you must speak and answer only when spoken to or asked a question. Is that clear?

MR. HARBERT: Indubitably, Your Honor. I mean . . . yes.

Q: Mr. Harbert, have you ever worked at Global Fiduciary Trust Company?

A: Yes, I have.

Q: For how long have you worked there?

A: Approximately twenty-three years.

Q: During that time did you know the plaintiff in this case, CaroleAnne Winter?

A: Yes, I did.

Q: When for the first time did you meet her?

A: The summer of 1997.

Q: What was her position working for you then?

A: She was a secretary working for me and for the vice president that I reported to, whose name was Richard Podesky. Everyone did call him Dick, by the way.

Q: At any time after she first started working for both you and Mr. Podesky, did she work for just you alone?

A: Yes, she did. Your Honor, I assume that since it is the style of this particular barrister to force me to repeat testimony and facts that have already been entered into evidence on multiple occasions, it is my duty simply to answer with continued redundancies until he moves on to something more interesting?

THE COURT: Yes, sir.

MR. HARBERT: Thank you, Your Honor.

THE COURT: No problem.

MR. HARBERT: Why do people say that?

THE COURT: What.

MR. HARBERT: When did "No problem" become the accepted response to "Thank you"?

THE COURT: An interesting point. Mr. Morgenstern? Feel free to jump in any time.

MR. MORGENSTERN: For how long after she first became your personal secretary did she continue to work in that capacity?

A: A long time. Three, four years, maybe.

Q: Did there come a time when you no longer worked together with CaroleAnne Winter?

A: Yes.

Q: Approximately when was that?

A: About the middle of 2000.

Q: At that point did you get transferred to a different department?

A: Yes, I was transferred to a special project at Global.

Q: The truth is, you were sort of fired at that point, weren't you, Mr. Harbert?

A: Up yours, shorty.

THE COURT: Please, sir. I don't want to have to hold you in contempt.

MR. HARBERT: Oh, no. Please don't.

Q: My point is, you didn't need a personal secretary at that point, is that correct?

A: That is correct, yes. *(Unintelligible)*

Q: At any time during her long tenure with you, sir, did Ms. Winter make a complaint to you about your behavior toward her?

A: No. Which side are you working for?

MR. MORGENSTERN: Your Honor.

THE COURT: Mr. Harbert.

MR. HARBERT: Sorry, Your Honor. I'm just having a little fun with y'all.

Q: Mr. Harbert, did you ever learn that Ms. Winter had

made a complaint to Frederick Tell?

A: Yes. I sent her to him, for God's sake.

Q: How did you first learn that?

A: Tell told me. Came to my office.

Q: Prior to receiving the call from Mr. Tell with respect to the complaint that CaroleAnne Winter made, had you ever offered to assist CaroleAnne Winter in speaking with Mr. Tell?

A: Yes, I had, once. A week or two before the complaint surfaced.

Q: What was the context in which you contacted Mr. Tell on CaroleAnne Winter's behalf?

A: CaroleAnne had come to me and said that she wanted to resign and leave Global. Like the great, pompous fool I was, I believed in the myth of my own invulnerability and I guess also still had illusions about the decency of the person whom I had known so well for so many years, and I strongly encouraged CaroleAnne, attempting as I always had to vitiate her pain and suffering with my friendship, and counseled her to look both within the company and outside the company before resigning, and said that I would talk to Fred Tell, and I encouraged her to go and speak with him. I'm an idiot, of course. I plead guilty to that, certainly.

Q: When CaroleAnne made the request to resign, was that done in writing, orally, or both?

A: Initially it was an oral request.

Q: When she first made the oral statement to you that she wanted to resign, did you respond in any way?

A: Yes. I thought I said that a moment ago.

THE COURT: Yes, you did, sir. But Mr. Morgenstern is very verbose and repetitive.

MR. HARBERT: I see that. Okay, then, well, I said, "If you are serious about leaving, I strongly encourage you before you resign and take that step, don't be rash and impetuous, look for opportunities both within the company and outside the company."

Q: Did you ever ask why she wanted to resign?

A: Yes.

Q: What, if anything, did she tell you?

A: She told me that she had had an encounter with another secretary and that that person did not treat her with the dignity and respect that she thought was appropriate.

Q: Did she ever tell you who that secretary was?

A: Yes, she did.

Q: Who was that?

A: Her name is Louise Dwight. She's an excellent woman and had been a good friend to CaroleAnne.

Q: Did you ever attempt to work out any kind of rapprochement between CaroleAnne Winter and Louise Dwight?

A: I did not. Once CaroleAnne got something into her head, it was hard to shake it loose. I think perhaps you may have seen that in her testimony.

Q: Apart from Ms. Winter's statement about Ms. Dwight, did she give you any other reasons as to why she wanted to resign?

A: She did not.

Q: Did she follow up her oral statement that she wished to resign with any kind of writing?

A: Yes, she did.

Q: I show you Defendant's Exhibit H in evidence. Is that the resignation letter that she submitted to you?

A: Yes, it is.

Q: Were there any discussions that you had with anybody else at Global in that same interval about CaroleAnne Winter's resignation?

A: Certainly with Fred Tell.

Q: Did you initiate that communication?

A: Yes, I did. Gee, this is like watching paint dry, isn't it.

THE COURT: It is a competent if pedestrian examination, Mr. Harbert. Bear with it.

MR. MORGENSTERN: Mr. Harbert, what did you tell Mr. Tell on that occasion?

A: I mentioned that CaroleAnne had said that she wished to resign. I mentioned the incident with Louise Dwight. I said to him that I thought that was rash on her part. I was concerned for her that she leave without having other employment. We're in a recession, even if they don't call it that. I said she had been a very good assistant and had excellent skills. I said as far as our relationship, I said I think we had been together too long, the chemistry wasn't working as well as it once did, and this incident would be

186

an opportunity for her to explore other avenues within Global.

Q: What did Mr. Tell say to you?

A: He expressed the opinion that I was not in my right mind. He felt I should have accepted her resignation. I think it's safe to say that in retrospect he's been proved correct.

Q: What was your reaction when Mr. Tell told you about Carole-Anne's complaint against the company, and you in particular?

A: I was upset and hurt and angry.

Q: Did you deny the allegations?

A: I denied the ones that were inappropriate, yes. I did not deny favoring the plaintiff, because it's pretty clear I did so to an extent that now appears foolish and inappropriate. The idea that somebody can be abused by excessive kindness, however, is rather curious.

THE COURT: Like Ms. Winter, sir, you could probably opt for brevity in your replies now and then.

MR. HARBERT: Okay.

MR. MORGENSTERN: How long did this meeting take, by the way, approximately?

A: Perhaps an hour and a half.

Q: Did you inform Mr. Tell as to other avenues of investigating the complaint?[23]

A: No. He knew the appropriate protocol for investigating a complaint of this nature.

Q: I see. Just two corporate buddies sitting around working things out, huh?

MR. BIDDLE: Your Honor.

THE COURT: Sustained. Cut it out, Counsel.

Q: I'm sorry, Your Honor. After you were told the specifics, did you have any conversations with CaroleAnne Winter about the allegations in the complaint?

A: No, I did not.

Q: Did you ever learn whether Mr. Tell interviewed anybody else with respect to Ms. Winter's complaint?

A: Yes. Perhaps fifty people. Pretty much everybody in the extended corporate family who might have had dealings with CaroleAnne.

23. I don't know about you, but this line of questioning drove me bonkers.

Q: Did Mr. Tell ever tell you that he had concluded an investigation into these charges?

A: Yes, he did.

Q: Did he ever indicate to you that he had prepared a written report with respect to his investigation of the allegations?

A: I don't believe he ever discussed a written report with me.

MR. MORGENSTERN: Thank you. I have no further questions.

MR. HARBERT: That's it?[24]

Cross-examination by Mr. Biddle

MR. BIDDLE: Good morning, Mr. Harbert.

MR. HARBERT: Good morning—good afternoon. It's almost lunchtime, isn't it? I certainly hope so. There are quite a few good restaurants around here.

Q: Are you currently employed?

A: No, I am not. It's an odd feeling, let me tell you. Not totally unpleasant, but I have been pretty much continually employed for my entire adult life, and . . . well, there you are.

Q: What is your status?

A: I am involuntarily retired. It's pretty creepy, let me tell you.

Q: When were you last employed?

A: This morning. Or maybe it was yesterday.

Q: By whom were you last employed?

A: The circus. No, but seriously. By Global, of course.

Q: I would like to come back to the time period when you first met CaroleAnne Winter.

A: Okay.

24. A bright, wide, and boyish grin spread across Harb's face at the realization that the examination by his adversary was now over and had been so pointless and inept. And yet, could a specious, flatulent, long-winded moron have succeeded in spite of his incompetence? I looked at the six people in the jury box, and I simply wasn't sure. I didn't like the way the women in there were looking at my friend.

32

"Those were the days," said Harb with an ironical twist of the lip. But I could tell he wasn't kidding.

"And then you got the Quality job, right?" Biddle was gentle, leading his lamb through the meadow of friendly testimony.

"Approximately five or six months after CaroleAnne came into our lives, yes." Harb still had the glow of memory on him.

"Did she come with you when you changed jobs?"

"Yes, she did. Are you kidding? I couldn't have done it without her. She was an awesome assistant. I will never see her equal, for a variety of reasons, some of them obvious. At my age, for instance, the chance of my ever attaining any job outside of Starbucks is doubtful, and I'm not even talking about a management job, either."

He smiled another loopy smile, and good God, I thought my heart would break. There was a new note of resignation and sad cynicism in my friend's voice that I didn't like one bit. The sight of a soft heart growing cold and hard is an ugly one. It happens fast, and most of the time there is no going back.

"Did she willingly come to the new job with you?"

"She was excited for me. We were excited for each other. I don't care what she says now. There was nothing wrong with us then."

"Would you briefly describe your duties as head of the Quality unit?"

Harb settled in with obvious pleasure. Even now, I could see, it gave him a charge to talk about the work, the job, that thing we do.

"Sure," he said. "The unit was responsible for creating what is known as a Total Quality Management Process within Global, and without boring anybody with a lot of jargon, Quality Process had as its principal aim the establishment of an external focus on the customer, and the principal task was, how do we make ourselves as accessible as possible, provide hasslefree service in a fashion that would exceed the expectations of the customer? It is a very simplistic-sounding principle but very difficult to implement, as anybody who has had to deal with various large organizations can testify."

"Was this an existing unit?"

"No, it wasn't. I created it. I was the first employee. CaroleAnne was the second. Others followed."

"Did there come a time when you left this Quality unit?"

"Yes, when I was assigned to a special project at the company that had no reality and was in fact a demotion so dramatic that the loss of stature practically gave me a nosebleed."

"Why did you lose your status, Mr. Harbert?"

"Why? Because of CaroleAnne's complaint, of course. This is an important proceeding, no doubt, but the most important trial of all took place behind the scenes months ago." Harb said this without a trace of bitterness or regret. This very lack of animus on the subject did more to cut me to the quick than would a barrage of invective.

"Was there a lot of work involved in the Quality Process?"

Harb smiled. No doubt he was remembering all the seven A.M. meetings, the conference calls that regularly kept us at our desks well after nine P.M. The candy bars grabbed in lieu of lunch while running down the street. The fun of being too busy to do anything but work. "Yes," he said. "Well, it was a real job."

"What was Ms. Winter's work load during this period?"

"It mirrored mine. I now in effect was thrown back on my own resources and was reading books and going out and looking at companies that were reputed to be excellent companies, and had to create de novo, new from nothing, a quality process for the corporation. The cycle of work that we went through during those couple of years kind of ebbed and flowed. Sometime around the late nineties, having formulated the basic components of the process, we then went out to try to deliver the message to our employees nationwide. We had large-scale meetings that required a lot of logistical work. That lasted for a period of about a year."

It was a fun year. We all liked each other so much back then, or so I thought. Harb was going on about what a good Quality soldier CaroleAnne had been and tracing the outlines of her meteoric rise to importance and relative affluence within the bosom of the enterprise.

"During the period of the major implementation when we were traveling across the country to a lot of different operations, she played an instrumental role in the planning and logistics of those meetings," Harb said. "That's when I gave her the special recognition award during that period, a special bonus of, I believe, some ten thousand dollars, which CaroleAnne found so . . . what was the word?"

"Deceitful," said Biddle. The two just looked at each other for a while. "Did you give the ten thousand dollars to CaroleAnne in response to any complaint on her part?"

"No, I most certainly did not," Harb said, with equal portions of outrage and disgust. Biddle, who had been sitting, rose and meandered in the direction of the bailiff, who was stationed on the other side of the judge from the witness stand.

"Did Ms. Winter ever have occasion to discuss with you personal problems she was having outside the workplace?" he asked mildly.

"Yes," said Harb, as if it were the understatement of the year. "At the outset, she told me that she was having difficulty with an abusive spouse. That went on until we got her a new apartment."

"Did she ever make any requests concerning the telephones in the office?"

"She was very concerned that her husband was very jealous. Fred Tell sometimes answered my phone or her phone, and her husband was apparently surmising that she might be having an affair with Fred." At this point for some reason Harb decomposed into such a torrent of muffled hilarity that he could not continue for a time. Honestly, I didn't see what was so goddamned funny about it.

"Take a moment, Mr. Harbert," said Lerner, who appeared to be in danger of chortling himself.

"I'm sorry," said Harb.

"Do you need a recess?"

"No, no," said Harb, composing himself. "Not at all. At any rate, CaroleAnne requested that Mr. Tell not answer the phones. So I spoke to him and it was no longer a problem. The idea that Fred . . ." And Harb lost it again. I'm glad he was having such a good time with it, because I certainly wasn't.

"Did you ever discuss with Ms. Winter any problem that she had with respect to your supervision of her?" said Biddle.

"On one or two occasions," Harb said. He thought about it for a minute. Biddle did not prompt him. "Ms. Winter had come to me," he said at last, "and told me that she felt at times that I was overmanaging or micromanaging the work that she was doing, that as a result she felt I was not demonstrating appropriate trust and confidence in her abilities. I realized that she had a genuine complaint and I told her that I would try to correct that in the future."

"Did Ms. Winter ever discuss with you any other complaint that she had experienced?"

"Only once."

"Would you describe that, please."

"She came to me and declared that although she had been making our department's coffee for several years, she would no longer be doing so, because God had allowed her to see into my soul and saw there that I was not being sincere with my gratitude for the coffee she was making."

"I see."

"I thought I was appropriately grateful. But I guess God could see otherwise. I didn't argue."

"When CaroleAnne came to you and said that she was resigning, you discouraged her from doing that?"

"Yes, I did, God help me."

"Thereafter, you learned that Ms. Winter had filed a complaint?"

"That is correct."

"Did Mr. Tell discuss with you the different allegations?"

"Yes, he did. It was one of the most horrible meetings—no, strike that. It was one of the most horrible days of my life. The morning my father died, perhaps . . ." There was a cavernous silence that nothing could fill. Someone in the back of the room coughed. A siren far in the distance loosed its call. A chair in the jury box creaked.

"Mr. Harbert," said Biddle very quietly, "did you ever call Ms. Winter a prostitute?

"No, I did not, sir."

"Did you ever call her a bagel?"

"No. I fetched her one, however, on more than one occasion."

"A whore?"

"God, no. Why would I do that?"

"Ho?"

"Do you think I'm out of my mind?"

"Trash?"

"Like all corporate officers, I'm exquisitely aware of laws that hover over all interpersonal relationships in the workplace. I would never risk such idiotic utterances, even to make a joke, although such jocose speech has at times been my Achilles heel, I admit."

"Were you ever present when anyone called her such things?"

"No, sir. Not at all. Nobody felt that way about her. The idea that she thought anyone did, let alone me, hurts very deeply."

"Did you ever ask her to type a memorandum in which you referred to meetings with hundreds of employees of Global as a code for saying that she had sexual relations with hundreds of Global employees?"

"No."

"Did you ever say or imply that she used drugs?"

"No."

"Did you say or imply that she used alcohol?"

"No."

"Did you say or imply that she had a party lifestyle?"

"No. Well, maybe at the beginning, when she came in dressed like a fan dancer, reeking of gin."

"Objection." Morgenstern.

"Overruled," said the court.

"Did you ever hear anyone at Global make any such allegations about her?"

"I did not."

"Did you ever put your face in Ms. Winter's face to smell for alcohol or drugs?"

"Only once. At the very beginning. She was in a lot of trouble then, and I forgave her for her status that morning."

"Did you refer to her as fun loving and free spirited?"

"No. Although, you know, she was, back then."

"Did you ever say that Ms. Winter ought to have her head examined and she was nuts?"

"Certainly not. Perhaps I should have, given some of the testimony we've been treated to today."

"Objection." Morgenstern, up on his feet now.

"Sustained," said Lerner, rising in his high-backed leather recliner and glaring in a moderately avuncular way at Harb. "Mr. Harbert, I'm making some allowances for your obvious frame of mind at this juncture, but I'll ask you to limit yourself to objective responses to questions that have been asked and to omit your editorial comments, no matter how entertaining they may be."

Harb flashed a huge and satisfied grin. "Well, thank you, Your Honor," he said to Lerner. "Did you know that at the height of my powers I was able to get a laugh from the entire population of a crowded elevator within the space of six floors?"

"I can believe it," said Lerner. "You seem to be a very humorous fellow."

"Oh, I am," said Harb gravely. "I am a humorous fellow."

"Now Mr. Harbert," said Biddle sternly, "was there ever a time that you recall when as a result of hearing a noise you asked Ms. Winter if she had killed something?"

"Yes."

"Would you describe that, please."

"Yeah," said Harb, "sure. I was conducting a meeting in my office and there was kind of a loud, clamorous sound as if someone had taken a shovel and banged it against the wall." He chuckled, rubbed his face with one hand, and continued. "I went out and I found CaroleAnne trying to affix a plaque or something to the wall with a hammer, and I asked her if she was killing a raccoon or something to that effect. It was a slightly ill-tempered thing to say, but then again she was giving me one humongous headache and I was the senior officer of the department and as such am pretty much recognized as having the right within certain boundaries to say whatever I please."

"Did that have reference to an alleged abortion she had?"

"No, it had reference to whatever she was trying to affix to the wall with a hammer!"

Biddle returned to his desk and continued standing, both hands tented up on the tips of their fingers on the tabletop. "You learned of the outcome of Mr. Tell's investigation," he said.

"Yes."

"From that point up to the time that you left the Quality unit, did you have any further discussions with anyone concerning the allegations Miss Winter had made?"

"No. What was there to talk about? Was I to defend myself from this nonsense? Even to discuss it with another human being would have been to give it weight it did not deserve."

"And after that time, and until the time you left, you continued to grant Ms. Winter a succession of generous raises, did you not?"

"Yes, I did."

"Why?"

"Because . . ." Harb seemed at a loss for a moment. "Because

195

it was the right thing to do," he said, looking directly at CaroleAnne and offering a small, wan grin. She brightened at his gaze and smiled right back at him. Biddle looked at them both.

"No further questions," he said.

33

MR. MORGENSTERN: You mentioned that the chemistry between you and Ms. Winter wasn't there anymore. Did you mean sexual chemistry?

MR. HARBERT: No. I think perhaps we had been working together too long. You know what they say about familiarity.

Q: Was the actual working relationship deteriorating in any way?

A: It certainly wasn't as close as it had once been, but it was still pleasant.

Q: With respect to this incident in which you came out and saw Ms. Winter attempting to staple something to the wall, did anyone make a comment about the noise besides you?

A: No, sir.

Q: Was the wall in question the wall of your office?

A: Yes, sir. Thank you for pointing that out.

MR. MORGENSTERN: I have no further questions.

THE COURT: You may step down. We will break for lunch. See you at two-thirty.

34

It was a very lovely day, and I was determined on this occasion not to let Harb escape from the courtroom without some kind of invitation to companionship.

I shouldn't have worried. He came over to me the moment the judge's gavel came down and took me by the arm. His features were relaxed and friendly, and there was a muffled excitement about him that had none of the feverish desperation that had marked his attitude since the worst came down upon him. "Come with me, Fred," he said, fleeing into the street with his coat in his arms and me in tow. All I can say is that he was a completely different person than the last time I saw him. How do people effect these character transformations at varying points in their lives? I've never been able to be anything but my own consistently tedious self. When I try to be more interesting, I become even more boring. I didn't have an adolescent crisis. I didn't hit a psychological wall when I reached forty. I just keep getting older, that's all. Like wine. Or cheese. What's wrong with that? Why do people have to change?

I just say I was happy that, unlike many in a similar situation, Harb seemed to comprehend my HR role entirely and to blame me not at all for the function I was forced to perform the previous afternoon. It might have been my imagination, of which, I must admit if you have not ascertained this already, I have little, but he appeared to like me better for it.

"How long does my expense account hang in there with me?" he said over his shoulder as he strode three long steps down the street in front of me.

"It should be deactivated when your severance goes into effect next month," I said. It was hard to keep up with him, even though he was a good four inches shorter than I. He was really motoring.

"Can you bridge me to, like, June?" he said, as if the request was nothing at all. In fact, it was a very big deal indeed and something he should have brought up with me before he signed that paper flushing away his right to contest his deal.

"Yeah, okay," I said. What the hell, I thought. I am the executive in charge of expense account policy, and in the worst case scenario I could simply cover Harb's account under my own limitless umbrella.

"Don't break the bank," I said.

"My traditional load is in the area of ten to fifteen grand a month," he said, turning into a side street that led us down to the waterfront. "I don't think I could go beyond that if I tried. I'm not going to buy a car or anything."

"Well, make sure you don't," I said gravely, "unless it is a very small car indeed."

"I'm not going to be needing a car," said Harb, flagging down a cab and just barely allowing me time to cram myself in before flogging the driver into action.

In the taxi, he was preternaturally silent, refusing in quite annoying fashion to answer any questions. In about ten minutes we found ourselves standing in front of a small, simple, rectangular apartment building, dating perhaps from the 1940s, some four or five stories in height, with a character so nondescript that one might not have noticed it between the more substantial structures that were its neighbors.

"What's up, man?" I said. I had a funny feeling about this all of a sudden.

"I saw it listed in the *Trib* this morning and I had to take a look," said Harb. He was staring up at the building with a speculative, vague smile, as if the structure was a crystal ball in which he could see the future.

"I mean, hey," I said. I admit it was not the most probing remark available to me. Harb and Jean had been together for several decades. I knew they were having problems. After all that had happened, what couple would not have suffered some emotional fallout? But I had no idea it had gotten beyond the point where Harb was content to hole up in a nice hotel for a couple of days before going home.

"Don't get your panties in a knot, Fred," said Harb. He continued to stare up at the building. "It's not a bad place, really," he said and looked at me.

"For what?" I said. I was feeling kind of annoyed. I certainly didn't want to be his accomplice in midlife cliché-ville if that was what he was in the midst of planning.

"Whatever, dude," said Harb. He walked up the three steps that separated the building from the sidewalk and pushed open the outer door. "Come on, Furd," he said. I could never resist when he called me that. There was so much affection in it.

We went into the vestibule, where Harb, after a short search, found the button he was looking for and pressed it. The reply came immediately.

"Coming." It was a small, dry, uninflected voice on the other end of the squawk box. I couldn't tell much about its owner, but if one word can convey an impression, this one did. This voice, I thought, belonged to a woman, between twenty-five and fifty years of age, educated, white, very tired, disappointed with the actualities of existence to the point where her life was now lived mostly indoors, mostly in the pages of books and on the Internet.

"We don't have a lot of time, Robert," I said.

"We don't need a lot."

A person was coming from the other end of the corridor. I don't have my job in Human Resources for nothing. As far as my analysis could go based on one lone word, I was correct. Her physicality did surprise me somewhat, however. I had been expecting fat. I was wrong.

She was indeed a woman of medium height, with shoulder-length black hair, very sleek, of medium build, somewhere between thirty and forty. Everything was medium about her, in fact. Her chest and hips were full, but not ample, and her waist was quite small. She was dressed, if one may call it that, in a leotard and tights, with a runner's bra stretched over her upper torso. "I was just going out for a run," she said. "You almost missed me." Her voice was very pleasant.

"I apologize for my tardiness, but my friend here is a poky puppy," said Harb with a grin.

"Okay," she said cordially. She was sizing Harb up, not grossly, but looking him over frankly to see as much as she could about her potential tenant.

"Do I know you?" she said.

"I'm Harbert," said Harb, putting his hand.

"I'm Emily Lassiter," she said. "I worked for the people who planned your meeting in Aruba that time."

"Yes," said Harb. "I remember you." They looked at each other for several seconds. I felt like a fifth wheel, I can tell you that.

"Well," said Emily Lassiter, "let's have a look at the space. It's not much." She turned and led us to a small elevator at the back of the building.

"My friend here is Fred," Harb offered to her back.

"Hey," she said without turning around.

The elevator was very small but very clean. There were no touches inside, no little bench or scrollwork above the panel that lit up as we climbed higher. This building was all about function over form. I started to like it. I also noticed something else: the quiet. There were no dogs barking, no screaming infants. No intense cooking smells, either. I caught a faint whiff of sandalwood incense, then that too faded. It might have been coming from an apartment somewhere nearby . . . or it might have been coming from her, I couldn't tell.

"Here." She opened a door at the end of the corridor.

We walked into the apartment. It was stripped bare, quite literally an empty shell. Two rooms, areas more than rooms, really. A small kitchenette between them.

"I'll take it," said Harb.

Five minutes later, we were out in the street.

"I'd like to know what you think you're doing," I said.

"She was a very good meeting planner," said Harb. "I wonder what she's doing home in the middle of the day." He started walking in a rather desultory manner down the street in the direction of the courthouse. I said nothing. What was there to say. "I guess it's her building," he added thoughtfully after a time.

I was scheduled to testify after Blatt, and as two o'clock struck we were nowhere near the courthouse. I have always hated being late to things, and my own testimony would certainly have been high on my list of things to which I would have liked to be on time. We stood on the sidewalk in the blistering cold, the wind whipping off the river. I was filled with a terrible anxiety: that I would not be present when my name was called to the stand. What would happen then?

I also realized that I was very, very hungry and about to be locked into a desiccated courtroom with no food in sight for several hours. Fortunately, on the corner where Emily Lassiter's street met Michigan Avenue, several miles away from where we needed to be almost immediately, we found a hot dog vendor stirring a vat of greasy, gray water with a slotted spoon. Somewhere in its depths, the hairless heads of a few pale, lifeless meat sticks bobbed to and fro. "Make me one with everything," said Harb.

I had two.

The hand of my Piaget swept forward relentlessly, but Harb, munching on his hot dog and staring off into the near middle distance, showed no signs of undertaking a return to the scene of the crime against him. He seemed to be in the throes of deep cogitation.

"Harb, man," I said, "we gotta fly if we're gonna be back at the court in time."

"I'm not going back there," he said. He seemed to be serious.

"My testimony is in, like, half an hour." I was getting increasingly annoyed with him. This . . . what was it? This sloughing off of the situation as if it did not exist was irritating.

"Then you'd better hump it, Horatio," he said. This was a new one on me. Who the hell was Horatio?

"Harb, man, you ought to be there for appearances if nothing else," I said, addressing him as if he was a small child in need of gentle instruction before a spanking was required. At the same time I was scouring the streets for any available means of transportation that would convey me back to the courthouse, a knot of anxiety twisting ever tighter within my gut.

"Yeah, see, that's the thing," said Harb. He was walking up Lake Shore Drive, his hands in his pockets, staring ruminatively at his shoes. "I don't think I'm gonna be doing a whole lot of things just for appearances anymore. That's sort of what I decided at the hotel last night. I couldn't sleep. I watched a movie. I had a couple of drinks from the minibar. I ordered a sausage and anchovy pizza from room service. It was very good. I looked through all my stuff again to see if I could find my keys. And I couldn't, you know, find them at all. There weren't in any pockets. They weren't in my briefcase. They weren't in my office, because I went back there and looked."

"You went to the office?"

"It was very quiet."

"Maybe you left them at home," I said. I was beginning to get hysterical. How could there be no cabs in the entire city?

"You know who I ran into in the lobby on my way out?" Harb was staring into the sky now, like a kid looking at skywriting.

"Who?" Six town cars in about three seconds rolled past. But no cabs.

"The Old Man," said Harb. This sort of floored me. The Old Man is rarely seen. "He was just standing in the lobby by the big plate glass windows and staring out into the street. I went over to him. 'Hi, Harb,' he says, without looking at me, you know. 'How are things going?' he says after a while. So I don't know what to say to the guy. The last time I saw him he hugged me. He was near tears about the success we were achieving. So I said, 'Just fine, sir. And you?' and he turns to me and I see this big juicy tear in his eye, just one, and he says to me, 'We gave it the good fight, didn't we, Bob.' And I said, 'Yes, sir. Thanks for the opportunity.' And then he hugs me again. It was very sweet. I'm not totally sure what it meant . . . but I'm sort of moved by the fact that he had retained who I was after not seeing me for several weeks."

And then, just as I thought I might explode in a shower of concentrated aggravation, an elderly Chevy Caprice with about 150,000 miles on its odometer crept around the corner and rattled up to the curb where I was standing. I leaped at the moldering conveyance and wrested the rear door open. It cried out with pain and age like the rusted portal of a subterranean tomb.

"More to the point, my frickin' keys aren't anyplace," Harb observed informationally. "I called Jean at, what, maybe two, three in the morning?" He chuckled at the naughty memory. "Boy," he said, "she was pissed."

"Get in, Harb!" I said, my patience altogether snapped. "I have to be at the courthouse right now and I want to talk to you, so get the fuck in the fucking cab!"

"Okay," said Harb. "Since you ask me so nicely."

We got into the motorized Conestoga and it got under way. I felt bad immediately about the vocabulary I had used in exhorting my friend to shake a leg. I had never expressed myself to him in that fashion before, and I wondered if it had anything to do with his recent loss of title and position. I hoped not. I felt I should say something to excuse myself, but he spoke before I had a chance to do so.

"So anyhow," said Harb, "I'm sure my keys are somewhere, but they might as well be nowhere. And then it occurred to me, very late last night, that I have no need for keys as such anymore." He had been wearing his normal garb of suit and tie, dressed for success for his stint in the witness box and later for the review of his potential new pied-à-terre, and while he spoke now I noticed his hand move absentmindedly up to the button at his neck, which he undid. Then went the tie, which he ripped off and shoved rudely into the pocket of his trench coat. "I mean . . . what do I need keys for? The office? I don't think so."

"I guess not," I said. "Louise will be there as long as you need her, to let you in and whatever." The cab was making pretty good time. If we kept along at this rate, I might just make it into my assigned location without any bump in the judicial proceedings.

"And I'm not sure if I really will need the keys to my house for very much longer."

"Why the hell not? Like, you still live there, don't you?" He didn't say anything. "What's up with that, Harb?" I said when it was clear he wasn't going to add anything.

"Right now, I don't live anywhere," he replied. He was staring out the window with genuine interest, as one who is being taken out on a fascinating junket into countryside he has never seen. Once again, I was struck by his aspect of extreme . . . youth. "There's something about that I find sort of . . . invigorating. I'm gonna keep that going for a while, now that I've got it started."

"But what about Jean . . . the kids . . . your whole, you know, life?" I realize I sounded kind of stupid, inarticulate and bourgeois. But when people start talking like Harb was talking it puts you in a funny position. You want to be supportive and New Age about the whole thing, but still, there's something conservative inside you that's revulsed and wants to slap the miscreant around.

"You don't have to tell me about my responsibilities, Fred," he said, and a coldness descended in the space between us in the back of that smelly cab. To my credit, I let it hang there. There are times, even in affairs between men, when a real coldness is better than a false warmth.

"I've been unhappy but I didn't know it," Harb said after about half a minute, and for the first time in our whole history together I realized there was no corporate veil between us. It was nice. "Then, you know, I became aware of it. Now it's all I think about. Look at me, man. Somewhere along the line I acquired a little potbelly. I get headaches. I sleep for a couple of hours and then I'm up for the rest of the night. I don't even know what I think about. I spend hours poring over boating magazines. I'm unhappy. And you know what? I'm not going to be anymore. That's the big experiment I'm going to try now that I've managed to get out of the web for a little while. Hey. We're here."

The cab had stopped. "But, Harb," I said, "you can't just . . . get out of everything."

"Oh," said Harb. "I don't know."

Departure was critical, there was no doubt about that, but I was hardly satisfied with where matters stood. "I'll talk to you later, huh?" I said as I got out of the cab. It was not a rhetorical question.

"Yeah, definitely," he said. He put his right hand out the window of the cab, and I took it with mine in a manly handshake. Then for no reason I can think of, we did not let go and simply held onto each other's paws for a while. "We're still friends, Fred," he said. His face was framed in the taxi window, and his eyes were locked onto mine with an intensity that held me fast. "There's no reason things like that need to be left behind. That kind of stuff is also within our control. More than a lot of other things, actually." That made me feel a little bit better. "You better get out of here now," he said.

"Yeah. Jesus." What was I thinking about? I could almost hear the judge calling my name. I pulled my hand from his and turned toward the courthouse. "I'll call you," I yelled over my shoulder and humped it to the front door of the building as fast as I could run. I'm not a very elegant runner, and I heard some kind of rude chortle behind me as I went. "Glencoe," I heard him tell the driver as they pulled away from the curb, his voice still filled with laughter.

35

2:30 P.M.

Direct examination of Julianne Blatt by Mr. Morgenstern

THE COURT: Call your next witness.

MR. MORGENSTERN: I call as my next witness Julianne Blatt. Good afternoon, Your Honor. Good afternoon, ladies and gentlemen of the jury. Good afternoon, Ms. Blatt.

MS. BLATT: Hi.

Q: At any time when you worked with her, did CaroleAnne Winter ever complain to you that she was being treated unfairly?

A: Yes, she did.

Q: Can you describe when for the first time she made that complaint to you?

A: The first time I remember was last year around the holidays, in November or December.

Q: Can you describe the sum and substance of the complaint?

A: I had visited CaroleAnne's desk to go over some type of work issue and had made a request, and she said okay, fine, we'll take care of it. When I got back to my desk I got a phone call from her, and she was rather upset and was making some statements to the effect that she wasn't being treated fairly and that basically Harb and I were in cahoots, if you will, and I asked her, what is it that you are complaining about, and the conversation really went nowhere, and I asked well, if you can't tell me what it is that you're upset about I really would rather not continue this conversation. And she continued to go through the tirade, and I hung up on her.

Q: How long did this conversation take?

207

A: Probably two or three minutes. I was upset because she had made me raise my voice, and I'm not used to doing that.

Q: In the course of that conversation, did you ask Ms. Winter what specifically led her to make a claim that she was being treated unfairly?

A: Yes, I did.

Q: And?

A: She wouldn't say.

Q: At any time after that, did CaroleAnne Winter ever complain to you that she had heard Robert Harbert make comments that she found offensive?

A: No, she did not.

Q: In your deposition preparing for this case, did you not state that CaroleAnne Winter had told you Mr. Harbert had made several comments that were sexist in nature, that it was "in the realm of possibility" that such statements had been made?

A: No, I did not. In fact, when I was presented a copy of my deposition, I sent back a notice to say that that particular statement should be stricken because that is not what I said. The exact comment that I made was "it is *not* within the realm of possibility." I think you'll agree that's a significant discrepancy.

Q: Okay. At any time while you worked with CaroleAnne Winter, did you ever learn of her faith or her religion, what it was?

A: I knew she was quite religious. I didn't know what denomination she was, if that's what you're talking about.

Q: Did you ever have a discussion with people in the office about her religious beliefs?

A: On occasion, yes.

Q: Do you recall when?

A: Probably at the time she was disrupting the entire office with her bizarre rituals.

THE COURT: Let's try to stick with the facts, ma'am.

A: Okay. I thought I was.

36

Blatt's inherent MBA smugness was coming out on the stand, and that didn't do us one bit of good. We didn't want jurors to think that any employee of Global might be unlikable in any way.

"Are you saying that you never overheard jokes or comments concerning CaroleAnne Winter's religious beliefs?" Morgenstern was inflamed. You would have thought he was talking about the Salem witch trials.

"People were freaked out, you know," said Blatt evenly.

"So you do recall jokes, then," Morgenstern proclaimed. It was a genuine gotcha straight out of a police procedural.

"No jokes, but comments, yes."

"What kind of comments do you recall?"

"People were marveling at what was going on, that's all. You have to realize. This was a very buttoned-down environment. These guys were praying in there. Loud, sometimes. You weren't even supposed to raise your voice on the telephone, for goodness sake."

"Did CaroleAnne Winter ever complain to you about any statements made by a consultant named Buddy Keaveney?"

"Complain to me personally? No."

"Did Mr. Keaveney ever tell you that CaroleAnne complained to him that he was spreading rumors about her being pregnant?"

"Yes, he did."

"Can you describe that incident?"

"Basically," said Blatt, leaning forward in the witness box and directly addressing the jury, "at some point on a particular day, I crossed by to see Buddy about a business issue he was consulting with us about, and he mentioned to me that CaroleAnne had called him on the phone, even though he was officing only a few feet away from her, and complained to him about spreading rumors that she was pregnant."

"Did he repeat any of CaroleAnne's words?"

"I don't recall—basically Buddy was aghast. Like most consultants, he just wanted to go along as long as possible without attracting undue attention to himself that might threaten his marginal status in the organization."

Morgenstern reacted as if he had just found a particularly bad hunk of cheese at the back of his refrigerator. He slowly, and full of matter, went to his desk and extracted a document, which he paged through laboriously and then read aloud. "At your deposition," he said, "did you make the following statement: 'Buddy had looked into an issue that CaroleAnne had asked about. When he came back to her with the information, moments later CaroleAnne called him on the interoffice line and, as he put it, ripped him a new asshole. He said, "I don't know where it came from, but she said, "Who are you to be talking to the entire company about my medical issues and telling them I am pregnant?" He said, "I didn't say anything like that to anybody."' Now Ms. Blatt, and remembering you are under oath, were you asked and did you give that answer?"

Blatt look incredibly bored. "At my deposition?" she said.

"Yes." Morgenstern was evidently at the end of his rope with this uncooperative witness.

"Yes, I did. So what? It's substantially what I just told you anyhow."

"Uh-huh. Right," he replied in a voice dripping with irony. "Was it ever revealed to you what Buddy Keaveney's comment in the presence of that other secretary was?"

"I don't recall."

"I see. You don't recall quite a bit, isn't that true, Ms. Blatt?"

Blatt was blasé. "I don't know," she said. "I think I'm recalling most of what you're asking me about."

"At any time did you ever post a cartoon or clipping from a newspaper in the Quality area?"

"Yes, I did."

"Did you ever have any particular intent when you posted this clipping?"

"Only the intent that it was humorous and it basically conveyed some of the feelings of my associates for all the Quality meetings that we were either running or attending."

"And that is all?"

"Yes, sir. That is all. Don't you post cartoons in your office?"

"Whether I do nor not is immaterial, madam."

"Madam?"

"Did you have an interview with Frederick Tell concerning CaroleAnne Winter's complaint against the company?"

"Yes, I did."

"Did Mr. Tell indicate to you that any of the specifics in the complaint were directed toward you?"

"Yes, he did."

"Do you recall what specifics were directed toward you?"

"Just that I was somehow involved in a general sense."

Morgenstern looked down at his notes for a time. Then he looked at Blatt. Then he looked down at his notes.

"Well, Mr. Morgenstern?" said Lerner. He looked annoyed.

"I have no more questions of this witness," he said.

"Anything, Mr. Biddle?" said the judge. Biddle rose but stayed in his place and issued his very few questions standing.

"Ms. Blatt, you described the incident over the telephone where you raised your voice. Was her voice raised as well?"

"Yes, it was."

"Other than that, do you recall any instance when she came to you to complain about her treatment?"

"There probably were a few occasions. My advice to her at that time was if she felt that there was a problem or an issue, she should address it to Harb, that he would be very willing to listen."

"Would you describe the work that Ms. Winter did with you during the time you knew her?"

"It was impeccable. In fact, I wrote the proposal that gave CaroleAnne that ten-thousand-dollar grant."

"And were you motivated in that action by the fact that someone in Pittsburgh had received a two-hundred-and-fifty-dollar stipend?"

Blatt looked over at the jury and made eye contact with one. Who was it? I looked to see and was not surprised to find it was the burly man of property in the blue pinstriped suit.

"No," she said.

37

MR. BIDDLE: Ms. Blatt, did you ever call Ms. Winter a bagel?

MS. BLATT: No! Who calls another person a bagel?

Q: A hooker?

A: No.

Q: A whore?

A: No.

Q: Did you ever hear anyone say such things?

A: No.

Q: Did you ever walk past her desk, saying ho, ho, ho as a code word for whore?

A: No. I do believe I might have been infused with the Christmas spirit, however.

Q: Be that as it may. Did you ever say that she got wild when she got drunk?

A: No.

Q: Did you ever hear Robert Harbert or anyone else make such statements about Ms. Winter?

A: No, I did not.

Q: Were you ever criticized with respect to the disorderly look of your cubicle?

A: Yes. Basically, my workspace can be described as organized disorder. I know where everything is, but you'll never find it.

Q: Did anyone ever say something to the effect that you've got an awful lot of trash here, you ought to clear it out?

A: Every vice president who passed by.

Q: Did you or anyone else ever call her trash?

A: No.

MR. BIDDLE: I have no further questions.

MR. MORGENSTERN: I have nothing further, Your Honor.

THE COURT: You may step down. *(Witness excused)*

MR. MORGENSTERN: Thank you, Your Honor. We have no further witnesses and we rest.

THE COURT: Motions, we will take them later. Do you want to call your witnesses?

MR. BIDDLE: We call Frederick Tell.

38

Direct examination of Frederick Tell by Mr. Biddle
Afternoon session continued

MR. BIDDLE: Mr. Tell, what is your position?

MR. TELL: I am senior vice president at Global in charge of Human Resources.

Q: How long have you been employed by Global?

A: Nineteen years.

Q: Would you briefly describe your duties.

A: I'm in charge of employment, training, compensation, employee relations and EEOC requirements, and also affirmative action.

Q: Are you the top human resources official in the corporation?

A: Yes, I am.

Q: Do you know Robert Harbert?

A: Yes, I do.

Q: At the beginning of this period, when CaroleAnne Winter joined the company, where was Mr. Harbert's office?

A: I believe he was on the eleventh floor in what we called the Castle.

Q: Where was your office?

A: Down the hall from Harb's.

Q: Did there come a time when you and Mr. Harbert moved to a higher floor?

A: Yes, when we built the new Quality department with offices on the thirty-seventh floor.

Q: Where was your office in relation to Mr. Harbert's

office at that time?

A: Right next to him. To the left.

Q: Did you know CaroleAnne Winter?

A: Yes, I did. Miss Winter sat outside of Mr. Harbert's office, and on occasion she would answer my phone or take a phone message for me.

Q: Did you have occasion to evaluate Ms. Winter's complaint in your role as head of HR?

A: Yes, sir. I did.

39

Biddle settled comfortably in his chair. The judge did the same. The jury was looking at me. I won't lie to you: I felt nervous. This was for all the marbles. I wanted to do a good, fair job and at the same time help my company and my friend. My rank partisanship had appeared in its most obvious form in the midst of my investigation, when I realized how demented CaroleAnne was. It built from there, until it reached the fever pitch I feel to this day. Would that yearning for the right side to prevail discredit me in the eyes of those deciding our fate? Knowing the truth, was I now to be dispassionate? As the arbiter of the internal investigation, should I evince anything less?

Biddle opened. "Let me show you Exhibit L and ask if you can identify it."

"That is my report."

"And did you reach any conclusion about her allegations?"

"Based on my talks with more than a hundred people throughout the company and the quality of the complaint itself, I came to the conclusion that no one verified or could support any of the statements made by Ms. Winter in her letter."

"Did you convey the conclusion to Ms. Winter?"

-"I met with Ms. Winter, I believe it was on February twenty-fifth, and apprised her of my findings."

"How did Ms. Winter react to your findings?"

"Ms. Winter got angry. She told me that she was not surprised that I found nothing, because I was a spawn of Satan and was dedicated to the propagation of evil on the earth. She also said that we should terminate her."

"What was your response?" said Biddle.

"I had no response to her allegation of Satanic influence," I said. "That's very hard to disprove. I did, however, state that I had no intention of terminating her. We had no grounds."

"What happened then?"

"She quit. And sued us."

"Do you recall the circumstances?"

"Yes. Harb was immensely damaged by Ms. Winter's allegations, and the entire Quality Process was winding down, so Harb was given another assignment, as it were, one of those meaningless duties that people are given who are not in good favor with senior management. And Harb's unit kind of decomposed until there were just a few of us on the floor, and then I moved to another office on a somewhat higher floor and pretty soon there was nobody in CaroleAnne's area except her and a few functionaries at odd locations, and a lot of empty offices. I should note at this point, I think, that CaroleAnne had been offered many, many assignments that would have given her things to do and impact within the organization, but she chose to remain where she was. Ultimately, I suppose she could stand the inactivity and loneliness no longer, and she resigned. This time there was nobody to stop her."

"I have no further questions. Thank you."

40

Cross-examination by Mr. Morgenstern

MR. MORGENSTERN: Good afternoon, Mr. Tell.

MR. TELL: Uh-huh.

Q: At the first meeting that you had with CaroleAnne Winter, before she had handed you the written document, did she make any complaints about the callous and insensitive treatment that she received from Robert Harbert?

MR. BIDDLE: Objection.

THE COURT: Sustained.

Q: Did she complain about Mr. Harbert?

A: No, she wouldn't tell me anything.

Q: Did she give you a reason?

A: No, she did not.

Q: Did Mr. Harbert arrange this meeting with you, or did Ms. Winter arrange it?

A: I believe Ms. Winter called and came over.

Q: So in spite of the fact that she arranged the meeting or she initiated the meeting, she wouldn't give you any specifics as to why they wanted the meeting?

A: That is correct. Thank you for making that clear.

THE COURT: I'm sure we can do without the sardonic tone, Mr. Tell.

MR. TELL: Sardonic tone?

MR. MORGENSTERN: How long did that first meeting last?

A: First meeting last?

THE COURT: Hey!

MR. TELL: Probably half an hour.

Q: Was the letter the next communication you received from her?

A: Yes, it was.

Q: Before you talked with Ms. Winter about this letter, had you talked with Mr. Harbert?

A: No, I did not.

Q: Had you talked with Ms. Blatt?

A: No, I did not.

Q: Did you talk to Ms. Winter?

A: No.[25]

Q: Did you at least invite Ms. Winter to your office to discuss the letter?

A: Yes, I did.

Q: And she came, right?

A: Yes.

Q: You stated before that she wouldn't give the names specifically she was complaining about? Did she give you a reason for that?

A: No, she did not.

Q: Is it possible that she simply didn't want to get people in trouble or cause waves within the organization?

A: No.

Q: But is it possible?

A: Anything is possible. What is certain is that she did in fact succeed in getting as many people in trouble as she possibly could.

Q: Did you inform Ms. Winter at this second meeting that you were going to talk to Mr. Harbert about it?

A: I told her I needed to talk to her first, and then I would talk to Harb.

Q: And then?

A: Then we went point by point through her memo. It was quite lengthy and rambled quite a bit, but we went through it thoroughly, because, you know, that's my job and all.

Q: Did she give you information other than what was in the written statement?

---

25. I suppose Morgenstern was trying to portay me as an inactive do-nothing dedicated to sitting on my rump while others suffered at the hands of callous management. I am sure you realize that it was my role then simply to wait for CaroleAnne's complaint to sort itself out on its own and not to prejudice the process by premature horn blowing and arm waving before the matter coalesced into its tangible form.

A: No. If I asked a question, she answered it.

Q: Did you tell her that you were going to investigate these charges?

A: Yes, I did.

Q: Did you use that word, *investigate*?

A: Fact-find, investigate. Yes. What are you getting at?

MR. MORGENSTERN: Your Honor?

THE COURT: Mr. Tell.

MR. TELL: Sorry, Your Honor. I'm having difficulty figuring out what fine point Mr. Morgenstern is attempting to hone here.

THE COURT: Myself as well, Mr. Tell. But ours is not to reason why. Ours is to answer any legitimate question, until I, not you, get sick of their repetitiveness.

MR. MORGENSTERN: Thank you, Your Honor. So Mr. Tell, did you inform Ms. Winter by what procedure you would pursue your investigation?

A: I told her I would be speaking to everybody.

Q: Did you ever tell Ms. Winter during the second meeting that you would try and remediate the conflict?

A: I told her I would try to find out the facts. That is what I told her.

Q: Isn't it part of your job to remediate the situation? If it's unjust?

A: I am responsible for finding out the facts, and that is what I did. I'm not exactly sure what you mean by remediate, but it certainly is a juicy word.

Q: What if there weren't really facts but the corporate story just didn't jibe? Would you take any action?

A: I would try to have everyone work together to resolve the issue.

Q: In this case, did you attempt to do that?

A: No, I did not.

Q: What was the reason that you didn't?

A: Because when I met with Ms. Winter, she didn't want to discuss my findings. She just told me that she wanted to be terminated.

Q: So in your mind there was nothing to be remediated, nothing to be gained by having the people in conflict sit down and try to work out their differences.

A: Well, if you think about it intelligently, sir, I think you'll see if that were our attitude we would have accepted Ms. Winter's resignation when she offered it. It would have been a lot less trouble for us.

Q: Oh, and it's all about what's more or less trouble for you, is it?

MR. TELL: Your Honor?

THE COURT: Mr. Morgenstern?

MR. MORGENSTERN: Sorry, Your Honor. In your role, then, Mr. Tell, as a single-person jury, you essentially interviewed the people that you mentioned before, correct?

A: Correct.

Q: So you received a lot of denials, and ultimately you accepted the denials as fact.

A: Nobody out of that entire group substantiated anything in CaroleAnne's letter.

Q: Did you anticipate anybody admitting any of the allegations?

A: People are honest, sir, even if they do work in a corporation. And if somebody has overheard people saying nasty things about an individual, someone in such a large group would say so.

Q: Do you admit a possibility that somebody in your group might not want to reveal who was spreading rumors?

MR. BIDDLE: Objection. Calls for speculation.

THE COURT: Sustained. We deal in probability here, Mr. Morgenstern. Almost anything is possible. Go ahead.

Q: So you actually anticipated that if these allegations were true, somebody would admit to one of them, is that correct? Is that what went into your calculation in finding "I have found no evidence to support her allegations"? Is that the calculus that went into it?

A: The questions I asked were based upon a concept that people were saying nasty things behind her back. No one substantiated that. Perhaps I should moderate that. I did have evidence, when Ms. Winter's behavior began to decompose, that people were talking about her, but truthfully, given the depth of her strangeness, people would have to have been blind and deaf not to be talking about her. That

222

does not provide proof of harassment.

Q: Apart from the portion where they denied hearing rumors, did you anticipate that somebody would actually admit to saying something untoward about CaroleAnne Winter's sex life?

MR. BIDDLE: Objection, Your Honor.

THE COURT: Sustained. You asked the same question before.

Q: Was there anything else that went into your determination other than essentially accepting the denials and rejecting Ms. Winter's allegations?

THE COURT: Morgenstern, shut up.

MR. MORGENSTERN: But, Your Honor, I am asking whether—

THE COURT: You asked it already!

Q: Other than with the interim—

THE COURT: You made a summation first, giving over the certain things that you wanted the jury to hear again, and then said a whole bunch of stuff I disallowed because you put in certain things you know you shouldn't put in. That's not the way to do it.[26]

Q: Was there anything else that went into your calculation and conclusion?

A: I also looked at Ms. Winter's performance reviews and salary actions, which indicated a pattern of favor, not abuse.

Q: But that perfect work performance didn't play any role in your ultimate conclusion?

A: She was a great secretary. That doesn't mean her allegations were well-founded.

MR. MORGENSTERN: No further questions.

MR. BIDDLE: No further questions.

THE COURT: You may step down.

MR. BIDDLE: Your Honor, could we have a moment at this point?

THE COURT: Sure. We will take ten minutes.

26. Now I find the court's tirade virtually incomprehensible. At the time, however, it made perfect sense to me.

41

Harb stood in front of his house as the clattering, belching taxi pulled away. In a moment, there descended the suburban calm that hides within its virtual silence so many pleasant, discrete noises.

A solitary owl hooted in the distance. "Hoohoo," said the owl, and then again, "Hoohoo." A yappy little dog barked from inside the Rooney house up the block and was answered by the big, sharp woofing of the far more serious rottweiler owned by the Nachmans across the street. Down at the little park tucked away near the path that led to the lake, he could hear children shouting. A soft hiss emerging from the area behind his own house told him that their automatic sprinkling system was doing a bit of work even at this, the cusp of winter. Snow would be coming soon. But until then, why not continue to maintain the beauty and health of their lawn? A decent lawn was a year-round affair.

On the porch flanking their front door sat the twin relics of the Halloween just past—two gigantic pumpkins, faces sagging, quickly turning to mulch. The one that had been completed by his daughter was leaning over, its once frightening grimace and arched eyebrows transformed into a mask of woe. The jolly and demented pumpkin on the left, done by his son, was little more than a vegetable pancake, with just the hint of a leer peeping from beneath its ruined brow. Although they were both in their teens, his son two years senior to his fourteen-year-old sister, his children still clung to the rituals of their youth. Well, thought Harb. This would be the end of all of that.

The house itself was perfect, of course. Looking it over now with a highly critical eye, he could still find nothing he would do to improve or fix it. A new paint job had been accomplished the previous spring, with a subtle shift in coloration that had made Jean very happy and left him scratching his head. From some kind of off-white with gray shutters, they had moved to a virtually imperceptible light yellowish accented by shutters that could have been either a very dark bluish-green or a deep greenish-blue. Or maybe they were still gray, he didn't know. They might as well be. For weeks after the job was finished, Jean would stand in front of the house and just look at it, arms folded, while Harb sat on the front steps, smoking a cigar.

Owning such a structure was the fond wish of many a bourgeois gentleman, indeed, of any adult person virtually anywhere in the world. And yet all Harb wanted at this moment, as he regarded the leaders and gutters for imperfections and squinted at the little patch of weeds that had arrogantly asserted itself near the stand of bushes next to the driveway, was to escape from the confines of this establishment as decently and quickly as was humanly possible.

What had happened? Was this decision made last week? Last month? Or was it possible that it was made before he himself had been aware that the process was not only underway but essentially completed? All he knew now was that it was done. He had been a man with a job, a huge title, and many, many things to do. Now it was full daylight on a weekday, and he had no tie on.

The idea had occurred to him years before, perhaps ten years before, that there was an alternative universe where a certain Robert Harbert was living in totally different circumstances. He saw this Robert Harbert as if at a very great distance, and at first he did not envy him entirely. The other Harbert had a little apartment someplace, although after several years he did acquire a sailboat in the marina by the harbor. This Harbert read books, not reports, and smoked Cuban cigars and the occasional French cigarette after breakfast, which he enjoyed at a small table by an open window that looked out over a picturesque vista of some kind. Then he took a walk by himself that lasted until almost noontime, when he took a nap. In the evening, this Harbert went to a bar, maybe, and had a cheeseburger. Some weeks went by when he didn't really talk to anybody. He had been aware at the time that this Robert Harbert did not enjoy many of the good things on which the real Robert Harbert had come to rely. The nightly chats with his children, for instance. Would not this reclusive, somewhat silent Harbert miss those? Yes, he would. He would have to make sure that some things, then, were not lost. If that were possible.

The shadow of his wife suddenly appeared at an upstairs window. Jean was in profile, bending over to fetch something out of the wicker hamper that sat in an alcove there. Doing laundry, then. Just a few pieces so that she didn't fall behind and suddenly find herself confronted with a larger load than she could handle. Jean hated letting things back up, when she was well in her mind and not too perturbed of spirit. When she started to get depressed, when the soupy cloud was beginning its inevitable descent upon her, she would begin to neglect the little items in the bottom of the hamper, and after a while there would be no bottom anymore, just an ever-growing top. Then the complaints about the laundry would commence and blossom into dissatisfaction with other things. And then she would go downstairs into the basement and the door to the darkroom would close and that would be all for a while. Her father had been a depressed person, but not an unhappy one, and the same could have been said for all of his children, except for Roger, Jean's brother, who had semiaccidentally overdosed on a speedball one night in Los Angeles twenty-five years ago.

So it was good that she was doing the laundry.

A sharp, heavy stab of love for his wife hit him in the chest, rocking him back on his heels with its unexpected force. He was aware of a physical effort to thrust it away from him, get it off his chest and out of his body. That way lay sentiment and, with it, failure. He would have to get this thing done in spite of whatever love existed between them. It was there, he knew that. He would not deny it. But he would not be a prisoner of love. That chapter was over.

He walked up the brick path to the front door for which he had no key, brushing errant twigs and leaves into the dying beds of impatiens to each side as he went. And what of right and wrong? The question welled up from deep within his carapace of determination and made him so weak so suddenly that he could not go on.

There was no question that what he was contemplating, the leap upstream that he, like a salmon, was attempting, would be viewed by everyone, not least himself, as a despicable act. It *was* a despicable act. Totally despicable. Then why was this feeling of jubilation, hope, and raw anticipation bubbling like a waiting geyser in his breast? He thought about that for a while.

One clear thought rose to the surface: The first chance he got he would get a new stereo. There was a store way downtown that sold old tube receivers and manual turntables. They were expensive but very cool. There was a Marantz that reminded him of the one that had been owned by his father. It had incredible power. Drive them through four state-of-the-art Bose babies and a monster subwoofer and the effect would be mind-blowing. Yeah, thought Harb. That, at least, was settled.

"What the hell," said Harb. "Let's do it." He pushed the doorbell.

42

MR. BIDDLE: Your Honor, we have testimony from a witness who cannot be here today.

THE COURT: Okay.

MR. BIDDLE: It is in the form of an affidavit, which counsel has agreed can be read in because the witness has a health condition. That is Richard Podesky.

Richard Podesky, being duly sworn, deposes and says:

"I am currently a retired employee of the defendant Global Fiduciary Trust Company. I submit this affidavit in support of Global's motion to dismiss this action.

"Global's counsel has informed me of the wild statements Ms. Winter claims I either made or witnessed. Such happenings did not take place and such statements were never made.

"For example, I am told that Ms. Winter accuses me of calling her trash because I supposedly spoke with Ms. Julianne Blatt, an employee in Mr. Harbert's unit, about trash and clutter in the area near Ms. Blatt's cubicle.

"It is possible that I discussed with Ms. Blatt the condition of her work area. I may have said to her that it was messy and cluttered and should be addressed. But such discussion was about Ms. Blatt's work habits, and she worked in an area significantly distant from Ms. Winter, and I do not know how anyone could construe that as a reference to her. I never said or insinuated that Ms. Winter was trash. She appears to have taken out of context a statement having nothing to do with her and to have blown it up in her mind into an insult.

"Most important, I did request that Ms. Winter refer to

228

me with proper respect. While there are individuals who have earned the right to address me by my first name in a familiar fashion, Ms. Winter was not with the company for a period of time sufficient to have merited that liberty. I deny utterly the imputation that there was anything inappropriate, malicious, or abusive in this request.

"In short, I am appalled that my name is in any way connected to her complaint. I have spent years with Global and the record shows that I have an unblemished reputation for dealing with employees in an appropriate manner. Accordingly, I ask that this court recognize the charges as the false product of Ms. Winter's imagination, a malicious imagination capable of doing the people who trusted her the deepest of harm. Thank you."

43

Harb rang the doorbell for quite some time, and nothing seemed to be happening. Of course nothing was happening, he told himself. Jean was upstairs, vacuuming. He stood at his own front door, his finger on the bell, feeling like a traveling salesman. Then there was suddenly a very slight change in the quality of the air around him, and Harb knew that the vacuum had gone off inside the house, and that there was silence around his wife at that moment, and that she was listening for a doorbell that she thought perhaps she had imagined while she had been at work.

He rang the bell again.

A light, musical tone issued from upstairs. "Coming!" it said. It was a lovely voice, a generous, earthy, sweeping voice that had a ton of muscle in it. This was one of his wife's most striking qualities, a voice that ensnared and fascinated people, made them feel comfortable and merry no matter what their mood, and hearing it inflicted upon him a tremendous feeling of affection that he noted but did not allow to penetrate.

In some way, in fact, the love made what he had to do easier. Of what value would the struggle be if it was conducted from a foundation of bitterness and disappointment? When he cooled off, he would have to do the whole thing over again. And he never wanted to go through anything like this again. He wished he could avoid it, even though he was the one who was doing it.

Jean had come to the front door and was looking at him through the glass. "Yes?" she said suspiciously.

"Hi," said Harb. "It is me."

"Ah, yes," said Jean without a trace of emotion. "I remember now. You 'lost' your keys." She made tiny quote marks in the air with the index fingers of both hands when she said "lost."

"That's right," said Harb, with absolutely no impatience whatsoever. He had determined that he would not allow this discussion to turn into a fight. That was the old thing and he was on his way to the new thing. "My keys have *disparu*," he said sadly. "I am sure there is a psychological explanation for it, but a simpler possibility also suggests itself."

"What."

"I've been under a lot of stress and was very preoccupied."

"Well that's just peachy," said Jean. She looked at him through the glass, darkly.

"Are you going to let me in or what?" said Harb.

"Where were you last night?" Jean peered at him intently to see if he was about to lie.

"I took a room in town."

"Uh-huh," she said.

"I took a room in town because of the whole thing, and because I had some thinking to do. I did my thinking and now I'd like to talk to you, Jeanie. Open the door now." He was firm, but by no means angry, having decided he would absolutely not allow himself to lose his cool or become overly bossy about the situation. The time for emotion had passed. The time for logical, kind, compassionate discussion was at hand. He closed his eyes and willed his wife to open the door.

"Open the goddamned door for chrissake," he said at last.

"Poopy," said Jean with some pique. It was an expression she favored when she was slightly but not seriously pissed off. He had always liked it. She twisted the lock and pulled the heavy front door open. Then she just stood in the doorway, looking at Harb.

"Thanks." Harb politely sidled around her well-known and comfortably large form and made his entry into the foyer that immediately preceded the great center hall of the house. Then he turned and looked at his wife. "Let's have a drink," he said.

"Now?" said Jean. Her hair was pinned up on top of her head

like a gigantic sno-cone, and she smelled of Pledge and Windex. "I was cleaning."

"You can clean later." Harb looked exquisitely uncomfortable. For the first time, the idea occurred to Jean that something out of the ordinary was happening.

"Clean later?" she said. "Why should I have to clean later? I need to clean now." A wave of apprehension swept through her. She moved then as if to leave the scene entirely, brushing past Harb toward the staircase to the second floor. "I have to vacuum up the carpet-cleaning stuff or it will get all weird," she said as she went.

"We need to talk, Jeanie honey." Why was he calling her Jeanie honey? Was that the way to begin this kind of a thing?

She turned to face him, her hand on the banister. Her face, which had been ruddy from the hard work in which she had been engaged, had instantly drained of color. He was using that inauthentic tone of pompous command that she had always loathed, but that wasn't the worst of it. Historically, he never used the phrase "Jeanie honey" unless there was very bad news indeed. She had last heard it when Pud, their beloved border collie who had graced them with her sainted presence for more than thirteen years, had been hit by a car and died. God, the horrible sadness they had experienced together on that endless nightmare of a day! Now . . . what could this news be? Something about the trial? Or his severance package, the terms of which she was aware were even then being negotiated? Something . . . worse? She both didn't want to know and wanted to know instantly.

Then, suddenly, nothing was happening. They stood there in the foyer, which is not really a room at all but just a space. During the indigestible silence that fell on them, she took some time to regard him closely. He did not meet her gaze. The house around them breathed but said nothing. Somewhere in the depths of the kitchen, the cat was pulling on her scratching post. Ah, thought Harb. To be that cat would be the very best thing of all.

"What is it, Robert?" she said at last. He looked down at the floor but said nothing. "Bob?" she said again and reached out and touched his arm.

"Okay, well anyway, I'm gonna be moving out for a while," he said. Then a very great, dark silence fell between them that neither of them wanted to break.

"What?" she murmured, very tiny indeed.

"I'm gonna have to . . . you know, because I'm too unhappy." At this last word, his façade of adult manhood slipped abruptly away from him entirely and he transformed before her eyes into a blubbering, sobbing baby who could barely articulate his words through his snot and tears. It started with something that almost sounded like a hiccup, then a few more, and then he was wracked with a grief so intense that his legs could barely support him. And yet he still did stand there, trembling. "I've been . . ." he paused, gasping and burbling like a bereft toddler. "I've been so unhappy, Jeanie, I can't be unhappy any longer now."

"You've been unhappy?" said Jean. "When?"

"I don't know," howled Harb. And with a howl of pure despair he turned and went into the kitchen, where she heard him slamming around in the cabinets and hooting to himself in a caricature of despair. In a few seconds, she heard ice in a glass and the sound of liquor being poured. And still she remained there in the foyer, one foot on the first step of the stairway to the second story of their house, where their bedroom stood, empty, blinds raised to let the sunshine in, the room in that stage between messy and neat, smelling heavily of furniture polish and window cleaner. She was not sure whether she wanted to have this conversation then or ever, or in the kitchen, or in another room that might give the whole thing a different perspective. What room would that be?

"Are you going to come in here or what?" he cried out in anguish. Who was he to display such ostentation of grief, thought Jean, he who was the author of it?

"Yeah," said Jean. "I'm coming." She went into the kitchen because there was nowhere else to go. Harb was running things now, in his own weird way, and not for the first time in their lives her curiosity overcame her resistance.

He was sitting at the long kitchen table, drinking scotch on the rocks from one of the tumblers they had picked up the last time they were in Paris. His head was down almost between his knees. He muttered something toward the linoleum that sounded like an apology of some sort, but she wasn't sure she made it out correctly.

"You're upset, Bob," she said. He didn't reply. Restless but uncertain how to proceed, she found herself slowly circling the room, not really looking at him, moving an object here and there into its exact optimal position. After a while, he raised his head and looked at her with a deep, moist gaze she couldn't quite read. There was a distance in it she didn't like.

"I'm not upset," he said. "I moved beyond upset about ten days ago. I'm just, like, looking through the window at the world now outside of my tidy situation here and I realize that I can get there all of a sudden. I didn't realize that until a little while ago, when everything, you know . . ." He rubbed the flat of his hand across his forehead as if attempting to smooth out the creases that had been there as long as she had known him, back when that spot was part of his hairline. "Fell apart," he said. "And then when everything . . . loosened . . . that way, it scared me, you know, but I still went on, tried to, going to the office and carrying my briefcase all over the place. Do you know how much I hate that fucking briefcase?" he barked and glared at her with a surprising, sudden animus. For the first time she felt like crying.

"You asked for that briefcase on your fortieth birthday, Harb," she said. "I thought you loved that briefcase. When that bird shat on it a couple of years ago I thought you were going to have an aneurysm."

"Then all of a sudden it didn't scare me anymore, this not knowing. It excited me, while at the same time filling me with this weird, you know, dread . . . but I realized I had to ignore that and just do it, because it was the right thing to do. And so . . . now I'm doing it." An enormous sigh shivered through him, and he once again dropped his head almost to the floor under his nearly fatal weight of misery.

"'The right thing to do'?" she said in a tiny little voice that made him want to reach out and put his arms around her. But he did not. That would be the cruelest thing! Or so he told himself.

Filbert walked on her stiff little stumpy legs to a patch of sunlight on the floor and stretched out in it. She seemed to be paying no attention to either of them, but in too studious a manner, like a spy overhearing a critical conversation while shrewdly appearing to butter a roll. And what about that cat? He loved her so much! Was he never to see Filbert again?

Still not looking at him, Jean took a seat at the other end of the table. A big, juicy, salty tear had formed under her right eye and plopped onto her cheek, but Harb did not see it, even when she did not brush it away. "You don't love me anymore," she said. "All this other stuff is rationalization, but that's what it all boils down to."

"That's not true," he said, and that was all. The words seemed thin and insufficient to him, even in the midst of his resolve. "I do love you, Jeanie. Don't say I don't love you."

"You don't. Don't tell me you do because you don't."

"I can't . . . go back," he said. "And . . ." He made a stab at going on, but then a surprisingly large bolus of pure unhappiness exploded from the depths of his stomach and stopped his mouth from speaking for a long time, an intolerable amount of time to her. She let it go for a while and then decided to move things along a little. If the conversation progressed at this pace, they would both die of respective broken hearts before it could reach a conclusion.

"And what, Bob."

"And I'm unhappy," he said and burst once again into the violent tears of a child who has lost all hope.

She had been trying to be the sane one, the quiet and restrained one during the entirety of the conversation, since he was so intent on being a madman, but at this point she simply covered her face with one large, slender hand and allowed herself to cry. "I can't believe you're doing this to us," she said.

They both sat at the table for perhaps three minutes, perhaps five, each sobbing in solitary grief.

Within this riot of emotion, Harb's monkey mind continued clambering around inside his skull. How could she be so shocked? It wasn't like this was coming out of nowhere. They had been in parallel, comfortable mental and physical spaces for years, and after a brief attempt at counseling perhaps a decade ago that only made matters worse, they had established an unspoken agreement to suck it up and let things be. They were happy enough, really, particularly on weekends, when they could at least be in the same room for longer periods of time and, in the evenings, drink wine together, happier and more congenial with each other than a lot of couples they knew. Look at the Sterlings, they were completely fucked up!

But seriously, could she possibly have thought that situation could last forever? Why should she want it so? Didn't she desire more for herself than this quiescent, structured, somewhat arid existence? What was the matter with the woman? Well, this was the best thing possible for both of them, even if she did not see that now.

"You had to know something like this was coming," he said finally.

"Well," she said, "I didn't."

"Okay, well," said Harb with a bottomless sigh, and she knew he was trying to wrap things up and then it would be over.

"Give me a reason or two, Robert." She got up and pulled a few tissues from the autumn-themed Kleenex box near the telephone. "Is it a woman? Do you have a . . . a little girlfriend?" She said this with enough contempt and incredulity for him to notice it and resent it. Why should he not be as likely to have a girlfriend as anybody else?

She did, however, consider this possibility highly unlikely, for a number of reasons both intuitive and evidential. Until recently, he had been at home, right on time, every evening, plopping himself immediately before the great plate of food and flagon of grog she had prepared for him, her returning lord, and when he wasn't in his chair as expected she had pretty much known the details of his out-of-house agenda: drinks with friends, the occasional game of poker. He didn't smell any different, when she had happened to take the opportunity to smell him. There were no unexplained credit card receipts, and no crazy midnight phone calls from "nobody," or "wrong number." She didn't feel another woman in him, maybe that was it.

"Naw," said Harb with a touch of annoyance, as if the suggestion in some way demeaned him. "Gimme." He extended one hand and wiggled his fingers at her. She handed over the tissues and got some more for herself. "I don't wanna come up with a whole lot of bullshit reasons, Jean," he said and blew his nose. "But it's not that. I'm too old and sedate for that now. Maybe that's a reason."

There were so many, really. Each one was both sufficient and a ridiculous excuse for what he was doing. The thousands of hours she spent in her darkroom, time in which he was left to contemplate the emptiness of life, particularly the bourgeois brand? The powerful fantasy life he had constructed for himself that centered on dreams of quiet and isolation, far from the demands of their life together? Yes, that too. But could he chide her or blame her for that kind of stuff? He didn't think so. Their separateness was part of what had enabled them to survive as a couple for as long as they had. It was so deep a part of them that it could not be changed without some kind of tremendous, painful, and probably impossible upheaval. He had always hated scenes like that.

Harb looked over at his wife. Once again a wave of pity and regret swept over him, along with the desire to apologize, fall at her knees, and begin the slow reconstruction of their lives, and he again thrust this feeling from him. He was doing so well! Why blow it now just because under the weight of current events she looked like hell?

Sex? The idea hit him like a howitzer shell. Was it that simple? He blew his nose again and stared down at his shoes, considering. Certainly not. While there was nothing wrong with it in any way, there was certainly nothing so compelling about their sexual relationship that would qualify as a reason either to stay or to go. Sometimes it was good. Sometimes it was not. Either way, it was no big deal. Maybe that was a reason too?

What good would it do to tell her that? What would that information do but bring her pain?

Did he want sex with other women? Sometimes he had thought so. But not really, no, except when he was very drunk. In fact, when he thought about it seriously as more than a passing mental vapor, he found himself frightened of the whole notion of physical contact with unknown sexual partners. Whatever the ailment he was suffering, partying hearty with the local babes was not the suggested prescription.

But . . . romance? Ah, that was something closer to the marrow. "I want to remember who I am!" he suddenly blurted out. Why? It was not what he was thinking. Why couldn't he say what he was thinking? Why did he have to be such a fucking liar?

"That is such a cliché, Robert," she said, and he could hear anger germinating inside her, a malevolent weed that would soon take over all other emotions, at least for a time. That would be good, he thought. Let her be angry with him. It would drive away all hope, all desire for reconciliation. Of course, it would also cost him a lot of money. "You suck," she added as if as a pleasant after-thought. A bubble of mucus formed at one nostril and quietly popped.

"I know I do," he said. "That's part of my plan. From here on in, if I want to suck, I'm going to."

"A laudable ambition!" Jean said and threw the ceramic cow they had picked up in Pennsylvania Dutch country across the room. It hit the wall and shattered, the head going in one direction and the body scattering. A fair-sized piece of Amish crockery flew in a high parabola and landed in the middle of Filbert's food dish. The animal got up, concerned, and walked with stiff dignity over to her kibble.

"I liked that cow," said Harb.

"Fuck it," said Jean.

The kitchen screen door slammed open and Kiki came in. "Hey," she said. She dropped her backpack, slipped off her Birkenstocks, which she wore with socks in winter, and went to the refrigerator. "Whuzzup," she added, her head in the icebox.

"How ya doin', Stinky?" said Harb.

"I gotta read sixty pages of the *Inferno*," she said, munching on

238

something she had grasped with one hand while rooting around with the other in the depths of the cold, white enclosure.

"You better get busy, then."

"No shit," said his daughter, emerging with a stalk of celery wrapped in a greasy, rubbery fold of no-fat bologna.

"Do your homework, Keek," said Jean to her daughter's back. Kiki was gone. The sound of music, if you could call it that, seeped down from her room upstairs.

"That's going to be a bitch," said Harb. "The kids are going to hate me."

"Yeah," said Jean. She raised her tear-stained, sweet, and oddly not angry face and looked at him with an expression he couldn't quite fathom. It's possible he had never seen it before, which was in itself quite astounding. "Let's make love," she said, with a weird little grin.

"Now?" said Harb.

"Sure," said Jean. "We're still married, for the time being. I want to."

"Okay," said Harb. He stood up. "It's not going to change anything in the long run," he added, not unkindly.

"I'm not worried about the long run right now," said Jean. She went to the door of the kitchen and turned to face him. "Hang up your coat in the closet before you come upstairs, will you, Harb?"

And he did, too.

44

Direct examination of Louise Dwight by Mr. Biddle
Afternoon session continued

MR. BIDDLE: Good afternoon.

MS. DWIGHT: Good afternoon.

Q: Ms. Dwight, are you currently employed?[27]

A: Yes, I am.

Q: By whom?

A: By Global. In a few weeks, I will begin a new job at St. Barnabas Church.

Q: How long have you been employed at Global Fiduciary Trust Company?

A: I started in 1992.

Q: What was your position?

A: Primarily I was Dick's secretary.

Q: When did you first meet CaroleAnne Winter?

A: On the day she joined the corporation.

Q: Did you become friendly with her?

A: Yes, I did. I mean, I thought I did. Now, you know . . . I don't know.

Q: Did Ms. Winter confide in you personal problems that she was having?

A: All the time, yes. Mostly, you know, marital kind of stuff at home.

27. I include Louise as the representative of some six or seven that Biddle called in support of our case. As I listened to this litany of right-thinking people, I relaxed just a bit. God bless America and its system of courts. It is flawed, since it is it run by human beings, who so often fall short of our expectations. But if you wait long enough, true things will be said, and even if they do not prevail, the fact that they get out at all is deeply satisfying to those who have been wronged. Unfortunately, Harb was not there to see it.

Q: Could you describe the relationship that you saw between Ms. Winter and Mr. Harbert?

A: It was always friendly and businesslike. I thought they were friends, as much as you could be in that kind of relationship of boss and assistant.

Q: Did you see Ms. Winter's interaction with Ms. Blatt?

A: At times, yes.

Q: Would you describe what you saw there.

A: As friendly as you could be with Ms. Blatt, since she was sort of a jerk.

Q: Did you ever hear Mr. Harbert say anything inappropriate to or about Ms. Winter?

A: No.

Q: Did you ever hear Ms. Blatt say anything inappropriate to or about Ms. Winter?

A: No.[28]

Q: Did you hear Mr. Podesky say any such thing?

A: No.[29] Dick was a tough boss, though. You had to know him to appreciate his good side, and even then it wasn't easy all the time.

Q: How did Mr. Podesky treat Ms. Winter?

A: He didn't have much contact with CaroleAnne. Maybe CaroleAnne would answer my phone and give him messages. Mr. Podesky was pretty much to himself. He would come in, and he spent a lot of time in his office.

Q: Did you ever hear anyone call CaroleAnne Winter any names or make fun of her?

A: No, sir.

MR. BIDDLE: I have no further questions.

Cross-examination by Mr. Morgenstern

MR. MORGENSTERN: Good afternoon, Ms. Dwight.

MS. DWIGHT: Good afternoon.

Q: In the course of any conversations that you had with

---

28. This was a little too pat. Everything Julianne said bordered on impropriety.
29. For his part, as you have seen, Dick was not loath to criticize CaroleAnne quite harshly over stuff that annoyed him.

CaroleAnne Winter, did she ever complain to you about her treatment at Global?

A: Beyond normal employee complaining? No.

Q: How frequently would you have personal conversations with CaroleAnne?

A: We spoke every morning, you know.

Q: You said she would discuss some of the marital problems she had.

A: Yes. She was going through a time with her husband, with some physical abuse going on at home. Also drugs. I suggested that she report it and probably not to be at home any longer, because he was physically abusing her.

Q: You said she confided in you. Can I assume by that that you didn't repeat that to anybody?

A: No. But you didn't have to. You didn't need to be a detective to see somebody had punched her in the face the night before.

Q: And isn't it true, Ms. Dwight, that in addition to her talk about her husband, Ms. Winter complained to you many times about the treatment she was receiving from management, and Mr. Harbert in particular?

A: No.

Q: I will remind you that you are under oath.

A: No, she didn't.

Q: Come now! She never complained to you about the treatment she was receiving from Mr. Harbert?

MR. BIDDLE: Objection. There's a difference between cross-examination and interrogation, Your Honor.

THE COURT: Sustained.

MR. MORGENSTERN: I have no further questions.

MR. BIDDLE: Nothing further.

THE COURT: You may step down. *(Witness excused)* I believe in consideration of the hour and my own personal predilection at this point that we will adjourn for the day. Be back bright and early. Don't discuss the case.

45

I had been fitfully sleeping the sleep of the exhausted, bored, and irritated. Everyone was filing out of the courtroom. I was determined to find Bob and ascertain what he intended to do with the rest of his stay on this planet.

I discovered him, as I knew I would, in the beautiful bar of the Ritz-Carlton hotel, where quite a nice suite of rooms still being paid for by our shareholders awaited him upstairs. I must speak to him about that, I thought. But not now.

On the table before him were the rag end of two martinis, with nothing left in them but their olives. In his hand was a third, which he was sipping from carefully, lest he lose a single drop of the precious liquor. With his other hand, he was wrist deep in a bowl of mixed nuts. "The best are the cashews and macadamias," Harb said, rooting around in the mixture with his index finger, a look of total concentration on his face. "Maybe that's why there are so few of them."

"Louise was just up," I said, popping a cashew into my mouth. Harb was right, it was delicious. "It was more of the same," I added into the silence. "Not one witness has helped CaroleAnne at all, including herself." Still Harb did not answer. He seemed more interested in the identity of the next nut on his agenda than he did in the outcome of the trial at that point. I can't say I blamed him. The nut selection process was almost certainly going to work out better for him, at least in the short and intermediate term.

"Yes, things are certainly coming up roses all the way around," he said after a while and popped what looked like a filbert into his mouth. I looked at him closely to see if there was any bitterness or hostility in this comment but found none. He leaned into me suddenly and produced a small, brown object that he held in front of my nose.

"This is a filbert," he said with a certain demented solemnity. Then he ate it and sat back in his club chair. "I have a cat named Filbert, did you know that Fred? And . . . and . . . I love that cat. Even though . . ." He leaned forward and peered at me as if he was imparting a very great secret indeed. ". . . she does stink a lot." I felt strongly that some sort of dispositive comment was required, but I had none to offer. Perhaps I said "Ah," or something like that, but that was pretty much it.

I gazed at Harb, who was already slightly potted, not obstreperously so, but discreetly, his cheeks and nose a little red, a comfortable and inattentive slouch in his comfy chair. His demeanor was odd, combining almost equal measures of relaxation, amusement, and some form of antic, boyish anticipation for what lay ahead, the source of which I could not then comprehend. Underneath it all, I felt an overwhelming sadness about him. I don't mean to say that he himself was melancholy, because he wasn't. Far from it. As incredible as it might seem, in spite of all that was arrayed against him, he appeared . . . happy. If you had told me that he had just received tickets for the seventh game of a fictional World Series, one in which the Cubs were participating at long last, you would not be too far from the affect. No, Harb showed all the signs of a man who was content with the world and what it had to offer. God help him, it wasn't my friend Harb who was sad. It was I.

What a man he had been!

"Yes. I'm going to have some fried shrimp from the appetizer menu," said Harb quite decisively. "You want some? They're very good. They roll them in salt before they deep-fry them."

"Harb, man," I said, feeling very much at that moment like a cardiologist, "that stuff will kill you."

"You're right," he said, motioning for the help. "I'll have one last martini to cut through all the grease." He gave his drink order to a young woman in black and white, who was looking him over with some dubiousness. "And my friend will have . . ."

I ordered a cabernet. They had quite a nice little list of wines by the glass, so it took me a moment or two.

"In addition," he went on with a coherence and precision that compared favorably with that of the judge with whom we had been spending the last several days, "I believe we'll get a couple of appetizers. This fried shrimp looks very good. Is it good?" The young woman, who appeared to have a pressing appointment elsewhere, assured him it was excellent, but I could tell by the way she said it that she had never eaten one of them. She was thin and obviously conscious of her health, which seemed very good, if one could tell such things by the ruddy color in her cheeks and the firmness of her little tummy. I caught myself looking at her perhaps too speculatively, and to regain my composure ordered, without really intending to have done so, a small andouille pizza. In a world full of harmful pleasures, none is a happier means of shortening one's life span than andouille.

"What's with the cabernet situation?" Harb said to me after she had left. He seemed slightly annoyed. "You gonna wimp out on me here, Fred?"

He challenged me, you see. I've never been one to shrug off a challenge.

I woke up that next morning with one of the worst headaches I have ever experienced in my adult life. The room was keeling this way and that. I was simultaneously hot and cold. My teeth were chattering.

What had we done the night before? As I pulled on a sock with the heel toward the front of my ankle and then strove to realign it without starting the difficult process over from step one, I plumbed my brain for coherent images. I was in the Ritz, for starters. This meant we had gone late and I had received spousal dispensation for an overnight stay in town. My wife still loves me well enough after long years of marriage, and this affection expresses itself in the desire to see that I am well fed and physically removed from potential harm. She has expressed a fear that I will be mugged or murdered on public transport one late night as I am reeling home from an evening of mandatory corporate intoxication. I have done nothing to allay this fear, since it is not unreasonable, and sometimes it is appropriate to stay in town. I have a change of clothing at the office, and the three or four hours of sleep I get in the arms of the Ritz or some other fine establishment are often among the most fully restful of any.

So I slept in town. What else had happened? I did not have the creepy, disconsolate, vague feeling of having committed some atrocity while in my cups. No shameful altercations of any sort, apparently, either physical or social. A good night of wassail and male companionship, then. But what had we done? There was the bar at the hotel to start with, then certainly others. The picture of an air hockey game suddenly materialized in my head. By the feel of it, I had downed my puerile little cabernet at once and then immediately moved to a heavy, single-malt scotch, Laphroaig, perhaps.

I smacked my tongue against my palate and remembered, in a flash, the andouille that had come on top of the personal pizza I had ordered. It had been grilled to perfection. In addition, I very barely recollected a large plateful of mussels and a veal chop, butterflied and covered with cheese. I sat on the bed with the other sock in my hand, trying to keep my insides from coming out.

And what of Harb? Why could I not remember what Harb had been doing? I closed my eyes until the spinning threatened to lift my head from my body, and then I opened them. Yes, there was a picture of Harb there in the back of my mental steamer trunk. He was sitting next to me on a bench outside, and we were looking at the lake. He was smoking a cigar, his feet extended in front of him, and he was talking. What did he say to me? Why couldn't I remember?

It didn't come back to me until I had my suit on and was slipping my feet into my loafers. Stereo equipment. He had been talking

on and on about stereo equipment, about the differences between digital and analog and in this dreamy voice laying out all the alternatives he was determined to explore. Stereo equipment, that was it. For his little apartment.

What else? Nothing more came through, until halfway to the courthouse that morning, as the Lincoln was pulling into the courthouse square, another glimpse, very faint, was granted to me. It was less than a memory, more like a subliminal hint. Harb, once again in the bar of the Ritz-Carlton. It was very late now, and his remaining hair was flying in all directions from his overheated head. He was all but reclining on the burnished mahogany and gold surface of the bar, in an attitude of jaunty ease, another lit cigar between his teeth, a small group of younger business types gravitating around him. Everyone was very drunk. Harb was wearing a semidemented grin. All those around him were laughing at something he had just said. Who were they? What was the content of their discourse? It was all gone. It was a nice picture, though. It was Harb as I remembered him, regaling a full audience of receptive businesspeople with his very special brand of charm and nonsense. As a final image, it made me happy. I didn't try to remember any more but went about clearing my mind for the difficulties of the day that most certainly lay ahead.

And then, as I climbed the long, long splash of stairs that led up to the doors of the federal building, one final startling mental vapor, clean and true, utterly stripped of the fog of drunken amnesia, was presented to me. It stopped me cold, and I just stood there in the bitter, clear November sunshine. Amazing that I had not remembered it before. Perhaps I had been striving not to do so.

Last night again. Almost morning, actually. We were standing in the lobby of the hotel, Harb and I, waiting for the elevator to come that would bear us to our rest. All around us, the hotel slept. At the other end of the gigantic lobby, a very elderly man in a white shirt and black vest was whisking a cigarette butt over and over again into one of those little metal receptacles on a stick, trying to make it go in, but it would not. "You know, Fred," said Harb,

"nobody wants to hire somebody my age if they can help it. The idea has occurred to me that I will never really work again. Do you think that's possible?"

"No," I said. But I did. It's hard to get back in once they kick you out, and the older you are the harder it is. At a certain point it becomes impossible. Whether my friend was, at that point, so expensive to hire and maintain, so mature, so set in his ways as to be inconceivable in any other role than that which had previously performed was anybody's guess. Possibly, he was. "You'll find something, man," I said.

"Yeah," said Harb. But he didn't sound very certain.

The elevators on one side of the bank went to the lower floors of the building. Those on the other skipped those floors and delivered passengers to the very topmost stories. I was on a lower floor and Harb was up high, is my point, so we needed different elevators. His arrived first. "I'll be going," he said. Then he turned to me abruptly and said to the carpet between us, "It's been nice working with you, Fred." He put both arms around me, a much shorter man than I, even on his tiptoes, and embraced me stiffly, patting my back with both his arms. The hug lasted for just a moment, then he backed away from me, turned, and bolted into the depths of the waiting elevator. The doors closed and I was alone. It struck me that I would never again see Robert within the context in which I had always known him. We would never again be part of the same family, dependent on the same people, reaping our food from the same harvests, fearing the same foes and superiors, dreaming of the same good things dispensed from the same bountiful font. We could see each other. Have lunch. Play golf. Get together for a little dinner now and then. But the brotherhood born of pain and pride and common interest . . . that was over. The ache smote my heart like a fist plunged directly into my chest. He had hugged me. We had said good-bye. That was what had happened last night.

Harb was not in court. I wish he had been, since we were now at the crux of what was wrong with his nutty former friend and associate. But I imagine he now thought he had other things to do,

248

and perhaps he did. The man who was Robert Harbert no longer existed in any meaningful sense of the term. What we had now was somebody else, perhaps not inferior, a man without standing, responsibilities, and societal definition, a man now in the process of determining upon what foundation he might begin to build his new persona. While he did so, the rest of us had no choice but to go on living the lives that had been given to us, since those, for better or worse, had not been ripped from their moorings and set to drift in the blackness of space the way Harb's had been. We could go on, and so we did, and my job was to be in court.

As I gingerly sat myself down in my customary seat on the third-row aisle of the gallery, I looked around the room to see who still felt it was important to be there to see how the case was finally, on that day or most certainly the next, to be disposed of. Our counsel, naturally, was there, as was his responsibility. No other corporate officers or working representatives of the company were there, except for myself. And this did not surprise me. Robert was no longer of the body, and his memory already was being expunged from the central nexus that ties us all together to the brain stem of the enterprise.

One unexpected individual, however, was seated in the back row, her attractive, focused, intelligent face glowing with the intensity of her anxiety and bewilderment. It was Jean Harbert. She was dressed quite nicely, in semibusiness garb, with a pretty scarf around her head all but obscuring her features. I caught her eye and gave her a little wave from my seat up front, and she tinkled her fingers back at me, but with less than a brimming fund of affection, I could tell that quite easily. Jean was not a woman adept at concealing her feelings. Why should she be? She was not in business.

I was disappointed but not surprised. I could comprehend and forgive her for any animus she might bear me as a member of the company that had now cut Harb loose for the worst possible reasons. Still, I had to feel she was a tad unfair. Had not she, too, recently upbraided Harb herself for his excesses? Harb had related the content of their discussion to me, and while I certainly identified with Jean's annoyance at her spouse's stupidities and very public indiscretions (particularly about the car), was not Jean, to some extent, a party in Harb's unmooring? Were not both of us now in the same position, trying to understand what had happened to the exemplary fellow we once knew? Were we not, each of us, trying to break down barriers of anger, confusion, and disappointment and find our way back to the person we thought we had known and, in different ways, loved? To find our way back to Harb?

Was there still a Harb to find?

46

"Good morning," said Biddle.

"Good morning," said the psychiatrist, whose name was Berkowsky. Our lawyer and our hired shrink then settled down to the slow process of establishing the latter's credentials. I was looking forward to this testimony, by the way, not the least because I truly wanted to know what the heck we were dealing with in the person of CaroleAnne Winter. Clearly, those of us in her workplace were ill equipped to have made that diagnosis when we needed it most.

For those who believe in psychiatry, Dr. Berkowsky's résumé was almost comically impressive. The man went to the University of Chicago, after which he attended law school at Harvard, and practiced law. He then attended medical school, where he received an M.D. degree, interned at an inner-city hospital not unlike the one on *ER*, did his psychiatric residency at the best hospital in New York City, studied at the New York Psychoanalytic Institute, and so forth. I'm paring down this list to keep things moving. But it gives you a flavor. He was also a member of the American Psychiatric Association, the American Society of Psychiatry and the Law, and the American Psychoanalytic Association, of which he had recently served as president.

"I am also chairman of the ethics committee of the APA here in Chicago," Berkowsky concluded, very dry, without a hint of arrogance. "And I recently noticed that I am listed as the only forensic psychiatrist in the volume *Best Doctors in the Midwest*."

"I offer Dr. Berkowsky as an expert in psychiatry," said Biddle, with a small, imaginary blast of trumpets.

"You may proceed," said Lerner, who looked like he didn't much care one way or the other.

"Dr. Berkowsky, you were retained by Global Fiduciary Trust Company to examine the plaintiff CaroleAnne Winter and to prepare a report in this action, is that correct?"

"Yes."

"Are you being compensated for your time?"

"Yes, I am."

"How are you being compensated?"

"I am paid eight hundred and fifty dollars an hour."

Wow, I thought. I wish I could make $850 an hour. Over the course of the next several minutes I tried to work out how much per hour I do make, and was unable to do so. My bonus is at least 40 percent of my overall compensation, and you can never tell what that might be, and the value of our stock options vacillates considerably. Still, I wasn't crying for Berkowsky. Of course, if I had gone to school as much as that fellow, I'd want to be making a lot of money for my time. It's possible that no amount of money would be enough.

Biddle then went through in tedious fashion the particulars of psychiatric examination of CaroleAnne, which had taken place over a three-hour period in late September. In addition to his tests, he had required the company to retain a forensic psychologist, one Sanford Globb, who administered psychological testing and provided a report. Biddle toted a sizable tome to the front of the room and introduced the scientific data into evidence.

"Dr. Berkowsky," Biddle said. Walking away from the bench, he turned and faced the witness. "As a result of your examination of Ms. Winter and your review of these materials, do you have an opinion held to a reasonable degree of medical certainty as to whether Ms. Winter has any mental illness that affects her ability to perceive and report upon actions that have occurred in the work-place?"

"Yes, I do," said Berkowsky. He had been wearing half glasses, and at this point, purely for emphasis and drama, he removed them

252

and focused on the jury. "I have come to the conclusion that Ms. Winter is suffering from a major delusional disorder with erotomaniac, grandiose, and persecutorial features."

I was suitably impressed. There was no question in my mind that this guy was a pro at the testifying business. I hoped his obvious experience in these matters didn't turn off the jury. It wasn't doing a whole lot for me. I've always hated pompous doctor types who try to make us believe that the human personality can be objectified and studied as one would a bug or a grape. His diagnosis did seem rather evocative, though.

"What kind of person are we talking about here?" asked Biddle, playing the role of the consummate layman.

"It's a person who has a fixed belief that cannot be changed by reason," said the doctor, staring at the jurors as if they were a bunch of students with dunce caps on their heads. "That is the definition of a delusion. In this particular situation, I also found evidence of what we call erotomania, which does not mean that someone is intensely in love with someone else, but rather it is the opposite, in which one becomes sexually interested in a person she hates. That is called erotomania. The other thing I found was what we call grandiosity, where the person believes that she is very special. Often the person believes that she has special powers, and in some cases that she has a special mission from God or something like that. Finally, I also listed persecutory features, which means that a person who has that problem believes that there are efforts being made to do bad things to her or criticize her in some way."

Well, I thought, that about sums it up.

"What effect does this have on the ability of the person to perceive and describe in an objective, factual way what occurs?"

"The delusions permeate a person's entire perception of her life around her and people around her," Berkowsky said. He was growing expansive in his role now and beginning to enjoy himself.

Biddle walked over to the evidence table and put his hand on the enormous tome that he had recently placed there. "Were your findings corroborated by the psychological testing?" he asked.

"Yes, they were."

Returning to his chair, Biddle added, almost as an afterthought, "Oh. Dr. Berkowsky, there has been testimony that Ms. Winter ably performed her duties as a secretary. Is this inconsistent with your findings?

"No, it is not. Not at all. Many neurotics are very highly functioning."

"Thank you very much. I have no further questions."

Biddle sat. Morgenstern did not rise. He remained at his post with the plaintiff by his side, looking at Berkowsky as if measuring him for a casket. I saw him consider several lines of approach and then settle on one. Only then did he get up, walk behind CaroleAnne's chair, and place his two hands on her shoulders. To her credit, she did not cringe or flinch.

"Good morning, Dr. Berkowsky," said Morgenstern.

"Good morning."

"You performed an examination of Ms. Winter?"

"Yes."

"Can you describe what that examination entailed?"

"It included a personal history, family history, marital history, employment history, et cetera, as well as an effort to discuss if possible the symptoms and how they came about."

"How long did that interview last?"

"About three and a half hours."

"About three and a half hours," said Morgenstern with intense sarcasm. He left CaroleAnne's side and wandered into the area in front of the witness box. "Can you tell the jury with specificity what particular things Ms. Winter said to you that confirmed your belief that she suffered these symptoms? Take her supposed persecution complex, for instance."

"Well, she described various things that were said and done that had a particular meaning to her, and I tried to explore whether she could possibly imagine that what was happening might not be what she thought was happening."

"And presumably if she couldn't change her judgment, she was considered delusional, is that right? But never mind. Let's focus on the erotomania. How'd you come up with that?"

Morgenstern could barely contain his contempt for this portion of the proceedings. It occurred to me that, with anyone who had an inherent mistrust of psychiatry, he might be scoring points. This did not make Berkowsky's testimony any less true or compelling. It was interesting to me that, throughout his rather blasé recitation of diagnoses, the doctor was confirming that not only was CaroleAnne a certifiable type of troubled person, but that somewhere out there there were more of her.

"There were various terms and situations," said Berkowsky, "that she interpreted as referring to sexual situations that other people might regard as neutral."

"Can you give me an example of those?" Once again, you could cut Morgenstern's attitude with a chain saw. Like everything he tried, he was overdoing the act, and it was growing tiresome.

"Trash, for example, was regarded as a wholly sexual term. Somebody said, take out the trash, and she viewed it as a sexual insult that could barely be tolerated. There were other terms, like the word *gang*, for example. Somebody would use it in regard to the working group in the corporation. She would impute the accusation that she had slept with a large number of fellow employees. I pushed her a bit to see if she could see any other possible interpretation of those words."

"And?"

"She just said no, this is the way it is, this is the fact. What I was actually trying to do was to test to see whether her mind would be changed by an effort to reason with her, and it couldn't."

To my mind's eye rose up an image: CaroleAnne, breathing through her mouth, her eyes dazed and glassy, staring off into the middle distance as the world swirled and turned around her.

"In the course of your interview with her, did she describe other phrases and behavior that she believed to be suffused with sexual innuendo?"

You may have noticed that once again Morgenstern seemed to

be doing his utmost to shine a bright light on the facts and occur-rences that placed the weakness of his case in the highest possible relief. Why I do not know. Perhaps you can work it out.

"Yes," said the shrink cheerfully. "For example, she said body language or a look—this is in addition to the words that disturbed her. Yet when I tried to ask her whether another interpretation was possible, she said no, she said, 'I know.'"

"When you first interviewed her, was it your intention to debunk the notion that any of this body language—"

"Not at all. No." Berkowsky seemed highly offended by the idea. "That is bad medicine," he added as if an unpleasant taste had just suffused his mouth.

"Uh-huh. I see. With respect to grandiosity, what did CaroleAnne say that led you to form that opinion?"

"She convinced me that she feels she has a special knowledge of the truth as contrasted to the way most of us derive the truth by human means. Her strong religious beliefs are perfectly normal, but the overlap into the belief that she was special and had a special mission and a special connection to God—that's different."

"If I said to you that many people who follow Pentecostal Christianity or evangelical Christianity claim to have had visions of the deity or Jesus Christ, would you consider all of them delusional?"

"No. In fact, psychiatry specifically excludes those beliefs from the concept of delusions."

"You said you read the depositions of CaroleAnne Winter and I assume that you read the portion in which she describes some of the visions—"

"Yes, and she described some of the visions to me, too."

"Did you take those into account in coming to your conclusions or opinions?"

"Were they the basis of my opinion that her beliefs were delu-sional? No. But I took them into account in terms of her general character."

"Based on the interview alone, could you come to the opinion that the behavior she observed in the workplace didn't happen?"

"You know, I never would say there is zero percent chance in that regard. But I can say that I have my opinion with a reasonable degree of medical certainty that they did not occur."

"With respect to the testing that was provided to you by Dr. Globb, do you know what tests did he perform?"

"Well . . ." said Berkowsky.

I'm going to spare you the details here, except to say that Globb, which was really and truly his name, conducted a battery of tests including the Million Clinical Multiaxial Inventory; the Minnesota Multiphasic Personality Inventory, which is known as the MMPI; the Rorschach test, a very well-known projected test; and a whole bunch of others.

Morgenstern, for reasons best known to himself, then led the psychiatrist down a merry itinerary of each and every test, forcing him to describe the methodology and utility of each. I'm going to skip most of it.

"The MMPI showed something very, very interesting," said Berkowsky, under the urging of the attorney. "It was positive for faking, but what it showed was that Ms. Winter was trying to fake being good, trying to present herself as appearing more healthy and more normal than the rest of the tests showed. She was in reality a lot sicker than she succeeded in appearing. Sort of the mirror image of malingering, if you will." What most of us do at the office every day, I thought.

Morgenstern regarded the shrink with equanimity. "Based on your review of the testing and reports of Dr. Globb," he said, "can you state with a reasonable degree of medical certainty—"

Lerner, who had been somnolent to the point of entropy, suddenly went erect. "I wish both of you would stop using 'reasonable degree of medical certainty' and all that," he barked. "That's mumbo jumbo that we teach in law school. He is a doctor. If he wasn't a doctor he wouldn't be testifying. He is not a shoemaker. I get tired of that. No more of it."

Morgenstern appeared for a moment on the brink of total consternation. Then he pressed on. "Dr. Berkowsky," he said, as if he was spending his last shell in the operation, "what is the basis for your opinion that the diagnosis you made months after these events took place applied during the time period in question?"

"I don't think I understand you."

"It's simple. What's to say that Ms. Winter, having suffered a great deal from the treatment she endured at Global, did not subsequently develop the symptoms you and Dr. Globb discovered?"

It was a good question, and it chilled me to the bone. The psychiatrist was unmoved.

"People do not suddenly develop symptoms and complaints like the ones under discussion here," he said. "They begin in childhood, and develop over time, improving at times and decomposing at times. I had a sense that these symptoms came upon her in earnest as her life became more stressful over time, as she separated and divorced, her very stormy relationship with her husband—these symptoms gradually increased in intensity."

"And yet you believe that the stress at Global had no effect on her mental health?"

"I didn't say that. I said the stress caused increased symptomatology. The illness is there. Whether it is manifest or provoked depends on the stress. When there is more stress, generally there are more symptoms. When that stress is taken away, there are fewer symptoms."

Anyone who has ever worked for a dysfunctional senior officer knows this to be true. CaroleAnne was a little bit sick from the moment we met her. I knew that now. But it took the pressure-cooker existence of corporate life to turn her into what she had become.

"Do you know," Morgenstern said, "whether any of the diagnoses that you reached would make a person bring a lawsuit?"

"It could be. The delusion is often focused on some injustice that must be remedied by a legal action."

"It is not your testimony that anybody who brings a lawsuit should be examined for a psychiatric disorder, is it?"

"I don't think the lawyers or the judges would want me to say

258

that. No." I could tell Berkowsky thought he had launched a peerless witticism, but nobody laughed.

"Do you conclude that?"

"I want to answer your question seriously. There are people of a particular psychological mental disorder type who use the legal system in various ways to vindicate themselves. For example, years ago we had a diagnosis that is no longer being used called the litigious paranoid. A person who was paranoid believed he was always being persecuted and always brought lawsuits as a result of that. So we have those types of people that we have thought about."

I looked over at the jury. I was pleased to see that all were leaning forward with the greatest of interest, eagerly—hungrily—sopping up the testimony of the psychiatrist. The bourgeois gentleman in the pinstriped suit looked particularly savage, although it was impossible at my distance to ascertain at whom his ire was directed. At the same time, CaroleAnne sat at the plaintiff's table, frowning slightly at the psychiatrist and pulling a ring on and off the fourth finger of her right hand. It occurred to me that in bringing this action CaroleAnne had shown not only her delusion, ingratitude, and greed, she had also demonstrated a fair amount of courage.

"In your interview with CaroleAnne Winter," said Morgenstern, "she did indicate her reluctance to have brought a lawsuit, did she not?"

"Actually, no. She seemed to evince a kind of zeal for it."

Morgenstern, who had been easily strolling before the bench, suddenly whirled on the witness and nailed him with a steely gaze. "In total," he said, "how much compensation have you gotten in this case?"

"I think it was so far about ten thousand dollars, but don't quote me."

"Prior to today, have you ever testified in a court before?"

"For much of my professional life I was the psychiatrist in charge of the psychiatric prison ward at Mercy Hospital, and in that position I testified hundreds of times. But in civil cases like this, perhaps a dozen times."

"Thank you very much, Dr. Berkowsky."

"You may step down," said Lerner. The psychiatrist did so. "I assume both sides rest?" Nods all the way around.

"We will now break until two P.M.," Lerner said, and I could almost taste the cheeseburger in his mind. "At that time," he said, "you will hear the summations of the lawyers and I will give you a short charge on the law and you will go out and deliberate. In the meantime, the lawyers and I have to work on things, so if we are delayed a little, it is because we are still having some problems. I don't think we will. I think we will move along."

47

The shrink and the case were done. Was there now anybody in the courtroom who doubted that a tremendous atrocity had been committed on the body of the corporation—not to mention the life and career of my friend Harbert—not only by this deluded individual but also by a social and legal system that made such things possible? There would be no retribution for the crime that had been visited upon us, I assumed that . . . but possibly a late and insufficient form of justice might prevail? Only the jury could tell. And how confused and prone to individual prejudices were they?

It was lunchtime, and I had no one with whom to share my midday meal. This was intolerable to me. I went back to the office to see if there was anybody who wanted a little companionship. After canvassing several floors and the usual conference rooms, I ended up breaking bread with Maltby and Fallante, a pair of management information guys who needed my support as they tried to expand their department. They paid.

As I masticated the aggressively raw tuna in the ubiquitious salade Niçoise that is now the mandatory luncheon of the day, listening to the cybertechnological drivel being emitted by the gentlemen across the tablecloth, I considered. Never would I have allowed myself to be entertained by a pair like that if the corporation had not stripped me of my most meaningful form of human interaction. What was my life going to be like without my best friend around? With whom would I hang out at the idiotic retreats, conventions, and off-site meetings that make so much of our corporate agenda across the years? Upon whose desk would I place my feet over my morning cup of coffee? Who would send me messages on my

BlackBerry wireless communicator from across the conference room at the many long and meaningless meetings, telling me, YOU SUCK? Who would grab a drink or two after work with me on days when nothing was doing and we could knock off a couple of minutes early? Who would be there with me late at night when crunch time was upon us? Who, in short, would be my friend in the one place I was consigned to go each day, the place that defined me, made me what I am, would do so until I could do it no longer? I am too old now to make the kind of friend that Harb was to me. My life was suddenly smaller somehow, sadder, and infinitely more businesslike. I didn't appreciate the change.

"The networking implications in a closed-circle system such as ours are profound," said Maltby, or possibly it was Fallante. "If we don't maximize the potentialities at this time they may slip away and be lost to us until the next paradigm shift comes along."

"And that takes low-cost head count to crunch the code," said Fallante, or possibly it was Maltby.

"Uh-huh," I said, tearing into a third sourdough roll, one over my limit, out of sheer ennui, grief, and exasperation.

There was nothing to be done for it, except to live with my . . . diminution . . . as Harb would have to live with his. We were bound, he and I, and I didn't even know it until it was too late. I thought this was strictly a business problem we had been dealing with. Is there really any such thing at all?

I thought about Harb and Jean and their two kids, now apparently being thrust into the cauldron of familial collapse. These things happen so suddenly, or at least it always seems so from the outside. Jean appeared to be fine in the courtroom, but you can never tell how people are functioning from the face they put on in public. And what about the Harbert children, Chas and Kiki? They were nearly grown. Is a person ever old enough to be divorced from the suffering of his mother and father? Which of their two parents would grab their sympathy? Who would appear to be the criminal and who the victim? I thought I knew. Harb would be the bad guy. And perhaps he was. The fact that his actions were the product of

262

an inexorable fate that had conspired against him would certainly not let him off the hook. Which miscreant did not have a similar rationale for his villainies?

As I was leaving the courtroom before lunch, I was approached by Jean Harbert. She was the embodiment of politesse and affable social friendliness. This cut me to the quick, but I did not let on. As I said, I accepted her feelings about the corporation and all those who were creatures of it, myself being the primary example. With all the goodwill in the world, and every fine intention to view me otherwise, I knew she could not overcome her aversion for those who had laid her husband low.

"Hello, Fred," she said. She was pulling on a pair of light gray kid gloves with black stitching. "I wonder if you have an idea where I might find my husband."

"Hi, Jean," I said.

"I think he's at the Ritz," she continued as if I had not spoken, "but his voice was kind of garbled when he called me last night so it was rather hard to tell. That, and the fact that it was two-thirty in the morning."

"That was inconsiderate."

"Oh, we're way beyond issues of consideration at this point." A crease of annoyance cut into the space between her exquisitely crafted eyebrows.

"Yeah," I said. There was a small pause. Then I blurted out, in spite of an intention not to do so, "I'm sorry, Jean. I had no idea what was in his mind. I still don't. I mean . . ." I stopped, flummoxed.

"Yes, well . . ." she said. "I guess if he's at the Ritz you haven't cut off his expense account yet . . ." She smiled a little, and the ice pack melted somewhat. I saw that at this juncture, in addition to everything else, her concerns were at least in part monetary in nature. That is, she was worried that Harb was not now in his right mind and would willy-nilly begin to burn through the personal funds it had taken them a lifetime to accumulate. That in the uncertain future she would be not only alone, but poor as well. I could set her mind straight on that, at least.

"His plastic is good through the end of the year, and probably even longer, you know," I said. "It's possible those in charge of the corporate Amex may sort of forget to cancel his privileges for six or seven months after that as well. These things happen. Besides that, all seems to be in order for quite a substantial pension, at least for one of his relatively young age. It's not as if he had retired at sixty-five, you know, but it's not peanuts. And then there are his options . . ." I didn't know how far Harb would want me to go into that issue at this time, so I stopped.

"Well. That's a blessing," said Jean and just stood there for a while looking at me, through me. Whatever human motor keeps us running during our waking hours seemed to have stalled in her for a moment.

"I don't think it's necessary for me to keep saying how sorry I am about everything, is it, Jean?" Incredibly, with enormous embarassment, I felt myself welling up with tears, and worse, blushing like a schoolboy. For whom was I blushing? I had been nothing but a friend to Harbert! Had I internalized the corporation to the extent that I now instinctively felt myself to be responsible for its antisocial, inhuman actions?

"You're not to blame," she said, reading my face. She was adjusting her gloves now and looking at the floor, as if that face were too dangerous a place to focus her regard. "Fred . . ." she said. I realized she was about to let the veil fall a bit, and I was afraid. "What do you make of this whole thing with Harb? You know . . . him leaving and everything. Can anything be done to stop it? To bring him back to himself?" She looked up at me then with the full force of her eyes, and I felt something roll over inside me. What a woman my stupid friend was giving up! What could possibly be wrong with the man?

"I don't really understand why guys go nuts like this," I said. "It makes me want to punch him. His world has been blown up and I think the organization man in him wants to start things off with an entirely clean slate. There's something in that that appeals to his sense of order." I really can't say why I decided to tell Jean what

I actually thought. Perhaps I was too tired and disgusted to put a gloss on the situation, I don't know.

The court was now completely empty except for we two. A man with a push broom came in for a moment and looked about the room, which was by no means clean, turned with a certain air of satisfaction at a job well done, and left.

. "I've been trying not to cry," said Jean thoughtfully. "But I cry and cry. It's ridiculous. Why didn't I see this coming? Of what use is being an intelligent person when for all intents and purposes you're a complete nitwit?"

"He's at the Ritz, Jean. Go see him." I didn't know what else to say and I felt quite strongly that the last thing she wanted was for me to put my arms around her, which was the only other thing I felt like doing.

"Okay," said Jean. She looked in her purse for a moment, extracted a set of keys, and showed them to me as if they were something special. They were hanging on a key chain that read, I'M THE DAD. "I'm gonna give him these. He lost them, you know. I figure if he has another set it's one less impediment to him just sort of slipping in the side door one of these days."

"He will if he's smart," I said. And then I kind of blurted, "He doesn't know himself anymore. The signposts by which he identified himself in the past have pretty much been removed."

"Uh-huh," she said wistfully and placed the keys carefully back in a compartment in her purse. "I haven't been removed," she added, almost in a whisper.

"No," I said. "I know you haven't."

"Yet," she said. She reached up then and touched me on the cheek with her gloved right hand. "Bye, Fred," she murmured, "Thanks for everything." She turned and left me alone with my thoughts.

And that was the last time I saw her.

48

At two P.M. on the dot the court reconvened for the lawyers' closing arguments. They were pretty hilarious, or rather Morgenstern gave his last bravura display of imbecility.

"Good afternoon, Your Honor. Good afternoon, Mr. Biddle," he intoned. "Good afternoon, ladies and gentlemen of the jury. First I want to thank you for listening to the past two days of testimony and listening to the reading of exhibits.

"The way I look at this matter, a few years ago it came out that there were several officers of Texaco who had made some fairly disparaging remarks about black employees and Jewish employees. The comments, if you recall, were about black employees being like black jelly beans stuck to the bottom of the jar. This Texaco official was complaining that first the Jews came in and took away Christmas from us, and now the blacks want Kwanzaa."

Good Lord, I thought. We had nothing against Hanukkah or Kwanzaa at Global. In fact, last year we had a little menorah in the lobby and an African cultural festival in the employee cafeteria.

"Had somebody told you before that came out in the news that a vice president of one of the largest corporations in the world would be making statements like this in front of other people," said Morgenstern, "you would have said come on, that's not possible."

I was wrestling with my emotions, and losing. The continuing lies, distortions, and exaggerations weren't even the worst aspect of Morgenstern's river of blather. It was the transparent presumption of the stupidity, prejudice, and gullibility of the jury that made the whole peroration so desperately nauseating and sad. Do lawyers believe the things they say in pursuit of their payday? I hope so. The alternative is really too terrible to think about.

Our Clarence Darrow then went through the situation from his point of view, masticating over each morsel of testimony that we had seen. I don't think we need to go over it now. He spoke for nearly an hour. Several jurors appeared to be on the verge of weeping.

"They spoke about the abuse she suffered at the hands of her husband!" he cried at one point. "Everyone knew about it! One person saw bruises on her. Ms. Winter readily admits that that was a major stress in her life. But, and this is a big but, the fact that she was going through this should have led to sympathy and instead you heard Ms. Winter testify that what it led to instead was more jokes about her background."

Would the jury buy this drivel? Does O. J. Simpson walk the streets a free man?

He mentioned Gretchen Kurtz and the prayer meetings. He mentioned Edgar and how Harb's interference had put their sainted matrimonial bond in jeopardy. He mentioned how many people went by CaroleAnne's desk and said "ho ho ho" and other suggestive comments. Did he believe this? It's hard to say. He once again plumbed into Podesky, who did not wish to be called Dick, and her party lifestyle and Mr. Harbert's jokes and finally, when the hour hand on the courtroom clock had moved one full divider, and Morgenstern had just said, "Now I want to talk about Ms. Winter's religion," the judge roused himself as if from a long and terrible dream and, leaning over the bench and pointing his gavel at Morgenstern, said, "Are you coming to a conclusion?"

I am sure I am not the only one in the room who blessed him in our hearts.

"Yes, Your Honor," said the lawyer, his feelings mildly injured. "I will touch on the psychiatrist's testimony and wrap up."

"Because you are way over your limit," said Lerner.

"I apologize," said Morgenstern, then he launched into a new tier of bloviation about the psychiatrist. You don't need to hear about it. The crux was that psychiatry was an inexact science and so forth. He then sat down in his appointed seat. There was silence. Was he finished? "Ms. Winter is a reluctant plaintiff," a voice said softly. Could it be? Yes! It was Morgenstern! He was still talking! Would this never cease? Who would save us? "She is not the kind of person who goes around suing people," he murmured. "She brings this lawsuit with absolutely no malice. She still has fond feelings about the people she worked with. She brought it because specific things happened to her and specific events affected her and specific things needed to be aired in court."

"Counselor," said Lerner, with the most menacing tone imaginable, "your time is up. You want rebuttal, don't you?"

"Yes, Your Honor." The lawyer seemed abashed. "You ladies and gentlemen of the jury, I hope you will retire to your deliberations, look closely at the allegations, look at the credibility, the denials. I think if you do so, you will come up with a verdict for plaintiff and that you will fairly and adequately compensate her for the sexual hostility in her working environment. Thank you very much. Thanks for your indulgence, Your Honor."

"Thank God," said the judge. "And now for the defense. Mr. Biddle, you have every excuse to be as long-winded as Fidel Castro. But I hope you won't be."

"Thank you, Your Honor," said Biddle, with mild amusement. "I will try not to be as verbose as my learned colleague."

I sincerely hoped that was his intention.

"Good afternoon, everyone," said Biddle. "First, on behalf of Global Fiduciary Trust Company, we too would like to thank you for your time, your effort, your patience, and the attention that you paid so far and that you will pay when you go back in the jury room.

"In order for the civil rights acts to work properly, they have to protect an accused as well as an accuser, and where there is no proof of discrimination, then the courts and the jury functioning in them have to come back and say it just didn't happen, and that is what happened here: It didn't happen."

I got a feeling Biddle was about to launch his own dirigible. That would be bad. All the animus that opposing counsel had accrued would be dissipated if we abused the jury in a similar fashion.

"The problem Global faced in defending this case," said Biddle, "is the problem of how you prove a negative. How you prove that something *didn't* happen. One thing we did was, we saw that you had the opportunity to hear from all of the principal people who were accused. You were able to observe them on the stand, and I trust you came to the conclusion that they were speaking truthfully when they said it didn't happen.

"How else could we show you that it didn't happen? Well, we did our best not to object during CaroleAnne Winter's testimony. We wanted you to hear out of CaroleAnne Winter's own mouth her allegations, because those allegations are . . . fantastic. Gossip about her in the elevator in code. People walking past her desk saying ho ho ho, meaning that she is a whore. A memo about meetings in the office and that meant sexual encounters with hundreds of employees. Cake and pie. Bagels. The vision of Robert Harbert with . . . a bloody wedgie."

Biddle, who had effected a very subtle but highly effective pause on the word *wedgie,* here took a deep breath and perambulated right up to the edge of the jury box. From this vantage point he scanned the small cluster of people who would determine the outcome of this case.

"Ladies and gentlemen," he said, "you heard the testimony, you saw the documents where we were able to come up with a tangible document that related to it. You can apply your common sense. You can apply your experience. You have seen the witnesses. I trust you will come to the conclusion that it just didn't happen.

"Finally," said Biddle, "we brought in Dr. Berkowsky to testify. We wanted you to understand how it could be that CaroleAnne Winter could work for Global for a long period of time, that she could be a very, very good secretary but still come up with these charges that really are unbelievable. How could this happen? Dr. Berkowsky explained to you how it could happen. He explained to you the nature of her condition, how it impairs her ability to understand and to recount what is taking place in the workplace.

"One last point for me to bring up to you. Think about Robert Harbert and the way he treated CaroleAnne Winter. It's any boss's nightmare. He gave her top evaluations, generous salary increases. He made special efforts to get her money when she wasn't going to get money otherwise. CaroleAnne Winter came to him one day and said, 'I want to resign.' The irony is that if he said, 'I'm sorry to hear that, but okay,' we might not be here. Instead, he said, 'Go to Fred Tell,' and she went to Fred Tell . . . and here we are today."

That hurt, but could not be argued with. She came to see me. I did all the right things. And here we were.

"Ladies and gentlemen, we ask that you go back to the jury room. Remember the testimony, look at any exhibits you need, use your common sense, and come back with the verdict that justice requires. Thank you."

Lerner was leaning back in his chair, his eyes closed, his fingers tented over his robed midsection. "Now it is time for the rebuttal. Keep it short, Mr. Morgenstern. Or I will cite you."

Morgenstern rose and gave a short bow to the judge. "Thank you, Your Honor," he simpered. "In rebuttal I just want to mention that you should also be quite cognizant of the fact that the people who testified on behalf of Global, most of them still have an interest in the outcome of this case. You should take into consideration the fact that people who are lower down on the corporate totem pole at Global may still owe their jobs to saying the right thing in this forum. With respect to Mr. Harbert's economic behavior toward CaroleAnne Winter, there has never been an allegation that she was treated unfairly with respect to her salary, her bonuses, and her benefits. It is not unusual where an employer really likes an employee that he also looks at that as a license to take other liberties with the employee because he is being so kind in the area of salary, bonuses, and evaluations. One question that plays in my mind with respect to Mr. Harbert's behavior is, when CaroleAnne Winter came to him and asked to resign after all those years, instead of saying why do you want to resign, is there anything we can work out, his first instinct was not to try and work it out but to get her to go to Fred Tell and see if there was another place in the company. Instead of reviewing his own behavior and trying to modify it, he tried to pass the buck. If you look at the circumstances of all this—"

At this point the judge literally stood up on his dais—which made him slightly shorter—and screamed, "I've had it with you, buster!"

Morgenstern turned very pale and blurted out so quickly I could barely make out the words, "I leave this dispute to your judgment, ladies and gentlemen, and thank you very much."

And except for the judge's instructions and, of course, the verdict, that was that for Harb's trial—the portion that took place in the courtroom, at least. The rest could pretty much proceed without our assistance.

49

THE COURT: All right. Now that the evidence in the case has been presented and the attorneys for the parties have concluded their closing arguments, it is my responsibility to instruct you as to the law that governs this case.[30]

It is your responsibility and duty to find the facts from all the evidence in the case. You are the sole judges of the facts, not counsel, not myself. I want to impress upon you again the importance of that role. It is for you and you alone to pass upon the weight of the evidence, to resolve such conflicts as may appear in the evidence, and to draw such interferences as you deem to be reasonable and warranted from the evidence or the lack of it.

The parties are equal before the court. This case should be considered and decided by you as between parties of equal standing in the community. All parties are entitled to equal consideration. No party is entitled to sympathy or favor. You must judge the facts in applying the law as I shall instruct you, without bias, prejudice, or sympathy either to the plaintiff or to the defendants.

The burden of proof. In a civil case such as this, the plaintiff has the burden of proving that her case is more likely true than not. If the plaintiff is to win, the

---

30. The judge, who had seemed something of a good-natured buffoon for the greater part of the trial, suddenly seemed to, as it were, grow in physical stature before us even as we watched. His body shifted in its heretofore somnolent position on the bench and sat itself upright. His head, which had tended to loll off to one side, suddenly righted itself and rested firmly on his shoulders like a boulder niched between two smaller stones. And his general expression, before this hovering perpetually between sleep and ridicule, suddenly cleared, revealing an aspect altogether serious, thoughtful, and stern. The jury, in subliminal response to this dramatic change, also sat taller and bent its attention in a new, more formal fashion.

evidence that supports her claim must appear to you as more nearly representing her claim than the evidence opposed to her claim. If the evidence weighs so unevenly that you are unable to say there is a preponderance on either side, then you must find in the defendant's favor.

We now come to the law portion of this case. This is the law. Racial and/or sexual discrimination under Title VII. Your verdict must be for the plaintiff against the defendant if:

- defendant or its supervisors or employees engaged in a course of conduct consisting of intimidation, ridicule, or insult.
- such course of intimidation, ridicule, or insult was motivated in whole or in part by plaintiff's sex, or consisted of sexual innuendo.
- the course of intimidation, ridicule, or insult was pervasive.
- a reasonable person would find said intimidation, ridicule, or insult to have created a hostile or abusive working environment.
- plaintiff herself perceived that the course of intimidation, ridicule, or insult created a hostile or abusive working environment for her.

We now go to damages generally. In a race and/or sex discrimination case, damages are meant to put the plaintiff in the economic position she would have been if the discrimination had not occurred. You can award damages for pain, suffering, humiliation, mental anguish, and emotional distress for the period of discrimination and for no more than six months after plaintiff left her employment.

Nominal damages. If you find that the defendant discriminated against the plaintiff but that plaintiff suffered no monetary damages, then you must return a verdict for the plaintiff in a nominal amount of one dollar.

Punitive damages. The purpose of punitive damages is to punish a defendant and to deter a defendant and others from committing similar acts in the future. If you find that punitive damages are appropriate, you must use reason in setting the amount. Punitive damages, if any, should be

273

in an amount sufficient to fulfill their purposes but should not reflect bias, prejudice, or sympathy toward any party.

In conclusion, I remind you once again that it is your responsibility to judge the facts in this case from the evidence submitted during the trial and to apply the law as I have just given to you. Your deliberations should include a rational discussion of the evidence in this case by all of you. In other words, it is now finally appropriate for you to talk about the case.[31]

Listen carefully to each other. Your oath sums up your duty. That is, you will, without fear or favor to any persons, conscientiously and truly try the issues before you according to the evidence produced in court. Start your deliberations, and good luck.

---

31. Here there was a little ripple of laughter throughout the jury box, and I saw that whatever decision they came to, this group, it would be unanimous. There was a feeling of amity and cohesion among them that was interesting and even slightly moving.

50

It was late afternoon when the jury repaired to the room dedicated to their task. As a place in which to spend an undefined amount of time, it wasn't much to speak of. Just big enough for an enormous, well-scratched table and nine or ten wooden chairs with capacious seats and curved arms. The arching windows were unadorned with any shades or blinds and stared out at the silent bustle on the street below through a film of ancient dirt and grime. Still, it was not an ugly room. Nor was it beautiful in any way. It was, in the deepest sense of the word, neutral.

There were, as I believe I have said, six jurors, four women and two men. I have now spoken with most, by the way, and from most conversations have a pretty fair notion of what went on in that nondescript room.

The women were a cross section of the ethnic makeup of our city and came in virtually all shapes and sizes. They ranged in age from thirty-five to fifty. All were dressed informally and for maximum comfort, mostly in slacks and blouses of one nondescript form or another. One of the younger ones may have opted for a navy blue jumper over dark blue tights. I'm not sure; I didn't see them standing up for any extended period of time, and for some reason the individuals seemed always to meld in my mind into one inchoate bunch. The men were in their forties. Both were as white as Dick Cheney. The younger of the two was generally dressed as a workingman would dress for a respectable job, in blue jeans and a blue button-down dress shirt, without jacket or tie. On this day of deliberation, he had donned a maroon crewneck, which lent him a jaunty and somewhat collegiate look. The older of the two men, as I noted before, was a pinstriped corporate animal of some two hundred and twenty pounds in weight, approximately five eleven, with a belligerent expression and perhaps six ounces too much jowl.

From the first day of the trial, this individual gave the impression of someone whose patience and ability to tolerate nonsense had been taxed to its absolute level of endurance and was now just about ready to snap with a twang and go flying around the room. During the jury selection, I could see that he was doing his best to come up with answers that would disqualify him in some way, but with pathetic ineffectiveness. I was certain at that point that the plaintiff would move heaven and earth to keep him off a jury in a case such as this one. I was wrong. About halfway through CaroleAnne's original testimony, as Morgenstern was grilling her about the many examples of how she had ostensibly been victimized, I saw every part of this fellow's face narrow to a point—his eyebrows, his rather small mouth, his nose, which was already quite pointed to begin with. And when CaroleAnne got to the juncture where the Lord began speaking to her personally, well before the incident with the bloody wedgie, the juror sat up with what I felt was clear indignation, looked about him as if he was the only person awake in the room, stared hard at the plaintiff, then sank back in his chair and allowed his countenance to assume the dark, foreboding expression I have already described to you. This it wore for the duration of the trial, except in the few moments right before lunchtime, when it took on a different, less truculent, and anticipatory hue. One time I heard him lean over to the juror next to him, a bright, plump younger woman with a Dutch boy haircut and a prevailing aura of pleasant amusement, and say with the utmost gravity, "Let's get some dim sum and a beer." That was the only remark I heard from him during the course of the trial.

Now the jury filed into the deliberation room one at a time, dumped their winter coats and jackets across a variety of chairs, and sat down. There was a silence. The foreperson, a nurse in her middle forties with a nunlike aura of calm authority, had quietly placed herself at the head of the table. "I'm not sure everybody sees this thing like I do," she said, "and I don't want to impose my opinion on anybody . . . but this sort of looks like a no-brainer to me. The woman is insane. Her suit has no merit. The sooner we take care of this the better."

"Oh, I don't know," said one of the larger women, about fifty, who was seated in one of the chairs near the window, her legs sticking out to full extension. She was in an inexpensive, shapeless turtleneck pullover, her winter scarf hanging around her neck and down her substantial bosom. The woman was looking calmly out the window, with none of the contentious tone that might presage an out-and-out disagreement. "The guy gave her a car. It's clear he thought a lot of her. Maybe she kind of . . . you know . . . misinterpreted the whole thing."

There was a thoughtful silence.

"You've got to feel kind of sorry for her," said the male juror in the nice maroon sweater to nobody in particular. "There's no question that she suffered a lot."

"I don't feel one bit sorry for her," said the upright man of property in the blue pinstriped suit. He appeared to be close to leaping entirely out of his chair and attacking the male juror in the nice maroon sweater with his bare hands. His face, once a rather pale, inexpressive mask of propriety, was now overly animated, an ever-shifting palette of emotions. The transformation from his prior demeanor of grouchy stoicism was complete, impressive, and executive. "I feel sorry for everybody but her as a matter of fact. That poor boss! What would happen to America if bosses like that end up getting the raw end of the shaft for the way they manage people? He hired her in spite of her noncorporate appearance because he saw her interest and value as a person. He championed her when others got into her face. He gave her a car! A car! And found her a way to escape from a husband who was abusing her! He raised her salary from fifty-three thousand to more than ninety thousand dollars in fewer than five years! And how was he repaid? With treachery and litigation! This whole thing makes me want to puke!"

"She's a troubled young woman, all right," said the female juror in the dark blue jumper. "And they're a very big company with a lot of money. What harm would it do for us to give her a couple of bucks?"

Two hours later, they retired for the night to their respective homes, having yet to reach a decision.

51

Harb sat in the large, comfortable armchair that the Ritz-Carlton provided for the workingman on the go, at least one who could afford an executive suite of rooms in the hotel. The seat of the armchair—more a single-person couch, really—was broad and comfortable, of a fabric smooth but not shiny, soft but not slippery, not rough like heavy tweed or corduroy but tender and yielding, with tiny blue nubs offsetting a field of dark maroon. His feet rested on a huge, square hassock that had been made to accompany the armchair. On his lap was the current issue of *Sail*, a copy of which always seemed to be in his possession these days, but he was not reading it. The armchair was angled so that Harb could look out the window of the sitting room and watch the lights of Chicago as they winked on for the evening.

A bottle of a heavy, peaty single-malt scotch sat on a little table at Harb's elbow, an ice bucket next to it. In his right hand, as he sat and gazed without expression through the window at the gathering night, was an ample, broad-bottomed glass bearing the crest of the hotel. In the glass was perhaps two inches of scotch plus one lone ice cube doing the backstroke.

At about eight-thirty or so, Harb rose and went to one of the night tables that flanked his ridiculously huge bed. After several long minutes of silent deliberation, he picked up the telephone and pressed one button.

"Yes," he finally said. "Room service?" There was a pause as Harb was placed on hold. He patiently bore it, looking neither left nor right, simply waiting, with the phone receiver in one hand and the glass of scotch in the other. Every now and then, he took a little sip. "Yes," he said at last. "I'd like the goat cheese and chorizo pizza, with some kind of starter salad. Uh-huh." He listened for a moment. "Does that have anchovies in it? No, no. That's fine. Make sure there are plenty. I like them. What's the least expensive decent Bordeaux you've got down there?" He sat down on the bed while he once again waited for the answer to his question, staring into the room and periodically drawing on his glass. "Okay," he said at last. "I'll have a half bottle of that. How long do you think this will take?" He looked at his wrist for a moment, then noticed there was no watch there. "Okay, that's fine," he said and hung up, downed the remainder of his scotch, flopped down on the bed, and grabbed the remote.

After a solid ten minutes of aimless flipping between channels, he got up, leaving the television on, took off his clothes, and went in to take a shower. In the quiet hotel room he had just left, the TV burbled on, the sound of cascading water filtered in from the enormous marble bathroom, and the phone began to ring. It rang once, twice, three times, and then flipped over into voice mail. The sound of water stopped. The silence in the darkened room was complete, except for the murmur of the unwatched television set.

Harb brushed his teeth. He was enjoying the steam and the quiet. Then, when the silence around him became too vast and deep for him, he turned on the small black-and-white TV that was placed to the right of his two sinks. A group of people on CNN were jabbering about the kind of inside Washington baseball in which Harb had no interest. He flipped on the bathroom heat lamps that were always one of his favorite features of hotel living, wiped the mirror with a hand towel emblazoned with the leonine crest of the Ritz, and started shaving.

Presently, he emerged into the main room of the suite, ensconced in an obscenely fluffy white bathrobe. He sat on the end of the bed and watched the television until a knock on the door announced the arrival of his solitary dinner. The pizza was crisp and very hot and the Bordeaux dry enough and not half bad. Harb ate slowly, occasionally working the remote with one hand while digging into the pizza and salad with the other. When the cart was cleared of everything but plates and cutlery, he got up, pushed the trolley out into the hallway, returned to the room, and stood in the middle of it, thinking.

It was only then that he noticed the winking amber light on the telephone. With a trembling in every limb and a sodden, heavy feeling in his heart, he dialed the two appropriate digits on the plastic pad that would deliver his unheard messages to him.

"Hey, Dad," said Chas from the bowels of the voice mail system. He sounded very far away, soft, as if he was making the call from a closet, so that no one could know or overhear him. Upon a moment of reflection, Harb decided this was possibly true. Although his wife was doing her best to keep the lines of discourse open, his daughter was terminally enraged at him and was at that moment declining all of her errant father's efforts to reach out to her. He was not sure he blamed her. Was he not the bad guy by any female measure? Was it not right in every sense for her to identify with her mother in this profound and abiding disagreement? He was in the process of destroying their world. He hated himself for it most of the time, too.

"It's Chas," Chas continued quite unnecessarily. "I was just, you know, checkin' up on you. I got back some test scores I wanted to tell you about." There was the sound of breathing then, the sound of someone realizing the futility of speaking with a machine. "Whatever," his son said after a moment. "I gotta go." There was a click and Chas was gone. Harb hung up, sat on the edge of the bed, put his face in his hands, and was quiet for a while. Perhaps the noises he made were the sound of a person clearing his throat repeatedly after having swallowed something the wrong way. It's impossible to say. He was very, very uncomfortable, that much was certain. But a man can cry for only so long. The supply of tears runs out long before the well of sadness runs dry. So Harb just sat there for a while, dry-eyed, in his borrowed bathrobe.

Then that look of decision we have come to know stole over him, and he rose, went to the bureau, then the closet, and dressed—khakis, a button-down shirt, an old raggedy sweater of coarse, loosely knit wool that had always been one of his favorites, and soft, virtually shapeless, very comfortable shoes he had recently purchased. They were strange and sort of bulky, with crepe soles. He liked them, not the least because they made him slightly taller. Of all the aspects of business life he was about to leave behind, the need to wear constricting and sometimes painful footwear was among those he would miss the least. Thus informally clad and shod, he pulled on his fifteen-hundred-dollar Burberry overcoat and made for the door, checking for the plastic cards that would guarantee his reentry to this sanctum of luxury. Then, after a moment of thought, he put the bottle of scotch in one of the overcoat's capacious pockets, thrust the glass in the other, and headed for the door.

On the way out, as if his body suddenly made a decision his mind knew not of, he veered back into the bathroom and picked up the phone. There was a ringing on the other end of the line, then, "Hey," said his son's answering machine. "You know what to do." And then it beeped.

"Chas, man," said Harb into the phone. Then there was a very long silence in which Harb found he could not speak. "I'll call ya later," he choked out at last. Then he hung up. For a moment he looked as if he might simply sit down in his coat on the cool tiles of the bathroom floor and stay there. Instead, uttering a strange groan that was more bestial than human, he leaned into the space ahead of him and launched himself out of the suite.

There was a groceria about half a block from his new apartment. He went in and looked around. There was a full panoply of soy-based foodstuffs and suspicious grains in barrels, but there was no Wonder Bread, which was his favorite, or any other commercial edible product he might recognize as an artifact of twenty-first-century America. So he settled instead on a loaf of something aggressively lumpy, grainy, and nutty, a hunk of soft, yellow Cheshire cheese clearly devoid of preservatives, some bottles of juice with tons of sediment floating in them, a few cans of soup he knew would turn out to be salt-, fat-, and flavor-free, and a nine-dollar chicken breast from a bird that had lived its life in a state of freedom superior to his. Then he had an inspiration of sorts.

"Peanut butter?" he asked the clerk, a very neat older man, bald with a small ponytail, dressed in jeans and a red and black checked flannel shirt.

"Several different kinds down the last aisle," said the man. Harb went down the cluttered final pathway at the far end of the store looking for the object of his desire, and there in the corner, looking at a rack of soy products, was Emily Lassiter.

"Hi," said Harb. "Emily, isn't it?"

"Hi, Harb," said Emily Lassiter.

She was in a high-collared shearling jacket, cinched tight at the waist by a belt that extended down to the middle of her thighs, and on her head was a woolen beret with a small, fuzzy pompom on top. Her dark hair peeped out from underneath the cap. Her cheeks were bright and rosy. She was eyeing him quite frankly with pleasant interest, not looking left, right, or over his shoulder. He wondered if he appeared substandard in any way.

"I've been wondering when you might show up again," she said. "The heat is on in your apartment, and the electricity. You can move in any time."

"I was thinking of kind of dropping in there right now," said Harb.

"Ah." She seemed to be amused. "Did you move some furniture in there when I wasn't looking?"

"I think I have a lamp in there, don't I?" Harb found himself looking at Emily Lassiter's nose. It was not a small nose. Not a beezer of any kind, certainly, but no button, either, and was covered with a small assortment of freckles. Her lips, too, were full, but small and well-defined, very pink without benefit of lipstick that he could see.

"No," she said, comfortable under his gaze, "I'm afraid not. Do you have a memory of bringing a lamp in there?"

"Sometimes," said Harb, "I conflate my wishes with reality. Maybe I sort of thought there was a lamp in there because I wanted there to be one."

"Well," said Emily Lassiter, "you know the old saying."

"No," said Harb.

"If wishes were horses . . . That one."

"No."

"If wishes were horses, beggars would ride." She looked at him sheepishly, as if she was sorry she had gotten herself into this mess.

"No," said Harb. "I never heard that. What does it mean?"

"Are you hot in here?" She suddenly appeared very warm indeed, and Harb realized that he too was building up a load of body heat in the small, close grocery store.

"They need to keep it like this to make sure all the organic vegetables remain tiny, sad, and wilted," he said.

"Let me just grab this and we'll go back to the building." Her fist, which had, he saw, ridiculously small fingers, child's fingers, closed around some form of supplement on a very high shelf, and he noted almost clinically how her body stretched to achieve its goal. Since she was wearing a pair of responsible, shapeless sweat pants and sneakers that had probably been headed for imminent retirement for the past two or three years, there was nothing prurient about his gaze. There was something about Emily Lassiter, however, that made him prone more to look than to speak and to be comfortable in silence. "Were you buying something down this aisle?" she said.

"Peanut butter."

"They have several. All are very healthy."

"Don't they have, you know, like . . . Skippy?" he said. "Or Jif?"

"No Skippy," she said. "No Jif."

Harb took a the nearest jar of inedible goo. They headed for the front of the store. "Put it on my tab, Omar," she said to the clerk.

"Have a good one, Emily," said the clerk. She left the store while Harb settled up, and as his goods were tallied he watched her on the street outside the store. She was simply standing with her little string bag, which clearly accompanied her on all her modest shopping expeditions. She was not fidgeting, not tapping her foot, although she occasionally chewed on the nail of her right index finger. Omar was very slow. "You moving into the neighborhood?" he said as he gave Harb his change.

"Yes," said Harb. "Into the Emily Lassiter Building."

"That's a very nice building," said Omar. "I hope you're very happy there and that we'll see a lot of you."

"I think you will," said Harb, adding with a smile, "unless I need some milk, I guess."

"Milk is bad, man," said Omar with a serious but not hostile intensity. "It's bad for humans and it's bad for the cows."

"I'm sure we'll hear more about that next time I see you," said Harb, and with a smile he left the store.

"I hope Omar didn't wear you out with the crazy milk stuff," said his companion as they made their way down the street and around the corner to the building. "He's a nice guy, but he's a little screwy on the subject."

"It's okay," said Harb. "Everybody's crazy about something or other."

They went into the little elevator without speaking much more, and on the floor below his, the door opened and she got out, placing her arm against the mechanism to prevent its closing.

"Are you going to be sleeping there tonight? I mean . . . You don't . . . have anything. Like, there's a couple of sconces there for light, but beyond that . . . it's mostly floor, you know."

"I'm just gonna sit there for a while," said Harb. Her tiny face under her silly hat was serious, radiating concern and a small bit of confusion. When she had known him professionally as a meeting planner, he had been a supremely powerful corporate Caesar. What had befallen him? He sensed that she would have liked to ask him a thousand questions but was refraining for a number of excellent reasons—their status as landlord and tenant, her innate tact and shyness, his obvious sense of dislocation and loss of coherence, of self.

For his part, Harb realized that whatever she wanted to ask him at some point in the future, he would be happy to answer.

"Um," she said. "Are you all right?"

"Oh, yeah," said Harb. Then there was a silence in which they looked at each other without blinking again. "I'll tell you about it sometime."

"Okay," said Emily Lassiter. "Good night."

"Good night, Emily," said Harb, and she removed her arm and allowed the elevator door to roll shut.

It took Harb a while to figure out the configuration of urban locks with which his door had been supplied. It required two keys, both of which looked the same but were not. After scrabbling around with the combination for another few minutes, he magically figured out the manipulations necessary for entry and found himself in the two barren rooms that had, in daylight, appeared to him so perfect, so appropriate for the future he was arranging for himself.

He turned on the light. It still looked all right, really. There was one long, flat wall on which he would place his stereo. On the other end of the two and a half rooms there was a fireplace that would come in handy, and in the middle of the far room sat a metal folding chair positioned before a large picture window.

No skyscrapers were in sight, not even the lake. Just rooftops, the measured backyards of his neighbors. After a few minutes at the window, he went into the tiny kitchen area and unloaded his groceries into the cabinets and the refrigerator. The booty hardly filled any space at all, but it made the place less naked and more his own.

Harb found the thermostat and raised the temperature to seventy-two degrees, four notches above where he was accustomed to set it at home in Glencoe, where even a degree of temperature in that big old house meant thousands of dollars in the annual cost of fuel. He felt the little folding seat to see if it would take his weight, and then carefully, gingerly, he sat. When the apartment grew warmer, which it did almost immediately, he opened his coat. Only then did he feel the weight of the bottle in his coat pocket. He removed it and fished out the glass from the other part of his coat as well. The glass he left on the floor. It was sticky and unappealing. After a moment, he got up, turned out the lights, and sat down again, the bottle in his lap. He opened it and then just sat some more. Occasionally, he took a sip from the bottle. After a time, to his surprise, he found that the bottle was empty, and he put it carefully on the floor beside him. He took off his overcoat and, folding it neatly, placed it on the floor beside the empty bottle. He was quite warm now.

At about two in the morning, his cell phone rang. The sound startled him quite a bit, and it took him a few seconds to find the little Motorola, but there it was in his hand in time for him to catch the call. He knew who it was. There were only two people up at that hour and one of them wasn't speaking to him.

"Chas, man," he said, flipping open the clamshell. "I was hoping you would call."

And Harb sat in the dark in the middle of the November night in that empty space on the edge of another long Chicago winter that would end only God knew when, and the future stretched before him like a vast ocean, unknown and uncharted, and he held the little StarTAC in his hand and talked with his son until the need for sleep overtook him and he said good-bye, at least for that day, and he slept, sitting upright in that hard little chair.

And that was how Harb spent the first night in his new apartment.

52

UNITED STATES DISTRICT COURT NORTHERN DISTRICT OF ILLINOIS

CaroleAnne L. Winter, Plaintiff, v. Civ. Global Fiduciary Trust Company, Defendant

Friday, November 22, 11:30 A.M.

THE COURT: We have been informed that the jury has a verdict. Will the clerk take the verdict?

CLERK: Madam Forewoman, please rise. Have you agreed upon a verdict? Yes or no.

FOREPERSON: Yes.

CLERK: Question number one. Did the plaintiff prove sexual harassment in the work environment? Yes or no.

FOREPERSON: No.[32]

THE COURT: Record the verdict. I will discharge the jury. Please go back, and I will join you in a minute. *(Jury discharged)*

Any motions?

MR. MORGENSTERN: No, Your Honor.

THE COURT: Thank you both. Nice trial. I appreciated the lawyers, and I normally don't say it.[33]

---

32. Subsequent investigation reveals that after a night of sleep, the jury had taken exactly twenty minutes to reach its unanimous conclusion.

33. And so it ended. No harm, no foul, right? The judge collected his papers, the jury rose with an air of quiet satisfaction. At the table reserved for them, CaroleAnne and her counsel rose, turned to face each other, and hugged. The plaintiff, dressed in a tight-fitting, lime-green, one-piece thing that came to just above the largest part of her thigh, her shoulders draped with a festive Pashmina scarf of green and golden hue, seemed overjoyed about the fact that the ordeal, however she perceived it, was over, and that closure, that most ubiquitous and annoying of current concepts, had at last been achieved. Biddle, at his work space on the other side of the room, was collecting the many files and other detritus of the case, and appeared to be patting himself on the psychic back, if such a thing is possible. I decided to join him immediately and help him along with that task. We had won! Sadly, I was the only one from the great Global Fiduciary Trust Company who could make that claim, except, at last, for my friend, the late executive vice president of the corporation, who had slipped into the back of the room to see the final adjudication of the case that had changed his life forever. He was wearing one of those navy blue pea coats we all wore in college, a big, riot-colored knit scarf around his neck. As I turned to leave down the center aisle, Harb saw me, smiled, waved a jolly greeting, then disappeared out of the back of the courtroom. He looked like he was going somewhere.

53

They met in a room off the chamber and forgave each other, Harb and CaroleAnne. Perhaps it was prearranged, I don't know. I was there because I followed him, and I can tell you that it was quite touching.

"It's okay, Ceece," said Harb, when she approached him with tears in her eyes.

"Thanks, Harb," she said.

They both just stood and looked at each other, and there was something big and sweet and sticky in the air around them. And then suddenly, there wasn't anymore, and all that was left was a dry, embarrassed void. Just like that, whatever feeling had existed between them, good or bad, was gone, and they each inhaled as if awakening from a deep sleep and, with individual quiet, apologetic smiles, drifted to opposite ends of the room for the donning of coats and scarves.

That's how things end much of the time, I guess. We think endings are going to be atrociously difficult and then the time comes for them, and we are looking at them in the rearview mirror wondering what all the fuss was about anyway. Thank God we are each issued at birth some measure of emotional amnesia. Life would be intolerable without it.

Edgar was present, by the way. Obviously having run out of the funding we had provided for treatment of his intense allergy to labor, he had returned to provide CaroleAnne support in her time of need. He was standing, bony and furtive in a dirty corduroy coat, looking out a corner window. I suppose he had come to pick her up and possibly to assist her in the celebrations attending a successful lawsuit. In this case, he looked understandably disappointed. I had no idea Smoking wasn't allowed in federal buildings, but nobody stopped him. We glared at each other a couple of times, but I had to quit it before I started laughing.

On her way out, CaroleAnne came over to me and, without speaking, stuck out her hand. I took it. "You were always a good guy, Fred," she said. "I'm sorry things worked out this way. You know I am."

"Yeah, sure, CaroleAnne," I said. And then she was gone. Last I heard, she had a very good job with a gigantic insurance company. Perhaps she is handling one of your medical claims right now.

I had one chore to complete before I could myself consider the matter of Robert Harbert over and done with, at least from a business point of view. I gave Harb an envelope. In that envelope were his stock options. Anyone in executive life will know what I mean when I say that, without question, I took care of him.

After that, Harb went home to his new apartment, or to a bar somewhere in the cool part of town, or to some lovely hotel or other, doubtless to raise a glass in victory, and I went back to the office. It was still only midday and there was plenty of light lifting to do before close of business.

The next morning, I believe, my friend Harbert drove his Z3 roadster into the BMW dealership that had sold it to him. They had him over a barrel. As a city person now, he would scarcely need a car at all and certainly not a state-of-the-art machine like that.

Today the corporation goes on, bigger than any one of us. I'm on the top floor of the building along with six or seven other guys. We're a nice bunch. It's fun up here.

I see Harb now and then, you know, but it isn't quite the same. I miss the Harb I used to know, but I recognize it's tough to maintain business friendships outside the milieu in which they were formed. Nowadays months might go by in which we do not hear from each other. I imagine him, sometimes, leaning into a stiff wind coming in from the north in his little Optimist sailboat, heading for the horizon. I wish that for him, anyhow.

But I don't know. What, in the end, would be best? For my friend to go backward into the past or forward into the wind? Is the old Harb and the life he constructed worth saving? Or does the new man have just as much right to life as the old? Is there some combination of the two that has a chance at emerging from the forge? What would that look like? Would that still be Harb?

For what is so fragile, and ultimately so inscrutable, as the human self? Does it exist at all, or is it simply a construct of the circumstances that collect around it and help to define it? And if, as is sometimes the case for the unfortunate or the unready, those circumstances are radically altered, what is to become of us?

What is to become of us in any event?

After the recession made its inevitable retreat, this turns out to be a good year for business. The market has been healthy. Revenue growth is in the high single digits, which translates to a very nice cash flow picture. We have a lot to look forward to. I myself will be eligible for early retirement in only five years. I plan to avail myself of that opportunity. There are places my wife and I would like to go, things we want to see before the darkness closes in. I have been inside these walls for so long it's hard for me to imagine what it will be like in the world beyond these doors, but I'd like to find out.